A MOVING SCREEN

ALSO BY KRIS ALLIS

A False Start

A MOVING SCREEN

KRIS ALLIS

This book is a work of fiction. Names, characters, places, and incidents either are the product of the author's imagination or are used fictitiously, and any resemblance to actual persons, living or dead, business establishments, events, or locales is entirely coincidental.

Published by T.S.W. Wordsmith, LLC
Powder Springs, Georgia

Library of Congress Control Number
2016907553

ISBN 9780986318443

First Edition

Printed in the United States of America

This book is for the loves of my life: Gilbert, Tishanna, Richard, Cassandra, Zico, and Georgie

No man has power over the wind to contain it; so no man has power over the day of his death.

Ecclesiastes 8:8

June 16, 2005 3:35 a.m.

Metropolitan Atlanta, Georgia

Prologue

A hot date with death was imminent for Meredith Payne. Literally. Not because she woke up with a premonition that this would be her last day on earth or because the skull and bones card was drawn by a psychic and placed in front of her. Meredith's appointment with death was being arranged by another person in the room, a dark figure whose facial features she could not see. As he spread gasoline on the floor of the tiny room they were in, he worked with the intensity of a floor finisher applying a final coat of polyurethane to wooden parquet. He sloshed the toxic accelerant against the walls as though he were an artist throwing paint on a canvas. Silent and deliberate all the while, as if planning to ignite a room with human kindling was kosher.

Nude and spread-eagled on a wooden table with splinters in her back, no amount of strain could produce movement from Meredith's arms or feet, giving her no option for escape. Nor was mental respite a viable alternative. Alert and aware, with a limited vista in which her shadowy companion moved in and out, seemingly unaware of her presence, she felt all of her body's silent distress signals. To make matters worse she had no idea who this ghoul was or how she had come to be in this place.

Before waking up in her present immobilized state, the last thing Meredith remembered was dressing for an evening out. She had been so excited to wear the new black dress she'd found in a boutique for 75 percent off the retail price of $450. It made her look thin and she felt beautiful. In her cache of free eye shadows that had been gifted with the purchase of a cosmetic product, she'd found a shade of lavender eye shadow that matched one of the alternating rows of sequins at the bottom half of the dress. A deep plum lipstick highlighted her pouty lips to give her face a lovely coordinating glow. The six-inch black pumps provided the perfect finishing touch, adding just enough height to make her interesting. She pivoted in front of the floor-length mirror, grabbed her snakeskin purse, and left her house for a night of fun at the church.

Now, having no fun at all, she lay in this small, dusty, dim, godforsaken room where the only light came from a row of seven candles on a mantel straight ahead. She'd counted them three times. She'd numbered the large fern leaves on the faded pattern of the wallpaper on the wall above the mantel—twenty-one. She spied water stains on the ceiling, and the ornate crown molding that had not suffered the wear and tear of the chipped, elongated shelf held in place by cracked, mortared bricks. She imagined that people who had once lived in this house made plans for the future, and sat around this table enjoying their meals without a clue that Meredith would end up as its centerpiece. The main course. It was certainly nothing Meredith had dreamed for her future. The smell of gasoline reached her nostrils. She tried to cry out, but her lips would not open, her tongue would not move. Only a low, hoarse, unrecognizable grunt came through. She screamed inside.

Michael, the ghoul, felt a surge of energy as he moved toward Meredith, stopping at the end of the table near her feet and looking into her eyes. He wanted to witness firsthand her fear by holding eye contact for a beat. Then, beginning at her feet, he poured a generous amount of gasoline over her body all the way to her face, down one leg of the table, and along the floor, making a trail to the door. He tossed the large plastic container aside, went to the mantel, and took one of the candles, feeling her eyes watching him. The next few minutes were critical, because once a flame touched the floor the fire would spread quickly. A careful glance over the room revealed nothing to prove he had been there and soon only ashes would remain as proof of Meredith's existence. He walked to the door, paused for a split second to take one last look at Meredith, and then touched the candle to the end of the trail of gas. The fire snaked toward the table and burst into flames worthy of an ancient funeral pyre. He tossed the candle into the room and turned to flee—leaving behind a beautiful, shallow, young woman on the way to meet her maker.

One down.

Michael ran swiftly through the next two rooms of the empty row house and out the back door. He stopped and looked back to see a scene from a horror movie: flames licking and devouring, the sound of glass window panes exploding from the intense heat, smoke billowing outward to fill every crevice and crack in the structure. The yard, filled with discarded debris that would soon be more kindling for the fire now raging on the inside, led to a huge thicket of weeds, shrubs, and young trees. Following a worn path through the undergrowth, Michael emerged into an alley that was fronted by a huge shell of an abandoned warehouse. The alley was empty, as he knew it would be—barred off from traffic by high concrete barriers. Michael walked toward the warehouse, reaching the barrier closest to the building where a space was wide enough to slip his toned body through. Strolling at a leisurely pace for about a hundred yards, he reached his destination and darted behind a tree, where his backpack lay. A quick removal of his black all-over-body suit revealed jeans and a T-shirt underneath. He kicked off the heavy all-purpose work boots and pulled out a pair of sneakers and slid them on. After stuffing the body suit and the boots inside the bag, he zipped it, slung it over his shoulders, and stepped back onto the sidewalk. The street, as usual, was deserted. He bid a silent farewell to Meredith Payne as he walked casually to his car, and prayed she'd had a good life in spite of its brevity.

He unlocked the driver's side of a dark sedan, slid behind the steering wheel, and started the ignition. Glancing into the rearview mirror as he moved away from the curb, he could see the flames as they flickered upward and brightened the night sky. No sounds of fire engines disturbed the night air. Not yet. Soon everything would be destroyed. Fire was like that. No fingerprints. No blood. No fibers. Not one single facet of evidence to implicate him in this fiery jewel of murder. The drive home was uneventful as Michael expected. Turning onto a street where all residents were most likely in their homes for the night, he sighed with the satisfaction of having successfully completed his task. His neighbors were probably sitting around a television enjoying late night entertainment, in bed, or getting ready to tuck in—completely unaware of the night's recent event that would no doubt be on the early morning news. Seemingly unaware that one person, unable to sleep, watched from a window, Michael turned off his headlights as the shiny veneer of the dark sedan moved along at the pace of a slimy night crawler, oozed into the driveway of the house two doors down, and stopped.

Three Years Later

Monday, June 16, 2008

Chapter One

While most people in the city were struggling to get those last few hours of sleep before daylight, Missy Kinner was endeavoring to stay awake. She needed to get out of bed and go home. Falling asleep in bed with a man in a house occupied by another woman who could appear any minute was hardly conducive to peaceful dreams. The lamplight allowed her to see perfume bottles sitting on the dresser; pantyhose hanging out of the dresser drawer; photos of a woman in various poses and outfits on the nightstand; and a bulging jewelry box on the chest of drawers with gaudy necklaces and big gold bangles bursting forth. She saw a pink shopping bag filled with lacy new bras and matching panties on the floor beside the chest. She had been too out of it to notice these things when she first entered the room.

To all outward appearances, Missy was the good-time party girl without a care in the world. But her life at age thirty-five had not gone the way she'd hoped. She'd fallen in love with her dream guy and married him. When the marriage failed she was forced to turn to alcohol, sex, and sleeping pills to face another day. Life became a game for her—getting high, getting laid, and coming out of a blackout in strange places. The object was to determine how much of any intoxicating substance she could handle so as to achieve mindless orgasm. The what, who, and where didn't matter—only the orgasm. After which there was brief oblivion.

She stumbled to the bathroom, sat on the padded toilet seat, and peed. As she came out of the bathroom she considered waking the guy to thank him for a lovely evening, but she was not in a polite mood right now. She found her purse, shoes, and the rest of her clothing on the floor, except for her panties. She tried feeling under the covers for them, but to no avail. She wasn't going to disturb this dude. She slipped quietly out of the room, giggling at the scene that would occur when the female occupant discovered a pair of strange underwear in her bed. Oh well, YOLO—you only live once.

The living room was pleasant, almost homey. A beige sofa with purple pillows scattered everywhere. Thriving green plants here and there were on double duty, decorating and oxygenating. She stood in the middle of the room and pulled on her black skirt, her bra, and lacy black top. She anchored her purse on her shoulder, opened the door with one hand, and put her shoes on with the other. Stepping out into the night, she closed the door behind her. A strong breeze hit her as she dropped her head to hide her face and went into flight mode just in case the hussy of the house turned into the driveway in the next few minutes.

She walked across the small porch and nearly tripped over a potted plant as she carefully descended four brick steps. She then turned right and crossed the lawn to the sidewalk, finally recognizing where she was. Trammel Court—a quiet, tree-lined cul-de-sac with sidewalks—where children rode bicycles and chased each other in the daylight. The backyards of the houses were bordered by trees and undergrowth. A U-turn brought her to the backyard where she could take a shortcut to Mulberry, the main street running east to west behind the subdivision. Taking the trail instead of the surface streets would shorten her journey by almost two miles.

Just before reaching the end of the trail, Missy stopped to get her bearings. She blinked, focusing her eyes in the darkness, as another heavy breeze swayed the young trees in the thicket and flapped the leaves on the mature oaks. She leaned against a huge tree and breathed deeply, assessing the distance left to travel. She looked across the way at Mint Leaf Manor, a new live, work, and play complex. The pale-green and white PVC plumbing pipe that stuck out of the ground along with huge cranes and tractors at rest resembled a set for a science fiction movie. The place was completely deserted. She released a sigh into the quiet night air, trying to sober up from whatever she had smoked and drank the night before. She was having a hard time getting it together. She ran her fingers through her thick brown hair and shook it loose on her shoulders. Just as she was about to emerge from the cover of the trees, she saw the car.

A dark sedan with no headlights turned into the site and drove about a hundred yards before stopping near a huge mound of dirt and what appeared to be a pile of discarded building materials. Missy strained to see clearly as a dark silhouette got out of the car, opened the trunk, and struggled to remove what appeared to be a rolled-up rug. After he dropped it on the ground, bent over, and rolled it toward the front of the car, he gave it a shove and it disappeared.

Missy saw a momentary flame, then observed as the flame was tossed forward and the person backed away. He stood with his back to Missy for a moment watching as glowing flames danced. Moments later he turned and a sudden burst of lightning followed by a clap of thunder froze him in a sinister stance. He hesitated, looking back over his shoulder at the fire as if he had a decision to make. The moment passed. He got into the car and backed out onto Mulberry, driving away with his headlights still darkened.

She stood stock-still by the huge tree for a few minutes to see if the car would return. She watched the flickering fire and concluded that if the driver planned to return, he would have done so by now. As she moved forward, the rain started coming down so hard that without the flame to mark the spot, she would have lost sight of it. The flames fought but gradually began to subside, soon becoming no more than a few sparks.

Her first instinct was to mind her own business and continue home, but it was no match for her curiosity. She decided to investigate in spite of being half drunk, tired, and wanting her bed. Arriving drenched at the spot where the automobile had parked, Missy almost fell as her feet became entangled with something. No sooner had she dropped to her knees to free herself than a flash of lightning revealed an old-fashioned fanny pack. The weight of it when she picked it up told her there was something inside. With any luck it would be filled to the brim with money. She stuffed it into her large hobo-styled purse and stood, noticing the torrential rain had quenched the flames.

She stumbled forward. Lightning flashed again as she glanced down into the ditch where the rug steamed. Did she see what she thought she saw? An arm protruding from the smoldering mass—from the elbow to the hand, its nails wearing glow-in-the-dark purple nail polish? She moved closer and nearly tottered over a rusted iron pole—the kind concrete finishers use for stabilizing the cement. She picked it up and stepped into the ditch where she used it to prod and push the smoldering and soggy material away from the body of a naked woman. As Missy leaned in closer, the acrid smell of burned flesh mixed with gasoline caused her to gag. She felt the woman's wrist for a pulse. She didn't know much about detecting a heartbeat, but she knew she was supposed to feel something. Somewhere. The woman looked like she was dead. Missy had seen dead bodies before, but never one like this. She threw the pole like a javelin as far as she could and climbed out of the ravine.

Missy realized that even though she'd intentionally avoided looking at the woman's face, she'd somehow captured a side profile that caused a sinking feeling in her stomach. The feeling was immediately followed by a strong impression she had seen the woman before. Alone in the downpour except for the "cinder girl," she shivered and turned toward her destination, her shoes caked with mud. The heavy rain made it hard to see ahead, but an occasional lightning flash as well as her familiarity with this shortcut soon brought her to Wellington. She lowered her head and shifted her purse to the other shoulder, aware that she should report what she had just seen. If not, hours might pass before another human being discovered that poor woman. Missy headed toward the pay phone at the gas station on the corner. Unlike most of her peers, she had no desire or need for a cell phone. It was just one more thing to keep up with.

Same Day

Chapter Two

It was still dark as Etta Wasp maneuvered her body so as to become more comfortable in her chair and ease the aching "catch," as she called it, which seemed to plague the right side of her back. She'd heard tell of people with the same ailment, blaming it on hours in front of a computer in a nonergonomic chair. She couldn't say the same. She rarely used a computer except for her occasional church duties and searching out things—like where to order the best tulip bulbs in the fall, or the crocus in the spring—and catching up with the daily headlines if one had missed the news three times in one day. That type of usage took only a few minutes not hours of sitting.

Weighing in at 174 pounds, she was by no means skinny, standing five feet four inches tall. Her small frame had carried a scant 107 pounds in her younger days, her hair had been brunette, her eyelashes thick and her brows naturally arched. She had grown into an attractive matron, but nowadays every hair on her body was gray.

She had not gotten much sleep. It had to be because of the green bean casserole that Pearl, her sister, had made for dinner. It had too many onions in it. How many times did she have to tell that woman that she couldn't eat onions? The smell almost gave her heartburn. Naturally Pearl did not force her to eat the casserole, but she was not about to blame herself.

Once she was positioned just right and pain-free, she turned toward the bay window and peered out. She was fortunate to have her master bedroom with windows facing the street. Watching life's parade go by gave her much pleasure, even in the wee hours of the morning, like now.

The street was quiet except for the rain. It was coming down as if poured from a huge water pitcher—too hard for any living soul to be out. She glanced at the clock on the table in the center of the window—4:15 a.m. Soon things would start stirring—folks leaving for work, newspapers being delivered, the dogs barking, and the five children next door running and screaming. Etta was just about to return to bed when she saw a figure weaving down the street through the rain.

"Missy Kinner! She's been out all night again!" she said, shaking her head from side to side.

Missy staggered along without a coat or hat. It's a miracle she had on shoes. Soaking wet. Coming home this time of morning, drunk as a skunk in all probability—or high as a kite as Missy liked to say. That girl had the neighborhood buzzing ever since she moved in with her aunt, Connie Henderson, three houses down on the left. Etta and Connie had been friends for years, being the oldest homeowners on Hydrangea Court, one of the first planned suburbs of Atlanta. Over thirty years now.

Connie was a hardworking Christian woman who'd taken in her niece—her only living relative—when the child fell into hard times, having promised her only sister, Missy's mother, that she'd always look out for the child.

But the child was now a woman, and she brought a lot of baggage—not the kind by Samsonite—filled with skeletons. She'd had problems with her marriage. Her husband left her and was awarded custody of the couple's only child, a little girl. Connie never talked about what happened, but Etta didn't know many men that could live with a drunken wife. Missy was a grown woman and she ought to do better. Etta was just itching to slap some sense into her. The way she was living her life she was never going to see her child again. It always saddened Etta when she thought about that.

She watched as Missy stumbled past. She was usually good for an outdoor show, because she could perform at the drop of a hat. All she needed was an audience—someone out working in the yard, walking along the street or even standing in the doorway. Missy seemed to think that everyone was concerned with what she did. As a result she challenged any and every one. She knew of Etta's habit of sitting in the window.

"Hey old woman! Whatcha looking at?" she'd yell at Etta whenever she caught a glimpse of her.

Etta never answered her of course because it would have involved too much. Etta would have to go into detail about what she thought of Missy. That would call for judgment and that just wasn't the Christian thing to do. Missy's waywardness would catch up with her soon enough. Etta watched Missy stumble up the steps of Connie's house and linger on the porch for a few minutes before going inside.

Same Day

Chapter Three

The 911 operator listened carefully as the female voice on the other end described a phantom, a fire, and a woman's body. Speech slurred, voice hesitant but calm, the caller identified the location of the cinder girl—Mint Leaf Manor construction site. The woman gave enough information to reveal that a terrible crime had occurred. The operator routed a call to the Peach Grove Police Department and Fire Department as soon as the anonymous caller broke the connection. Less than thirty seconds later, these emergency responders were rolling, their sirens blasting, lights flashing, and their speed steadily increasing as they made their way to their destination. Crime-scene technicians and paramedics with ambulances were dispatched along with Detective Dennis Cane, the lead detective of the police department. He was a highly trained, experienced investigator who had been on the job less than a year.

He was driving as if he would be the one to extinguish a fire. Water pooling from the heavy downpour and speeding at eighty miles per hour caused his car to hydroplane as he made a left-hand turn at a major intersection. He skillfully regained control of his vehicle, grateful there was no traffic, reached into his center console, found a peppermint, and popped it into his mouth. He had no way of knowing that he was racing to the scene of a crime he had been expecting. All he knew was that a woman's body had been found. He remained calm. Police work was his life and he never allowed himself to get excited and lose focus.

He arrived at the scene as the first responding police officer almost simultaneously with another Peach Grove police cruiser. The fire engine and paramedics were already there. He could see their lights focusing on a drop-off directly in front of him. Dennis bolted out of his car, push-button umbrella up and over his head. A few rubberneckers stood with umbrellas watching the action from the street. *Thank God they weren't on the crime scene*, Dennis thought.

Any evidence in all of this rain was going to be next to impossible to find.

He leaned inside his car and grabbed his radio to get an ETA from the investigation team. As he visually surveyed the scene, looking through the rain curtain, Dennis spied a heavy rod in the distance sticking up from the mud like a javelin.

"Hey, stretch that tape over beyond that pole," he ordered a police officer who stood ready for instructions. "Nobody enters! None of those people standing around, nobody who comes up asking any questions! Only my investigators. They'll be here in three minutes. You got that?"

The officer nodded his head and followed orders. Iron poles used by concrete finishers lay scattered around the area where Dennis stood. None of them were positioned as if they'd been thrown. There had to be a reason for this one. He went to take a closer look.

"You need help over there, Lieutenant?" one of the investigators called out.

"No, I've got this. You guys just go over this whole area with a fine-tooth comb. Don't be shy about the mud. If there's something else here I want it found. I need evidence like an aching tooth needs a dentist."

"So far the only other promising evidence is some muddy tire tracks. Someone drove a car up to this site."

"You're right. It looks like they drove up and stopped. Which means the victim was moved to that ditch," Dennis said, looking toward all the activity being carried on by the emergency medical team. He wondered about the someone who drove the car there. And the someone who made a 911 call.

Dennis reached the pole, leaned over, and saw some type of material stuck near the bottom above ground level.

"I need photos of this thing and I want it bagged and tagged!"

The investigator moved to follow orders as Dennis turned and hurried over to where the paramedics were down in the ditch, pulling a tarp away from and hooking an IV to a woman who was badly burned. At that moment a helicopter hovered over, then landed in a clearing about a hundred yards away. The paramedics, after lifting the woman's body onto a stretcher, climbed out of the ditch and rushed to where the helicopter waited.

"How's she doing, guys?" Dennis asked as he ran along beside them.

"She's in bad shape. Somebody marinated her with gasoline. They're airlifting her to the burn unit at Grady," a paramedic replied.

"Is she conscious?"

A look of chagrin from the other paramedic gave Dennis his answer. As badly as he needed information it would have to wait. He backed off.

Gasoline! Exactly what he'd expected. He went in search of the fire officer in charge to find out his official determination of what had happened and the conditions he witnessed upon arrival. He felt his adrenalin rising as he took another peppermint from his jacket pocket and put it into his mouth. This just might turn out to be the end of a three-year vigil.

Same Day

Chapter Four

Michael drove alone in the car. The rain had been predicted for the afternoon—not the wee hours of the morning. He fought the urge to go back and get the body, knowing that would be a foolish and dangerous decision. Everything could be ruined by this sudden deluge, but it was not worth getting caught red-handed. The heavy rains would extinguish the flames before the body could burn completely. But smoke inhalation would lead to her death because she was double-wrapped in the tarp.

Repetition had proven itself invaluable. He'd learned the first time the cruelty of looking at the person as he poured gasoline over every inch of the body. Rolling it up in the tarp solved that problem and made transporting it easier. It worked every time. No way his mission could be stopped by an act of God. It was God who directed him. Even if somehow the body was discovered right away, the police would never discover who was responsible. The fire removed all incriminating DNA that could have been left by the doer. And as for the victim—they usually can't match DNA unless they have someone to match it to. How can you match a shoe if you don't have the mate? How do you add a piece of a puzzle to nothing? And nothing is what they had. No identification and no way to match fingerprints because he was careful to select women who had no reason to have fingerprints on file in a police database. A thorough investigation would not be done because there was nothing to investigate. Just a crime scene, if one chose to call it that, with no clues.

It was good that the rain and subsequent muddy conditions would keep workers away for at least a day. Perhaps they would find the body somewhat intact if the fire didn't burn long enough to consume the flesh and erase any identifying facial features. With nature's fire hose aimed at it, odds were less favorable. A careful and prolonged stakeout of that construction site had all been for naught. But Michael did not despair.

The car entered the northbound lane of I-75 and merged smoothly into the flow of traffic. The interstate usually made for a nice drive this time of morning, but not when a curtain of rain adorned the windshield and splashed the side windows as other vehicles passed. Michael slowed down to fifty-five miles per hour and stayed to the right. Glancing at the clock on the dash, he noted that plenty of time remained to return the car and get back to a nice warm, comfortable bed.

Sighing with satisfaction, he leaned back to enjoy the ride until a glance at the passenger seat almost caused him to swerve off the road. What he did not see hit him like an unexpected slap in the face.

The sports pack was not on the passenger seat.

Where was it?

Did he drop it at the construction site? How in the world had that happened? Was there anything inside that would lead back to him? With a furrowed brow Michael played every possible scenario out to the end—finally deciding that there was nothing to lead back to the origin of that little handy carryall. No need for concern.

All is well.

This plan had been three years in the making. It had required time in prayer, time for research, hours of stakeouts, manipulation of people and paperwork, not to mention the effort to stay alert so as not to miss that proverbial golden opportunity. The bodies had to be burned in Peach Grove this time so they would be found. It was uncomfortable, and required more risk than the other times, but nonetheless it had to be done. Perfect execution required staying calm and focused so as not to be distracted by things outside of his control. Confident, ready, and eager to see the plan through, Michael adjusted the rearview mirror and relaxed as he set the cruise control at fifty-five miles per hour.

Same Day

Chapter Five

Merlot Candy awakened to the relentless buzz of the alarm clock on his night table. Realigning his six-foot four-inch body, he breathed deeply and reached over to push the snooze button. The sound of falling rain slowly erased the lingering irritation of a saleslady in his dream, and his thoughts turned to the day ahead. Traffic in Atlanta, which was bad on sunny days; would be even worse this morning. No need to rush. He could afford to keep his eyes closed for twenty more minutes. After all he was his own boss and would not punish himself for being late. He pitied those who'd already entered the fray, making their way to spend hours at various jobs around the city, but that was not his life. He was on his time clock, and he liked it that way, he admitted to himself as he closed his eyes.

Twenty minutes later the alarm sounded again. Merlot pushed the off button and sat up, placing his feet on the white alpaca rug beneath his king-size bed and opened his eyes wide as he looked around. The entire living space of his contemporary-style loft was a mélange in black and white. His bedroom, with its dusky faded black walls, black lacquered furnishings, and dark oak floors, was highlighted by white everywhere else—the comforter, lampshades, draperies, and various sizes and shapes of urns. He walked to the bathroom, his feet adapting to the smooth, cold surface of the wood floors. The black-and-white tiled surface of the bathroom floor always gave a frigid shock to his feet, but stark white plush rugs were strategically placed so as to allow only seconds of exposure of skin to tile. White fluffy towels and framed prints of sea and sand adorned the black tiled walls. He brushed his teeth and washed his face. He opened the door to the massive walk-in shower and turned the hot water on full blast.

He stepped out and closed the door to allow a build-up of steam. He left the bathroom, slid his feet into soft terrycloth thongs he kept beside the bedroom door, and headed to the kitchen. He flipped on the light, opened the cabinet near the stainless steel refrigerator, and pulled down a bag of freshly ground coffee and a filter. He poured in a sufficient amount, placed it into the coffee machine, and flipped the switch to begin brewing. Clad in absolutely nothing, which was how he liked to sleep, he returned to his bathroom and stepped into the shower.

Fifteen minutes later, he stepped out of his makeshift sauna and dried himself off in front of a full-length mirror, turning his face to the side to see if by some chance he'd grown facial hair. No such luck. He dried his curly brown hair as he walked into his well-organized, color-coordinated, walk-in closet. He dropped the hand towel and selected a green suit from the left side, where all his tailor-made suits hung, and chose a shirt of a lighter shade of the same green from the right. He hung those pieces on the special rack that held his selection of the day. After choosing a pair of black leather shoes and setting them on the floor, he returned to the bathroom for deodorant, cologne, and aftershave that was only for show. He'd never had a need to shave. From the huge chest of drawers in his bedroom, he pulled out his underwear and stepped into them. He returned to the closet and began to dress, starting with the green shirt—Merlot did not believe in undershirts—while thoughts of his first appointment ran through his mind.

He was scheduled to meet Louise Canola at 9:30 a.m. Louise had no idea where her sister, Chanel, could be. The last time she had talked to Chanel was Friday. Today was Monday and Louise wanted Merlot's help because she believed he was an excellent private investigator. She based her belief not only on Merlot's own opinion of his abilities but also in testimonials from former clients who endorsed him. And so had Anissa Lynne Strickland.

Anissa. It was because of her that he now lived in a 130-year-old, prestigious apartment building on the corner of Ponce de Leon Avenue; the reason that he'd been able to relocate his office to 100 Peachtree Street smack in the middle of downtown Atlanta; and the reason he was in love for the first time in his life. He'd earned an excellent paycheck from her husband who'd dug into his deep pockets to pay Merlot to find her—more than he'd ever earned from a client.

Almost seven years ago, Anissa Brogdon, as she was known then, came back from the dead. When her "widowed" spouse, Foley—grieving and confused—knocked on Merlot's door seeking help to find her, his outrageous story aroused Merlot's curiosity. Foley believed Anissa had perished in the attack on the World Trade Center on 9/11 until an anonymous phone caller tipped him off that Anissa was living in Powder Springs, Georgia, a suburb of Atlanta. Merlot had to ask himself why a woman would go to such lengths to get away from her husband when she could have easily divorced him and walked away with half of his assets.

"Why wouldn't she just divorce you?" he'd asked Foley. Who'd hesitated before answering. And then had manufactured a look of shame on his face.

"She had an affair and she was on drugs. Cocaine. She was ashamed and didn't want to drag me and my family through a scandal. She didn't think I could forgive her. But, Mr. Candy, I have."

Merlot sensed that Foley was not being completely honest with him, but he'd accepted the job at the behest of an old friend who was also a friend of Foley's father. And the money didn't hurt, either. Finding Anissa had proven to be a challenge, but he located her in Boston, where she was living with a new identity. He smiled at the memory of their first encounter.

"Are you a new student?" she'd asked when she approached him from behind as he stood in the center aisle of the foreign language lab.

"No, I'm looking for human resources." He'd somehow managed a quick response in spite of being completely taken aback at her lovely face and body. "I'm Marvin." He'd extended his hand to her and she'd promptly sent him on his way.

Pretending to be someone he was not to gain her confidence, he soon realized that Anissa was afraid, that she was suspicious of everything and everybody, including him, which was a good thing. The bad thing was that she nearly jumped out of her skin every time she saw a man who resembled Foley. She didn't act at all like a woman who'd sinned against her husband. Merlot returned to Atlanta determined to complete the job in spite of his misgivings, but as fate would have it, he never had to reveal her whereabouts because Foley paid him in full and then fired him. And of course, the marriage ended abruptly. A year later, Merlot contacted Anissa again to begin an open relationship.

"What will your name be next week?" she'd asked.

"I'm sorry about that lie. But I can't very well do my job if I am completely honest. I have to disguise myself."

"I guess I can accept that. I owe you for my life because of that tendency you have of bending the truth," she'd said with a laugh.

And that was the beginning of a long distance, platonic alliance with Merlot often traveling to New York to see her. Three years ago, Anissa moved to Atlanta, a few blocks away from Merlot. She began seeing a good therapist, and was slowly healing. They were still the best of friends and although he wanted more, Anissa was waiting. Her marriage had been a nightmare with a kaleidoscope of abuse—physical, emotional, and psychological.

"I want to know everything about you. I want to spend the rest of my life with you. I've never felt this way about any woman," he'd said.

"I don't know if I'll ever be able to be in a relationship with a man again," she began, her eyes filling with tears. "And never with a woman," she'd added.

"I can wait. I know you like me and that's a good start. We can work on developing the best friendship the world has ever known," he'd responded as he pulled her into his arms to comfort her.

He knew it would be hard for her to trust a man again and lovemaking was out of the question. She emphasized her intentions to avoid sleeping with a man and confusing lust for love. So they went to movies and ate together, and on Sunday mornings the two hiked up Kennesaw Mountain, part of a national park located in Marietta. It was on these long walks that Anissa and Merlot talked and listened to each other, becoming closer each time. They'd stand at the top of the mountain and watch the sun rise and showcase the tall buildings of Atlanta against an orange background. It was just yesterday morning, while they admired this view, that Anissa mentioned Louise to him.

"Merlin, would you do something for me?" she'd asked, with a worried frown as she pushed her blonde hair away from her face. Merlin was her nickname for him because he'd come into her life as one man and magically turned himself into another.

"Yes, I'll marry you," Merlot responded.

Anissa laughed. "Seriously, Merlin. It's my friend Louise. Her sister is missing. She reported it to the police, but feels like they aren't doing enough to find her. She wants to hire a private investigator. I told her about you. Will you help her?"

"Yes, I will. I can see her tomorrow morning if she wants to."

Anissa gave him a big hug and planted a kiss on his lips. "Thank you!" she said.

Merlot smiled at the remembrance of that kiss as he took one last look in an ornate full-length mirror. Satisfied he was ready to take on the world, he grabbed his briefcase from beside the oversize white armchair in his bedroom, walked out of the room and down a hallway. He turned right and entered his living room. Low, comfortable black leather furnishings with white fur pillows, glass-topped tables and odd-shaped floor lamps created an attractive place to come home to and to welcome his guests. He set the security alarm near the door and left the apartment, forgetting about the coffee he'd brewed. Luckily, the pot would shut off automatically, as it did most days of the week, leaving a full pot of perfectly blended, caffeine-laced, expensive java to cool.

Same Day

Chapter Six

Louise Canola—sleep-deprived, distressed, and almost at her wit's end about her sister's disappearance—was thrown another curve ball by Monday morning traffic as huge raindrops pounded against the windshield in a knock-out round with the wipers. Wind blew the rain across her passenger window when cars on either side rolled through water deep enough to create waves. Thunder shattered the quiet, with flashes of lightning electric in their intensity, as she moved into the far right lane to the shoulder, feeling no need to proceed any further without a field of vision. Several drivers joined her, having given up as well. The last thing Louise needed was to have another tornado barreling down with its forceful winds and destructive potential. She silently prayed that the city of Atlanta had gone through its proportion of severe storms for the next 100 years back on

March 14, when the first tornado ever for Atlanta roared through downtown. It had always been her opinion that rainy weather, storms, and tornadoes were not for driving but for staying inside and doing only the things one wanted to do.

"I want to go home, wake up again, Chanel will call, and everything will be back to normal," she said aloud.

But she wasn't going anywhere. Not anytime soon. Interstate 75 had become a parking lot. Traffic—the scourge of humanity. Louise looked at her watch. She was going to be late for this appointment. "If anything can go wrong it will go wrong." Those words floated through her head. *Who said that?* she wondered. *Was it Occam's razor*? For the life of her she could not remember.

With her dark hair, piercing blue eyes, and slender body, Louise was striking. Pretty in a different sense—the combination of everything about her working together—she'd come to think of herself as just okay. Her figure was not flawless, but good nonetheless. And she got double takes often enough to know she appealed to the opposite sex. Not that she was interested. She'd been in love once and that was enough.

She felt like crying as she pulled down the visor and scrutinized her makeup. A concealer hid the bags under her eyes that had developed over the weekend. A little eye shadow, a hint of blush, and a nice red lipstick took the edge off her strained appearance. The anguish she'd experienced the past few days did not yet show on her face, and she certainly did not need to start bawling now. She chided herself for vanity at a time like this, but her mother told her that the best way to fight back tears when you're sad or upset was with expertly applied eye makeup. After making sure that eye shadow, liner, and mascara were just right, any woman knew the damage tears could do.

"Where are you, Chanel?" she said. She felt her emotions going south and her eyes beginning to well up. She pulled a tissue from the box on the passenger seat and gently blotted the corners of her eyes as she noted the time. It was 9:15 a.m. and she was at least ten minutes from her destination and going nowhere fast. Merlot's business card and her cell phone were inside a pocket in her purse. She reached in, pulled both out, and dialed his number.

"Candy Detective Agency," the secretary answered.

"Murphy's Law!" Louise blurted into the phone, still

dabbing at the corners of her eyes. "Oh excuse me, I'm so sorry. I had something else on my mind. This is Louise Canola. I'm stuck in traffic on I-75. Please let Mr. Candy know that I will be late, but I am on my way," Louise said as she realized "If anything can go wrong . . ." was Murphy's Law.

Merlot's receptionist promised to inform Mr. Candy of Louise's delay. Louise disconnected the call and sat back against the smooth tan leather upholstery and closed her eyes. She was going to have to wait out this minihurricane until she could see and be seen. No point in hydroplaning or having an accident in these impossible driving conditions. A thought flashed through her mind. "*Whatsoever things are pure, whatsoever things are lovely and of a good report, think on these things.*" Where had she heard that? The Bible of course. Philippians. Her mother had read that aloud whenever Louise felt down about something. With a stockpile of positive quotes and mantras stored in her subconscious, Louise was always prepared for the barrage of negative thoughts that could trouble a mind.

Chanel Franco, Louise's only sister, telephoned on Friday morning as she sometimes did just to say hello and chat. Her plans for that day had included work of course, and a later meeting with a girlfriend for happy hour. She asked Louise about seeing a movie together on Sunday. That was the last time Louise had heard from her.

She'd tried to call Chanel on Saturday morning and got no answer. By Saturday evening she'd gone by Chanel's house only to find it empty—the bed not having been slept in. She'd called the police immediately and followed their instructions to go to the precinct and file a missing person's report. In addition she had contacted Chanel's friends to see if anyone had heard from her, as well as a news station who agreed to show Chanel's face with an appeal for information about her whereabouts. No one seemed to know anything. And the police had not contacted her. Louise was afraid that something had happened because it was so unlike Chanel not to call. Even when she had overnighters with men, she'd call Louise from wherever she was just to check in. It was routine for the two of them to talk to each other every day—no matter the circumstances. The sisters had made that agreement the day Chanel moved to Atlanta.

As images of her sister lying mangled, bloody, and beaten tried to form in her head, Louise struggled to push them away. She was prone to fits of hyperventilation, and could not allow negative thoughts to take root; otherwise, she'd never be able to breathe or to communicate coherently. Her nerves were almost shattered. A thought popped into her mind, something that someone had once said. "All the bad things that could happen that I've worried about never happened." Louise had no idea who'd said it, but was certain it was an elderly person.

She stared at her phone. Every time it rang she answered on the first ring, hoping to hear Chanel's voice. Should she call the police again? She'd called several times, but decided that she was annoying them. That's when she decided to hire a private investigator. Anissa mentioned Merlot. She must have talked to him immediately because the next thing Louise knew, Anissa was giving her an appointment time this morning. Anissa had told her that if anyone could find Chanel, Merlot Candy was the one person to do it.

Louise had confidence in Anissa. They were the best of friends. They'd met at the gym in a high-intensity step class that gave them an I'm-not-trying-to-do-all-of-this attitude. and they'd walked out at the same time. Almost collapsing from laughter at their lack of stamina, they'd headed for the fitness bar and had a smoothie together. That was nine months ago. Since then they'd become fit enough to make it through the entire class and had developed a strong bond as well. Louise admired Anissa. She had done something that Louise could never have done—stayed three years with an abusive husband without killing him.

Louise had waited till Sunday morning to break the news to her parents. She'd waited as long as she could, for fear of upsetting them. But she knew that somehow, somewhere, Chanel was in trouble and her parents needed to know. Her father had been stoic and clear-headed. Louise was certain that he'd telephoned every person he knew in the United States. Her mother, as expected, became emotional.

Their flight from Paris was scheduled to arrive at 10:00 p.m., and Louise was eager to see them. Her brother, Pierre, who played guitar in a band, had arrived in Atlanta late Saturday night for a gig and ended up staying at Chanel's place. He was upset, too, but this was a working weekend for him. He'd contacted everyone that he and Chanel knew, but got no news. The family would be reunited soon and, with any luck, Chanel would show up with a smile and explanation for everything.

Same day

Chapter Seven

Merlot Candy entered the lobby of 100 Peachtree Street whistling an unrecognizable, peppy tune. He folded the Velcro tab on his umbrella, plopped it into a plastic umbrella bag from the stand just inside the door, and unbuttoned his raincoat. The twenty- minute drive to work had taken twice that long this morning, but Merlot's day would not be ruined because of rain and traffic. As he approached the bank of elevators, he glanced toward the security desk.

"Good morning, Mr. Jasper. How do you like this weather?" he said.

Steve Jasper, a big man—taller and heavier than Merlot—stood behind the counter. He was head of security when Merlot moved in five years ago, and rumor had it that he started out as a janitor when the building opened in 1968.

"Good morning, Mr. Candy. I can deal with a few raindrops, just can't handle another tornado," Steve said.

The first tornado ever in Atlanta had been a shock to many, one that would remain a topic of conversation for some time whenever it stormed.

"It's more than a few, but I think we're safe. Plus it's June. Not tornado weather," Merlot said, glancing back at the huge glass windows. The building had sustained only minor damage when the virgin tornado blew through the city.

"We only had a two percent chance of having a tornado in March, and we got one anyway. Now when it rains hard like this, I watch the winds."

"Have a good day, Mr. Jasper," Merlot said, smiling to himself as he thought of congratulating Steve on being the first human to actually "see" the wind. But Steve didn't have a good sense of humor. Merlot continued toward the bank of elevators, remembering the night of the infamous tornado. It was a scary experience. He was at the Georgia Dome watching the SEC basketball tournament.

When the elevator doors opened, Merlot stepped inside and pushed the button for the nineteenth floor. He began to whistle again as the elevator made its ascent. He was happy working and living downtown. When the doors opened, he emerged and turned toward his office suite. He always felt proud when he stepped into the reception area. A couch and two armchairs in teal-green leather, glass-topped tables, a bookcase filled with volumes of *National Geographic* magazine, and urns of various sizes against a background of pale-green walls welcomed visitors. A huge painting of a fall forest scene with orange, gold, and rust-colored leaves on the trees and carpeting the ground beneath took up the entire wall space behind the receptionist desk.

Maude, his receptionist, had been with him since he opened this office. She sat behind her desk looking glamorous as usual in red. Men from several offices in the building seemed to gravitate to Merlot's office just to have a chat with her as she batted her lashes and giggled.

"Good morning, Maude. How are you today?" Merlot smiled.

"If I was any better I wouldn't be able to stand myself," she said with a wink. "How are you?"

"Fantastic! You're looking especially beautiful this morning. Did you do something different to your hair?"

"Thank you. I thought I'd try platinum for a change. And you're looking quite handsome yourself."

“Thanks. Any calls?”

“Louise Canola phoned to say that she would be late. The rain I guess. This is her first time here, right? She sounded a little off, but that’s all you've got so far. And you did remember that Wesley Cole is coming by after lunch?”

“I surely do. Thanks, Maude.” Merlot continued toward the conference room that was straight ahead behind Maude’s area and turned right down a short hallway to his office. Down the hallway to the left was the office of Glenn Bausch, his other full-time employee.

He hung his coat in the closet and then walked over to take in the view. All the windows in his office space and the conference room faced Peachtree Street. The view included Woodruff Park and the Flatiron Building. An avid fan of history, Merlot was pleased to have topics of discussion for his first time visitors to Atlanta by simply leading them to the windows. He had quite a few pilgrims, as his client list included people from thirty-five states and one client from Brazil. The view from his office allowed him to go back to the Civil War, thanks to the *Atlanta from the Ashes* sculpture in the park, created to celebrate Atlanta’s rebuilding after being burned to the ground. The Flatiron Building was another conversation piece, as it was designed according to the same school of design as New York City's Flatiron Building.

He admired his reflection in the window glass darkened like a mirror by the dark skies outside. He unbuttoned his suit jacket to reveal his shirt and tie that was flecked with the same color green as his shirt with little dashes of pink and gray on a green background. Pink was his favorite color and he had no problem with it. His black patent leather shoes were shined, his nails were manicured, his diamond pinky ring sparkled, and his cologne smelled exciting even to him. He was as impressive as a stately oak in a pine forest—one of a kind, but with panache.

He closed his eyes for a few minutes of meditation on the business of the day. His normal workday involved looking for people who did not want to be found—missing persons, runaway teens, husbands or wives sleeping around, or the occasional petty criminal. And as usual his meditation efforts were sabotaged by wandering thoughts. He was the chief operating detective of his self-made and efficient private detective agency. He'd started out in Boston working for a legal firm. When he crossed paths with the district attorney of Fulton County, the man had been so impressed with Merlot that he'd offered him a job in Atlanta. Merlot was a one-man force until Glenn joined him.

He'd met Glenn for the first time at a party when Merlot was a student at Harvard and Glenn at MIT. Most people at that party were mixing it up, while Glenn stood alone at the bar nursing a beer. Merlot took the seat beside him and ordered a beer before inspecting Glenn's attire, a habit of his whenever he met a man for the first time. Merlot was a true believer in the adage that clothes make the man. In a world of students dressed in jeans, tees, sweats, shorts, and sneakers, Glenn wore neatly pressed brown slacks, a white dress shirt with a brown tie, and sensible brown leather shoes that Merlot felt were just plain unfortunate and subject to cause extreme consternation to any fashion-conscious person. Unfortunate or not, Glenn's choice of apparel indicated to Merlot that the guy was full of self-confidence and wore exactly what he wanted.

Merlot started a conversation and liked him immediately in spite of those sensible shoes. The conversation was about basketball, and Glenn's knowledge was extensive. So was Merlot's. With a dad who had played professional basketball and always had his ball playing buddies around, Merlot, an only son, had had to learn the game. Although he'd learned, he never excelled. He knew he was not going to the NBA, but his skills allowed him to make the team in high school and at Harvard.

Glenn recruited him for one of his pet projects—a basketball camp for middle school boys in the summer. Although good at teaching the fundamentals, Glenn needed someone who could demonstrate what he taught. Merlot entered the gym that first day to find the boys grouped around the floor watching a power-point presentation on a portable screen and listening attentively to Glenn whose enthusiasm held the boys spellbound.

"You must set yourself in the screen far enough away from the defender so that he can see you," Glenn said. He then directed the boys' attention to the players on a short video, pointing out effective screens and highlighting the ineffective ones. "If you are setting the screen, it is the responsibility of the player receiving the screen to move, by faking or cutting. Not you. You don't move."

After the presentation was over Merlot took the boys onto the court and physically showed them what Glenn had just taught. He practiced relentlessly with them over the summer until most of them could plant their feet like a tree growing by the waters—not moving. He went back the next two summers and never forgot about those lessons with the kids.

Eleven years ago he was heading toward baggage claim at the Atlanta airport, when he spotted Glenn heading in the same direction. They walked together and caught up on old times. Glenn shared his passion for working with computers to gain knowledge about all kinds of things, his fascination with research. Merlot offered him a job as his investigator. Graduating summa cum laude, Glenn accepted the offer and proved himself invaluable. As a result, Merlot earned a sterling reputation as a private investigator. He and Glenn worked well together, they liked and respected each other, and both were thorough to the extreme. Sometimes they even thought alike.

At 9:45 a.m. the intercom on his desk buzzed.

"Mr. Candy," his receptionist said. "Louise Canola is here to see you."

"Send her in."

Same Day

Chapter Eight

Merlot turned away from the window and smiled at Louise Canola as she walked toward him. He couldn't help but notice the change in her normal demeanor. He'd met her once before briefly and at the time she seemed a bubbly person with smiles and giggles. She now had a very serious expression on her face. He had not given much thought to the reason she was seeing him until this very moment. She was clearly upset and trying to look normal, but it was not working. He moved toward her and extended his hand. She grasped it like a thirsty person reaching for water.

"Good Morning, Merlot," she said in her husky voice. "I'm so sorry that I'm late. The rain, the traffic—"

"I understand, Louise," Merlot said. "It's nice to see you again. Please, have a seat and tell me what I can do to help you." Merlot gestured toward one of the two red leather armchairs in front of his desk, as he moved behind his desk and sat down in his red leather executive chair.

Louise took a deep breath. “My sister is missing.” Her eyes welled and tears began to stream down her face.

Taking a few tissues and handing them over to her, Merlot became concerned. He leaned back and waited. He always waited for his clients to speak first while he observed their body language and their eyes. Eyes always told the story. Louise’s eyes were filled with pain. Her body, stiff and awkward, attempted to create a shield for the hurt she was feeling.

“I talked to her Friday morning,” Louise continued. “She didn’t call on Saturday morning. Or Sunday. I haven’t heard a word from her and that’s not like her at all. Something’s wrong. She wouldn’t do this unless she was . . . I hate to say it . . . unless something—”

“And when you talked to her on Friday did she say anything about going out of town or to a retreat of some sort?”

“No! She said she had plans for the evening, that she was meeting a friend, and that she’d see me Sunday for a movie. I was on my way out to work, we just had a quick chat." She sobbed, pausing to blow her nose again.

"What do you think has happened to her?"

"I don't know! I don't know what to think. I keep trying to be positive, but I can't get it out of my mind that something bad has happened. She never does this. She always calls to let me know that she's okay. We've always been close, even when we were younger. I would get this weird suffocating feeling. And each time Chanel had either broken her arm, fallen out of a tree and knocked herself out, or rode her bicycle into an embankment." Louise blew her nose and looked into Merlot's eyes. "And I've got that feeling now."

"Chanel. Nice name. Sounds like she's a bit accident prone. Have you checked the hospitals? Her apartment or house to see if she has a guest and is just not answering the phone?"

"Yes. I went to her house Saturday morning after calling and repeatedly getting a voice message. She wasn't there. She hadn't been there. Her bed had not been slept in. I've filed a missing person's report with the police. I've done everything I know to do. I've come to you because I'm desperate and Anissa says that you specialize in finding missing persons." Her voice trailed as she began to wring the tissue in her hand.

"Was she in the habit of making her bed every day?"

"Yes, she is. But not in the habit of getting up early on Saturday morning. She usually sleeps until the afternoon. I know she didn't come home Friday because there were no clothes on the floor—that's how she dresses for a night out. Clothes on the floor from trying on until she finds the right look. Chanel takes Friday night off and so does her house. She knows she can clean up after herself on Saturday. Her house was neat."

As Louise talked, Merlot continued to assess her reactions under his intense scrutiny. He had learned a lot about why people behave the way they do and how they think from his mother who was a doctor of psychology. Watching someone closely often disarmed them. Louise held his gaze as long as he held hers, but her body language said it all. She was truly distressed.

"Is there any reason that she would not come home and consequently feel justified in not telling you anything?"

Louise didn't answer right away. Instead she focused on the big windows, appearing to be in deep thought. After a few seconds, she turned to Merlot, the tears momentarily stopped.

"If you mean a man—if you're saying she ran away with a man to . . . I don't know . . . start a new life, if she somehow fell in love and lost her mind—the answer is no. On the other hand if you mean she was arrested for a DUI or for shoplifting or some other crazy thing, the answer to your question, no matter how you mean it, is no, no, NO!"

It was Merlot's turn to pause and think. Louise's response indicated that her sister was neither impulsive nor prone to mischief. Two scenarios ruled out. He waited, confident she had more to say.

"We have a brother, Pierre, who drops in unexpectedly when he's in town for a while," she continued. "He stays with Chanel when he's here. He tried calling her too and scouted around some of her hangouts. Like you just suggested, he thinks she's out on a long weekend. But Chanel would not do this. If she wants to do something, she does it because she knows she doesn't have to hide it from anyone. Something is wrong."

"Okay you've convinced me. I'll do everything that I can to find her. The next thing is my fee," Merlot added as he handed her one of his business portfolios.

"That's a good segue," Louise said. She opened the folder and carefully examined the itemized list of fees, services, testimonials, and contractual agreements. Merlot, in the meantime, pushed the buzzer on his desk. A male voice answered.

"Glenn, when you get a chance I need to see you," he spoke into the intercom. He looked over as Louise opened her purse and pulled out her checkbook.

"I see here that you accept a retainer up front," she said.

"Yes. You're billed for everything else."

"I appreciate your agreeing to help and I hope you find her soon." Louise quickly wrote a check and placed it on Merlot's desk.

"I want you to sit down with my assistant and answer his questions thoroughly. Don't hold back anything. The least little thing could provide a big clue. Do you have a picture of Chanel? And by the way, is her last name Canola as well?" Merlot asked.

"Yes, I do have a picture, and no, her last name is Franco. She did that married-too-young-got-a-divorce-but-held-on-to-his-last-name-thing," Louise answered. She took out her wallet, removed five photos, and gave them to Merlot. He looked at them and did a double take.

"My goodness, has anyone ever told you that you and your sister could pass for twins?" he asked with a twinkle in his eye.

"You wouldn't believe how many," Louise responded halfheartedly.

Merlot's weak attempt at humor failed. Louise was upset, and there was no need to further complicate the situation by trying to change her mood. He looked into the smiling face of Chanel Franco.

What rabbit hole have you fallen into? Merlot thought to himself as he gazed at the photos. Chanel had been gone for two days—and counting. The first place to look would be the hospitals. She could be on a slab labeled as Jane Doe or she could be a patient under the same name suffering from some sort of confusion, disorientation, head trauma, or memory loss brought on by an accident. Louise, like any caring family member, would shy away from the prospect of death or injury. She'd gone to the police who would go through an immediate routine that included hospital checks after the obligatory twenty-four hours missing, but this was going on the third day. Odds are they weren't visiting hospitals today. So that would be Merlot's first mission.

"Thank you, Louise," Merlot said as he stood and approached her. "I'm going to do my best to find your sister. I don't like to make guarantees, but trust me to handle this like I'm looking for my own brother or sister.

Come with me and I'll get you started with my assistant. And try not to worry." Merlot led Louise down the hall and past the conference room to a smaller office where Glenn Bausch sat, hovering over a computer. He looked up as Merlot entered.

"Good morning, Glenn. This is Louise Canola. We're going to find her sister. She's going to answer all of your questions so we know everything we need to know in order to do that."

Glenn stood eagerly, grasping Louise's extended hand and shaking it vigorously. "So good to meet you," he said. He had on brown pants, a white shirt with a brown and white tie, and sensible brown shoes. His brown hair was neatly cropped above his ears and the shrewdness in his brown eyes could not be missed in spite of his glasses. He appraised Louise quietly.

“Nice to meet you, Glenn,” Louise smiled.

“Please, sit down,” Glenn responded, pulling out a chair. Louise sat as Merlot left the two of them alone.

Two hours later, after Louise had gone, Glenn placed a file on Merlot’s desk and sat down in one of the comfortable leather chairs. He stared ahead as Merlot perused the pages. Once finished, Merlot regarded his friend and partner.

“Okay. Thank you very much. You go do what you do, and I’ll hit the street. I’m going to the hospital first, and then I’m going to visit this friend of hers, Mona Challis,” Merlot said.

“Roger that. By the way, Louise was pretty forthcoming. I may not have to dig very deep, but I’m on it. And you just may emerge victorious at the hospital. It’s been almost three days, and my sources reveal that a Jane Doe was brought in to the burn unit at Grady early this morning,” Glenn said.

“Really? I’d hate like hell for it to be Chanel. But if it is, this will set a record for us—shortest case ever. See you later.” As usual Merlot was confident that he’d find something. What he didn’t know was that it would be diabolically different from anything he’d ever encountered.

Same Day

Chapter Nine

Peach Grove, Georgia, twenty-one miles northwest of Atlanta, was incorporated in 1837 on land filled with fertile groves of luscious peach trees that inspired the name. Located in Cotton County it was a small mecca for some of the most affluent people in Georgia. The crime rate was nil and the mayor of the city wanted to keep it that way. An influx of citizens seeking a quiet place to live where they could walk along the streets at night without fear and raise their families had created a need for more housing. The newest effort to fill that need was the Mint Leaf Manor complex, considered by city leaders as prime real estate.

Arriving at the precinct, Dennis Cane dashed from his car to the entrance of the Peach Grove Police Station. Dripping wet from the rain, he pushed open the double glass doors and walked in. Gladys Duff, the receptionist and desk clerk when necessary, spotted him and quickly began to fan the smoke in the air around her head. Smoking was off limits and she knew it. She ground the cigarette butt out and began to explain.

"Sorry, Lt. Cane. I was going to take a smoke break, but it's raining, and—"

"You've got to give the cigarettes up, Gladys. And we've got a covered area," Dennis said.

"I know. It won't happen again. Where's your umbrella?"

"My umbrella was a casualty to that heavy downpour this morning. I had to tread the waters with just my hat and overcoat."

"My God, hasn't it rained! You get out of that wet coat and I'll see if I can round you up a fresh hot cup of coffee. I know you like it black. And I can get you a dry uniform if you want." Gladys stood, straightened her yellow blouse, and pushed a few strands of brunette hair away from her kind brown eyes. She smiled, clearly ready to do anything to make up for being caught red-handed breaking the no-smoking rules.

Dennis paused and looked at her. "Thanks, Gladys.

Don't worry about a uniform. Those are in my past. I'll just take the coffee. I didn't mean to snap at you. You know I love you."

"That's okay. I know I need to quit. It's just so hard. But on a different note, I heard you had an emergency at Mint Leaf Manor," she said over her shoulders as she walked away in pursuit of the promised coffee.

"Indeed we did. I'm just coming from there." Dennis continued toward his office. He'd stayed long enough to supervise the crime scene investigative team as they erected tents and roped off the area in order to protect the integrity of the crime scene and begin the arduous task of gathering evidence.

He sighed as he walked past Peter Millet's desk. Peter was the desk sergeant who secretly harbored a desire to be a news reporter—or so it seemed. The man was highly competent at telling everyone what was going on in the world, but slightly less competent when it came to police work. Hence the desk. But Peter could be trusted. The one thing that he was good at was listening and never repeating what he heard unless he was told to do so. Dennis loved that about him.

"Good morning, Peter," Dennis said as he continued to his office. Peter looked up, his signature lopsided smile, unkempt hair, and wrinkled uniform making him the same today as every other day.

"Good morning, Lt. Cane. I heard about that vic at the fire early this morning."

Dennis couldn't help but notice the morning newspapers stacked on one corner of Peter's desk, while his computer screen showed the headlines from an online news feed. But that was Peter—he read the news, made coffee, handled walk-ins when Gladys yelled at him, answered the phones, and sometimes filled in for squad patrol.

"Any more word on our burn victim?" Dennis asked, looking back over his shoulder. The paramedics had not been hopeful about the woman's chances for survival.

"Joe checked in from the hospital. He said the woman's still alive. The doctors were working on her at the time he called." Joe was the officer Dennis had posted there to maintain a watch near the woman. Just in case whoever tried to kill her came back to finish the job.

"Is she able to talk at all?"

"Don't know. Joe didn't say anything about that."

"Thanks, Peter. Anything in the newspaper about her?" Dennis knew the answer before he asked. *The Peach Grove Sentinel* was a selective newspaper. Any incidents involving high-profile residents, or God forbid, an attempted murder were either not reported or so whitewashed as to read like a fairy tale. Bad news could not be allowed to discourage future residents from moving to this small metropolis.

"Not yet. The evening paper will carry the story."

"Let's hope she pulls through. She may be able to tell us who did this to her."

"Good thing Joe's there. He'll let us know if there's any change," Peter added.

Dennis reached the door to his office, opened it, and entered. He removed his hat and placed it on the coat rack in the corner. He hung his wool-blend overcoat that reeked of soggy wool on a hanger. He stomped his feet on the tile floor to shake off some of the mud from his shoes and the bottom of his pants legs, resisting the urge to go back home and change clothes. It was his own doing. That pole-like object that he had discovered in the mud would go to the lab for close examination of the fibers clearly visible on one end. Perhaps this time he'd get some evidence he could use.

He opened the blinds, ran his fingers through his tousled blond hair, and focused his steely blue eyes on the weather outside. The weather report had been spot-on for the last few weeks. This hiccup that quickly became a deluge, turning his city into a watery blue blur, had been a surprise. But his theory about a torch murderer with a schedule that included a death on June 16 was on point. He had not expected it to occur before sunrise. And he had not expected the intended victim to live. And neither, he was certain, had the killer.

"And I was right." Dennis said softly. "I was right!" he repeated aloud.

"Right about what?" Gladys asked as she walked toward him with a steaming mug in her hand.

"Just a theory," Dennis replied as he turned from the window in time to take the coffee.

"I made a fresh pot." Gladys beamed, showing fairly white teeth, considering the damage that nicotine can do.

"Thank you, Gladys. What would I do without you?" He lifted the mug to his lips, feeling the heat, and took a huge swallow of the hot brew. "Just like I like it!"

"You're welcome. Can I do anything else? Like comment on your theory?"

"Yes. When those reports come in, let me know."

"Will do," she said.

Dennis took another sip of the coffee and turned toward the window once more. His torch murderer theory would have to remain his secret for now.

Same Day

Chapter Ten

Northern born and educated, Dennis began his career as a crime scene investigator in Washington, DC. But politics, snow, and cold weather made his days and nights longer than they should have been. With no family ties, Dennis woke up one morning and decided to move to Atlanta. He had some money put away in addition to a modest inheritance from his parents. He moved to Atlanta in 2002, and accepted a job with the Atlanta Police Department where he was promoted to homicide detective within a year. After that promotion he ran smack-dab into politics again. To survive he gave one hundred percent of his effort to his job.

Helping to bring murderers to justice gave Dennis a sense of purpose. The loss of his parents had put death in perspective for him, driving home two facts—life was preciously short and death was unpredictable. The audacity of killers to think that life was something to be snatched away by their particular whims was a pet peeve that quickly turned into unfettered contempt. He was fascinated and repulsed by them. Serial killers were a particular thorn in his side because they appeared to kill for entertainment, self-fulfillment, and without empathy or remorse—making them the most difficult of all killers to catch. Some were organized, others haphazard—all were elusive.

Dennis's thoughts traveled back to June 16, 2005, as he stared out the window. He stood in a rundown neighborhood in front of an abandoned house that had nearly burned to the ground. When the flames were put out, a human corpse was discovered inside. It was common knowledge that most people who burned to death under those circumstances were on the lower end of the economic and intelligence scale; otherwise, they would have been someplace else or not done something that stupid. Dennis's partner and lead detective at the time, Gus Alfred, said so.

"Okay. What kind of person would have been caught in this neighborhood, in this house, in a fire and not had enough sense to get out?" he'd asked Dennis. "Somebody with nowhere else to go and who was stupid enough to get stoned out his or her mind and fall asleep, that's who."

"So you think this was a homeless person?" Dennis asked.

"Yes. With a bad smoking habit."

"I think I'll wait and see what the fire investigators say," Dennis replied. "I learned a lot about those guys when my parents died in a hotel fire."

"I'm sorry, man. When did that happen?"

"I was twenty-three and I really don't want to talk about it. But I found out that those fire investigators are just as thorough as we are. Most of them have worked as firefighters."

The arson investigators ruled it arson and murder, as the fire was incendiary and the accelerant was gasoline. The medical examiner could not tell if the person was alive or dead when the fire started because all the lung tissue had been burned away. He could tell that the victim was a woman by her pelvic bones.

"We got nothing, Cane," Gus announced a few days later.

He came to this conclusion after exhaustive efforts that

included questioning onlookers at the scene, canvassing the area for someone who might have seen something, and reading the reports from the crime scene techs that contained nothing. The few arson suspects that fit the MO had alibis. None had ever been involved with murder. No witnesses. No leads. No evidence except the body and a platinum ring with the letters *MP* engraved inside. Nothing with which to prosecute an offender if they had one. Faced with another human being who'd died in an inferno, Dennis didn't want to let go so easily.

"We just need to dig a little more," Dennis insisted.

"If you want to dig more, be my guest. As far as I'm concerned this case has gone cold."

"Just give me a little time. I've seen cases like this turn on a dime."

"Like I said, be my guest."

Dennis reread the arson report and learned the investigators determined that the seat of the fire—the area where the heat was most intense and where the highest concentration of accelerant was used—was in the second room of the four-room row house. Several fires had destroyed houses in that same neighborhood, which would have added credence to the supposition that it was an accident were it not for the presence of gas. It seemed like the neighborhood had been chosen deliberately.

"I think I'll go back over the crime scene," Dennis said to Gus, who was busy hunting down an informant for another case.

As a crime scene investigator, Dennis had learned to look longer and harder, and that's why he went back to see if anything had been overlooked. He started with the outside because he believed the arson investigators had done a thorough job on what remained of the house. Whoever started the fire probably escaped unseen from the back of the house because that would have been the safest route according to the arson report, which detailed the way the flames moved through the house.

He found a path from the backyard that came out into an alley near an old warehouse. He retraced his steps and broke through another path, checking the bushes and trees for snags of fabric. His job description demanded that he keep tweezers, gloves, and small envelopes with seals on his person. For good measure he also had a camera. He found himself in the alley again as he snapped photos along the way. The arsonist/murderer could have escaped down one of these paths. At the end of the alley concrete barriers kept motorized vehicles from entering, but a person could come and go on foot through a narrow opening between the end of the barriers and the warehouse building. After a thorough search he found a black thread caught on one of the cement barricades. He took two snapshots of the thread where it lay stuck in the uneven texture of the concrete, then removed it with tweezers and sealed it in an envelope. He wasn't sure if it meant anything, but he was taking no chances. He drove back to the precinct, filled out a second investigative report, and took the thread and the camera to the property room. He was confident that this evidence would be enough to keep working the case.

But he was wrong. Unfortunately, the shooting that occurred in the Fulton County Courthouse in downtown on March 11 that ended with the death of a judge, a court reporter, a sheriff's deputy, and a federal agent had left its aftereffects. A major incident like that created an atmosphere where it became more expedient for detectives to work cases with some solvable potential. Why put an unnecessary strain on manpower and resources on a police force that was already reeling from the effects of four senseless murders by a belabored investigation into a case that lacked the required ingredients to prosecute? Like clues, a suspect, or a motive? The case went cold and Dennis put the burn victim out of his mind.

Until later, when the same thing happened again twice, and he discovered the killer had a pattern and a routine.

Same Day

Chapter Eleven

On June 24, 2006, Dennis happened to hear a news broadcast about a female body being found in Jolting County, approximately twenty miles east of Atlanta. The remains were found inside a burned- down house. This news caught his attention. Even though the crime had occurred outside of Dennis's jurisdiction, he decided to drop by the Jolting Police Department. A woman he'd dated a few times worked in the property room there, and she flashed a bright smile when she saw him. It didn't take long before he charmed her into giving him the name of the investigating officer in charge of the case. Not wanting to be a mere opportunist, he asked her out to dinner. She was thrilled and actually arranged for Dennis to meet the detective, Joe

Brady, a middle-aged, towheaded guy who, as it turned out, was eager to talk.

"I've got nothing to go on in this case," he said.

"We had a case like that last year," Dennis explained. "A woman burned to death in an abandoned house with gasoline used as the accelerant. It's a cold case because we didn't have anything either. Nothing but a black thread."

The detective's expression changed. He scrambled through some papers on his desk and located a file. He opened it and gave it a quick scan.

"A black thread was found on the gate leading into the yard of this house. You know that could be something," he said.

They both agreed to have the threads examined in their respective labs and get back to each other. Both lab reports identified the thread as the type used in leotards—90 percent polyester and 10 percent spandex. DNA tests matched. A nationwide search through the police database came back with negative results. Whoever wore the garment that left the threads had no police record—a ghost. Another dead end.

On June 16, 2007, another burned female body was found in a huge sewer drain pipe in a deserted area of Wilder

County, thirty miles west of Atlanta. Through several channels Dennis managed to reach out to the detective in charge of that case, Darcy Goodman, a serious investigator.

"Good to meet you, Dennis. How can I help you?"

"I wanted to see if you have a suspect in your arson/murder case?"

"I have absolutely nothing. No suspect, no motive, no clues. We can't identify the victim. The medical examiner is working on tracking down a knee replacement. A foreign job. All we've got is a damn black thread!"

He and Darcy agreed to have the threads tested in their respective labs and get back to each other later. The testing revealed that the threads were identical and had a high probability of coming from the same source. Unfortunately, there was no DNA. Which meant a serious lack of evidence to support joining forces.

"I can't deny that this looks like the same person is responsible, but what can we do with nothing?" Darcy asked.

She picked up a stack of folders on her desk with both hands, and broke eye contact with Dennis. She concentrated on stacking, straightening, and tapping the folders against the desktop. It seemed that she was ready to occupy herself with something else. Dennis got the hint, but he couldn't leave without giving it one more shot.

"You're right. I agree. But one thing I know to be true about murder is that it is contagious. He's getting good at it. He won't stop until he's caught. And I'll bet these victims are just the ones we know about. I think we have a serial killer who's working the metro area like a pro."

"I don't know about that, but I know I've got murder cases with identified victims and real suspects with records and fingerprints. These will have to take precedence right now. Sorry I can't be of more help. Thank you for sharing. It makes me want to get this perp badly."

She opened a folder, took out a piece of paper and immediately began to type in a number on the phone. The meeting was over. Dennis stood and took a deep breath.

"Thank you for your help. I'm a patient man. I can wait. This guy is going to make a mistake one day."

He knew there were hardly ever any coincidences where murder was concerned. Ironically, the one common thread in this small chain of evidence that spread out over three jurisdictions was literally threads. Black threads. There was no way anyone with authority was going to form a joint task force, not on a case hanging by threads. That's when he became aware of the pattern that was beginning to form. But a pattern is not evidence.

This time the killer made a mistake. He tried to kill someone in Dennis's jurisdiction. He had failed. Unless the woman died. If not he either had to finish the job and stay on schedule or never kill again. And Dennis didn't think he'd stop on his own volition. This killer was determined. His schedule called for another murder to be committed on June 24. Unless Dennis could stop him.

He finished his coffee and pulled the crime scene checklist from his inside jacket pocket and turned to his computer. In less than thirty minutes, he'd completed his investigative report and clicked to send it to cyberspace where all reports were filed. He glanced out of the window again and saw the sun. He was ready to take the next step.

"I'm on my way to Grady," he said to Peter as he passed his desk.

The woman in the hospital could shed some light on this whole thing and hopefully identify the person responsible.

Same Day

Chapter Twelve

Grady Memorial Hospital—Grady to Atlanta residents—had gained a reputation for being one of the best level one trauma centers in the United States. Most doctors and the resident staff come to the hospital from Emory University School of Medicine and Morehouse University School of Medicine. When Jane Doe arrived in the emergency room, the trauma team immediately went to work. An IV line for fluids and plasma was hooked up; a nurse gave an injection for tetanus; the patient's temperature was checked and documented; and the patient was checked for spinal cord and head injuries. No trauma was found. The emergency room doctors had done their duty—they'd begun to save her life. Their familiarity with burns let them know that the red, black, brown, and white quilt-like skin indicated the patient needed intensive care that could only be provided in the burn unit.

The burn unit team consisted of three doctors—two being surgeons—four nurses, four techs, and the residents. With the exception of the residents, everyone was experienced. Dr. Vincent Salada, the attending surgeon on the unit, read the report handed in by the emergency paramedics who were first responders. Jane Doe was an unidentified female found at a construction site shortly after being set on fire with gasoline. He noted that a liter of saline had been given on the way to the hospital. He carefully reviewed the documentation of the care received in the emergency room. The next step was to locate additional access to veins and arteries for fluids and medication to enter the body, and blood and other fluids to come out. Catheters would do the job, but avoiding going in through burned tissue was paramount. He instructed the burn tech to go in just below the collarbone on the right side where the patient had not suffered burns. Almost simultaneously Dr. Salada moved to circumvent one of the most dangerous conditions that result from a huge burn—suffocation. He performed a bronchoscopy, looking down into the patient's throat for evidence of smoke or soot. He sighed with relief when he saw a clear airway. That was a good sign. But her body was puffed up, which meant that edema was setting in. The woman's swollen lips, eyelids, and mouth were completely out of proportion as if an invisible air pump was slowly pumping air inside. The next danger could come from hypovolemia, the most common type of shock, caused by loss of blood. A patient could bleed visibly or internally, by fluids trickling out of blood vessels into tissues, which could lead to a drop in blood pressure. Vital signs would have to be monitored and more plasma and fluids given in order to keep shock at bay.

As the attending, Dr. Salada's major role was to make a diagnosis by determining the depth and the total body surface area of the burn. He drew in a deep breath as he began to examine the body inch by inch—front to back, head to toe. Unfortunately, the burns on the left shoulder and arm were circumferential—a wraparound formation of dead skin and tissue, or eschar as it was clinically called—requiring immediate removal before everything underneath began to swell. Some of the burns looked as though they were partial thickness, but it would take some time to know for sure. He determined that the burns covered thirty-five percent of her total body surface, mostly on the left side. The right side of her body suffered only minor burns, probably due to the way her body was positioned during the fire. The odor of gasoline was pungent, and yet she was in relatively stable condition at the time being. Stable but still very ill and in need of immediate attention. He scheduled the operating room and then gathered his staff together to run through what needed to be done.

Hours later the patient was wheeled from the OR swathed in bandages, her left arm extended straight out from her side, held in place by a splint. She was placed in the one empty bed in the Bacterial Controlled Nurses Unit, the intensive care unit for severely burned patients. Centuries ago, physicians learned that burns are not merely injuries, but a complex disease that signals all-out war inside and outside the body—bacteria being the major enemy. The bandages on her arm would remain for the next five days, but the rest of her burns would undergo dressing changes twice daily. It would take time to see which area presented urgency for the next round of skin grafts. The leg was his guess, but not enough healthy skin remained.

Same Day

Chapter Thirteen

Dennis Cane showed his badge to the receptionist in the emergency room and was directed to the burn unit on the third floor of the west wing. He got off the elevator, turned left, and approached double doors. The sign on the wall near the door directed him to push the buzzer for entrance.

"May I help you?" asked a female voice.

"Yes, I'm Lt. Dennis Cane, Peach Grove Police Department. I'm here to see a patient that was brought in early this morning."

He heard a loud buzz and the doors swung open. He walked forward, not at all relishing the sight of burned patients. Dennis hated hospitals. On the left, to his relief, was an empty room that looked like a place for physical therapy. To his right a small empty office. He relaxed a bit.

He continued to the end of the hallway and turned right,

heading toward a reception area. On the wall, directly in front of the counter hung a slab of marble engraved with the words "Grady Burn Center welcomes you." A young woman dressed in a blue T-shirt and pants stood looking quizzically at him.

"You the police officer?" she asked.

"Yes, I am." Dennis held his badge in hand so she could see it.

At that moment a woman wearing a blue lab jacket over a dress, her feet clad in the standard white nurse's shoes, came from one of the rooms into the hallway.

"Claire, we need to get this bed changed in here,' she said, indicating the room from which she'd come. "Now would be good."

The young receptionist made a move toward the room and then, as if in afterthought, turned to Dennis. "If you see a nurse, she'll help you. Anyone dressed in white," Claire said as she rushed into the room with the other woman.

Dennis stood there, looking around. It was quiet. That was a good sign. No screaming or agonizing moans. The desk behind the counter was more like a countertop and was very neat. Blue, white, red, and black binders stood at attention in the left corner near the wall; next to that was some type of ticker tape machine, balanced on several rolls of toilet tissue; a clipboard, a phone, and a fire alarm mounted on the wall; a fax machine; a computer and a few files. The wall above contained a large framed print of a green lush valley with the sun setting in the background. In front of him on the counter lay a binder opened to a page labeled "Burn Center Staffing and Treatment." Closer inspection revealed physician and patient names with their diagnosis and treatment plan. Dennis was about to turn a page and read further when a woman wearing white came around the corner pulling a red wagon. In the wagon was a young boy about seven years old with bandages on his arms and legs.

"Are you being helped?" she asked.

"Maybe you can. I'm from Peach Grove Police Department." Dennis showed her his badge.

"Okay . . ." the nurse said.

"A burned woman was brought in early this morning. I'd like to see her, please."

"You must mean the woman that was airlifted in. I'm afraid you'll have to speak to one of the doctors. If you'll come with me, I'll show you where you can wait."

"But I can see her?"

"Not without a doctor's permission." She smiled down at the child in the wagon who chattered away about something in the book he held. She nodded her head in agreement with whatever he'd said as she led Dennis to the empty office he'd passed on his way in.

"A doctor will be with you shortly," she said, continuing through the double doors with her patient in tow.

Dennis sat down. There was nothing on the desk and nothing on the wall. Not a single thing to focus his attention on while waiting. He reached for a peppermint and glanced at his watch.

Fifteen minutes later, a doctor appeared. He was tall, thin, and about forty years old. His hair was beginning to gray at the temples. He looked tired. Armed with a clipboard and a stethoscope, he focused pale-blue eyes on Dennis.

"I'm Dr. Salada. May I help you?" he asked with a slight accent to which Dennis could not attach a country of origin.

"Yes, I'm Lt. Cane." Dennis once again showed his badge. "I understand a woman came in early this morning with burn injuries. She was found on a construction site."

"Yes, Jane Doe."

"No identification? I'd like to speak with her, please."

"That's not possible at this time. She has some third- and fourth-degree burns and she is heavily sedated—almost comatose."

"Do you think she'll survive? I really need to question her, to find out who did this to her."

"We are working as diligently as we can to save her life. Only time will tell. If you have no questions for me, I'd like to get back to her."

Dennis sighed. "No, and I apologize for the disturbance. Thank you, Doctor."

Dr. Salada nodded his head, turned abruptly, and walked away.

Same Day

Chapter Fourteen

Dennis was a little discouraged because the woman was unable to talk—to even give her name, much less say who had done this to her. He flipped his little notepad closed and walked toward the double doors, reminding himself that at least she was alive. He heard the buzzer and the doors opened, allowing the nurse with the little boy in the wagon to pass through. She smiled at him as the child continued to prattle on. "Have a good day," she said over her shoulder.

"You, too," Dennis replied, shoving his notepad back into his pockets, his eyes cast down as he almost collided with a man.

"Excuse me," Dennis said. When he looked up at the taller man, a smile spread from ear to ear. "Great Scott! Winston Merlot Candy! How the hell are you?"

Merlot did a double take, recognizing his fellow

teammate from high school. Dennis Cane had been the point guard when the team won the state championship.

"Dennis Cane! How the hell are you?" The two men embraced giving each other solid pats on the back. They stood apart, each appraising the other.

"I'm doing great. What are you doing here?"

"I live here. I came here two years out of college and I've been here ever since," Merlot replied. "What about you? Don't tell me you live here, too."

"I lived in Atlanta for a while and worked for the police department as a homicide detective. Now I live and work in Peach Grove."

"The suburbs! With a wife, two kids and one on the way, a mortgage, and a dog?"

"No to everything except the mortgage. I do have a house. I got a great deal on a foreclosure. I couldn't believe my luck. That was one of my dreams. My own home with a lawn and everything. I love going home to my house!" Dennis grinned.

"Show a little more enthusiasm, will you."

"Get this. The day I moved in, the newspaper that was delivered to my front door was filled with headlines about the sudden death of the then-police chief."

"Don't tell me. You're the chief of police?"

"No. Listen to me. About a month later I was doing my duty as a new citizen by accepting an invitation to attend a town hall meeting where I was introduced to some key individuals, including the new police chief and the mayor. After some small talk and handshakes, it was suggested that I just might be the right man to head up their homicide division."

"So you're the chief of homicide?"

"I'm the lieutenant of homicide. With two other officers who have no experience whatsoever with murder investigation."

"That sounds like a challenge." Merlot patted Dennis on the shoulder.

"It's too easy. But what about you? It's good to see you. I always thought you'd end up playing pro basketball like your dad."

"How do you know I'm not?" Merlot asked.

Dennis laughed. "I keep up with the game and I haven't seen your name on any team roster. That's how I know."

"Speaking of basketball, who do you think is going to

win? Lakers or Celtics?"

"The Celtics! As long as they keep playing smart, it's all over." Dennis grinned. "The team is already up three games. They'd have to try to lose to not take that trophy."

"I like the Celtics, too."

"So what are you up to these days? How do you earn your paycheck?" Dennis asked.

"I play hide and seek," Merlot smiled.

The two men moved over to allow the nurse to come through with her wagon again. The little boy stopped his chattering long enough to stare at Merlot, standing almost a foot taller than Dennis and a giant from his tiny viewpoint.

"Hide and seek?" Dennis asked, looking puzzled.

"I'm a private investigator. I look for people who don't want to be found. And you're a homicide detective? Not at all what I'd thought you'd be doing either. How's that working out for you?"

"I got myself assigned to homicide in a town where no one has committed murder for the six months that I've been there. Until this morning. Someone tried and failed." Dennis's face suddenly became serious. "Say, let's have a cup of coffee and talk over old times. And maybe I can tell you a secret."

Merlot sighed. "I wished I could, but I'm on a case. I'm looking for a missing woman and I heard that they brought in a Jane Doe to the burn unit early this morning. I wanted to see if she's my lady."

"The burn victim? Found at a construction site?" Dennis asked.

Merlot opened his notebook and checked his notes. "Yes," he replied. He looked perplexed as he regarded his old friend. "How do you know that?"

"Because I just came in to see her. She's the woman somebody tried to kill this morning. The doctor's not letting anybody near her right now. She's in pretty bad shape. I came in because technically she belongs to my jurisdiction. The doctor says she's in a coma. You're not going to be able to see her either. So come on, let's go. We can catch up on old times. Plus I need to talk to someone and you could always keep a secret."

Merlot hesitated, torn between continuing his task or changing midstream, Dennis guessed. Minutes later he smiled.

"A secret, huh? That's just my game." He turned to fall instep beside Dennis.

Dennis beamed. It would be nice to catch up. The two had had that bond that comes from being teammates. Merlot had been his go-to guy with the ball. Perhaps he wouldn't mind being a sounding board for a little while.

Same Day

Chapter Fifteen

Seated on a couch in the unlit room made darker by the rain clouds outside, Michael, somewhat tired, took a long swig of lukewarm coffee and stared at the television. The news reporter was finishing up. “Breaking news! An unidentified woman was airlifted to Grady Burn Unit early this morning.” The reporter went on to describe the area where the female had been found, reveal that an anonymous caller had reported the body, announce there was no further news of the woman’s condition, and make a plea for anyone with information to come forward. Michael’s brow line wrinkled in deep thought.

An anonymous caller? Someone was out there. But who? If they saw the body, could they have seen me?

The thought caused his hands to quiver involuntarily, resulting in spilled coffee. He sprang up to make a quick trip down the dark hallway to the kitchen and retrieve a towel, allowing time for sensible thinking to return. Odds were the person had not seen him, because the reporter would have given a description and pasted a police sketch asking for help in finding the responsible party.

The missing pouch that contained the matches, the torch lighter, the extra gloves, and the paper could possibly complicate matters. *Did it fall off with the effort to push the woman's body down into the drainage ditch? Could it have gotten tangled in the tarp somehow? But surely there was nothing inside it to incriminate him.* Michael relaxed a little knowing there was no incriminating evidence inside the pouch—no fingerprints or DNA because he always wore gloves. All he needed to do now was think. The woman was still alive at Grady Hospital in the burn center, but she should not be able to tell them anything because of the Rohypnol. As he mopped up the spilled coffee, he deliberated the reasons for losing the pouch. That had never happened before. Why now? If they found her, chances are they found the pouch, too. How could something so purposeful and dedicated end like this? It could not. It just would not. If a smart detective put two and two together . . .

Oh God . . .oh God . . . oh God, please step in and reorder everything!

Michael felt his heart begin to beat like it would burst forth and splatter blood all over the darkened room. And just as quickly the peace that "passeth all understanding" overcame him and reasoning returned.

One would have to know to understand. Not knowing would make it impossible to put it all together. All was still well.

It had not been an easy decision to begin killing. And one wanted to be good at it, thus it took practice. A little blip like the rain and losing the pouch were just small obstacles that one encountered on the way to a successful climax. Soon the first stage of the plan would be over. Michael sighed.

Living a life filled with heartache, pain, and mistreatment could cause one to hate. To hate the sound of a voice, a touch, a smell, at times even the sight of something or someone that triggered a memory laced with fear and revulsion. But God had erased the fear, the hatred, and the revulsion, and replaced them with righteousness and entitlement. A child of the living God was supposed to have the best in life and to be joyous and free. And so it was for a time. Until the day that hatred entered again and morphed into revenge. And the plan was born. Now all that remained was the strength to carry it out.

Of the four elements—earth, air, fire and water—only fire and water could completely destroy or eradicate trace evidence. One had to know these things in order to successfully kill a person and leave nothing behind to trace back to oneself. If one wanted to remain free. Michael had chosen fire as the weapon because fire purged before destruction occurred. Plus he had no desire to linger and watch someone drown. What if they could swim? That would complicate everything. When a person was ignited after being soaked with gasoline, they were going to die. Nothing could save them. Michael had studied enough to know that even if a victim survived being set on fire, they would not remember anything. The drugs used in a hospital to ease the pain never failed to induce amnesia. Ironically, water was the element that could put an end to fire. That unexpected downpour!

Michael began to pray silently. After a few minutes he stopped praying and remained perfectly still. Waiting for the answer that always came.

There it is. Thank you, God.

An idea was forming. No use crying over spilled coffee and rain any longer. It was time to take action. And Michael knew just what to do.

Same Day

Chapter Sixteen

Merlot took a sip of his coffee as he pondered what he'd just heard. Dennis believed that a mysterious serial killer was on the loose in the Atlanta metropolitan area. Burning his victims to death on the 16th and 24th of June for the past three years. It sounded crazy to Merlot. He really thought a lot more information was needed before drawing a conclusion. But that was Dennis's occupation—making sense out of crazy. Merlot didn't look for killers. He limited himself to finding missing persons and occasionally spying on unfaithful spouses. A job he'd been doing for years and only once had he encountered a dead body. He could tell that Dennis was really involved in the serial killer incidents, but it had nothing to do with Merlot. He swished the coffee in his mouth as he tried to come up with a tactful response.

"So tell me, what evidence do you have to support this theory?"

"Black thread," Dennis replied, looking him straight in the eyes.

"So your theory is literally hanging by a thread?" Merlot began to laugh. "That's funny!"

"It's not funny when the same black threads were found in three separate instances at the scene of a female body being burned to death. In three different jurisdictions. All threads were the type used in leotards—90 percent polyester and 10 percent spandex. DNA tests on two of the threads matched. And all of the women were doused with gasoline." With his hands raised, Dennis looked at Merlot as if what he'd just said cleared it all up.

"You're right. That's not funny. But doesn't that mean you can now find out who is responsible?" Merlot asked.

"If the nationwide search through the database had come back with results. He's a ghost."

"So three women, burned to death, three jurisdictions. Can't you guys get together and form one of those task forces?"

"There's no way anyone will authorize a joint task force with two black threads. And how do you know about task forces? I thought you didn't do murder?"

"I watch TV and I have associates on the police force. Why wouldn't they? You've got means. You even have DNA."

"Just like everybody who watches TV, you think that DNA is the magic potion to solving a crime?"

"Well, yeah. What else is there in this high tech world we live in?"

"A suspect. Motive and opportunity. Witnesses. An identification of the victim. Forensics, man. None of which I have."

"It looks like you've got some work to do, Cane. Some problems that need solving. It sounds pretty mysterious to me, but I don't know what to tell you except wish you the best. Hey, did you ever marry that girl you were so in love with in high school? What was her name?"

"Lucinda. No, Lucy went her way and I went mine. So why are you changing the subject? Did you hear everything I just said?"

"Yes I did. But listen, I don't dabble in murder. I felt

like you needed to talk about it so I let you, but I can't help you."

"Seriously, Merlot, all of the jobs you've had and you've never encountered the dead?"

"Just once. And when I accepted the job, I didn't know she was dead. Most of my clients run in the best circles that don't include zombies. I lead a very sheltered life. I only see dead people at funerals and not many of them."

"Okay, once. That's all you need. Did you have to find out how the person died?" Dennis said.

"Yes, I did. But I still don't look for killers. That's not my thing. That's your thing. You go do your thing, and I'll carry on with mine."

"All I wanted was a second opinion. My precinct is like a country club where major crime doesn't exist. I know there's a predator out there. I can't get help from the feds because they get involved after three murders, and right now I only have an attempted murder."

"You said you suspected other murders. The operative word here being *suspected*. Why don't you wait and see what happens with this attempted murder? Maybe the killer will show up at the hospital to finish the job and you'll catch him red-handed!"

"Maybe. But this killer is smart or very lucky. He doesn't leave any evidence or DNA. I can't imagine him suddenly turning stupid enough to go to the hospital. But stranger things have happened. I just wanted you to hear me out, because if I'm right he's going to kill another woman on June 24. And then the trail goes cold for another year. This time it's in my city. I have to do all that I can to try to stop him!"

"How do you know these dates? How do you know any of this stuff?"

"I've been keeping a record of any woman reported missing in the past three years in the metro area."

Merlot held his hand up to stop Dennis. He got up and went to the counter to order two more cups of coffee. While he waited he thought about what he'd heard so far. Even though he was giving his friend a hard time, he believed him. And he was a little intrigued. And angry. Setting someone on fire was a horrible way to kill and the person doing this needed to be tied to a stake and teased with flames. For days, weeks, months. *But this is not my problem.* He returned to the table and sat a cup in front of Dennis.

"Forgive me, but what do missing women have to do with anything?" Merlot said. "Sometimes women just leave. That's my strong suit you know."

"Missing persons are key. Most serial killers choose victims that won't be missed like prostitutes, derelicts, homeless people, or frequent runaways. Thanks for the coffee."

"You're welcome. There are a lot of all of those kinds of people. How long is your list?"

"Beginning in 2005, on or near June 16 and June 24, one of the women in my chronological list fell off the grid."

Merlot took a long drink from his cup. *A chronological list.* That sounded menacing. And a little anal.

"Merlot, five of those women were identified as having died in a fire. All in separate jurisdictions. I was unable to get any information from the police in three of the cases."

Dennis pulled his chair closer to the table and leaned in close, lowering his voice as he continued his tale.

"This killer chooses women that are gainfully employed, upstanding citizens. Women who are missed by their families. He does just the opposite of what I'd expect.

The victimology is all wrong."

"So in other words, the victims are chosen haphazardly?"

"Yes. Exactly. In direct opposition to his methodical execution of the crime—not leaving a trace of himself behind except a random thread."

"Maybe he doesn't really care whether he's caught or not. And I wonder why he chooses to kill in June? The wedding month?"

"That's what I've asked myself a thousand times, Merlot. And why those dates? They must mean something to him."

"What if he's done? Maybe this last victim not dying will frighten him away. And in that case, it sounds like you'll never find him," Merlot said as he stood.

Dennis ran his fingers through his hair. His face was miserable, and yet Merlot could see steely determination in his eyes.

"If the woman survives she can tell you what happened," Merlot continued. "Then you'll have something concrete, like a description of your suspect and how he gets these women. You said they were all respectable, so your suspected killer has to appear harmless. Just be patient. And if the woman dies, be ready on the 24th. That's all I've got, man. That's not an easy puzzle you're trying to solve. You don't even have all the pieces." Merlot spread his arms wide and pasted a look of pity on his face as he stood. He had to get back to his work. He felt sorry for Dennis because he was clearly disturbed by the whole thing.

"So you think I'm on to something here? I respect your opinion. You were always smart, not all brawn, you know what I mean?" Dennis laughed, convinced he'd just made a joke. He got up and the two headed toward the exit.

Merlot ignored the joke. "I believe that you believe there's a serial killer. I don't know how you're going to stop him. You've got your work cut out for you. A lot of people play with matches. Anybody who drives has access to gasoline. You've woven a tangled web, my man."

"You've said you've found one dead person. Did this person die a natural death?

Merlot thought for a second. He had a good memory, but he tried not to memorize anything that he could check in his files. *Ah yes.*

"No. She died in a house fire."

Dennis stopped and grabbed Merlot by the arm. His face was beginning to turn red.

"In the last three years?"

Yes. 2006."

"What was her name?"

"Meredith Payne."

"Great Scott! She's the first name on my list. Reported missing by an employer. She has to be the first victim. We found a ring engraved with the initials *MP* at the crime scene. Merlot, do you realize what this means?"

"That you've identified a victim?"

"No. This is a sign. I mean you can't call it a coincidence. All of this was meant to happen. Our running into each other. It means you do look for murdered people. And it means we can work together to stop this killer."

Dennis never could give breathing room. Everybody had called him "Mitten" in high school. If you had the ball and Dennis guarded you, the only recourse was to risk overturning the ball or have it taken away. He was relentless, and it seemed that he'd held on to this trait for his police work.

"It is a coincidence. And no, we can't work together.

I don't look for killers. How many ways can I say that?"

"You'll think about it and then you'll call me. This is so fortuitous. There's no way you can't see that."

Merlot had heard enough. It wasn't that he didn't care that people were dying at the whim of what Dennis believed was a ruthless killer. It was that he had things to do. He had a woman to find. Chanel Franco. He took out one of his business cards and handed it to Dennis.

"I hope this all works out for you, Cane. It was really *fortuitous* seeing you again, man. Let's stay in touch. Maybe we can get together and shoot some hoops and talk about the old days. You still play?"

Dennis looked at the card for a minute and then took it without trying to mask his disappointment. "Of course I play. How else would I keep such a fine physique?" He extended his hand.

"Good answer!" Merlot replied, grasping Dennis's hand in a firm handshake.

"Good seeing you too, Candy" Dennis said. As an afterthought, he took out one of his cards and handed it to Merlot. "I'll be in touch."

"You do that! And good luck with your manhunt there."

"Thanks for that. I appreciate you listening to me."

Merlot walked away. It was a shame that he'd not been able to help him. Dennis was a pseudo-genius. They'd both loved a good challenge in high school, and had been the only two guys on the team that had taken accelerated classes. One of those classes had been criminology. After one semester, the class was removed from the curriculum. Professor Livingston, an inspiration, was the reason Merlot ended up in law school. He continued on his way, his thoughts returning to Chanel Franco.

Same Day

Chapter Seventeen

Dennis Cane ran this morning's police report through his head again as he drove back to Peach Grove. The woman had been completely naked, wrapped in a tarp. The heavy downpour had put out the fire before said tarp was destroyed. One piece of evidence. And the iron pole that stuck into the ground made two. According to the paramedics, the woman's left side was burned horribly. The fireman stated that the way the woman had landed prevented the right side of her body from exposure to the flames. It appeared as if someone or something besides the killer pried the tarp away. But why would a killer take the time to wrap the woman in a tarp, and then pry the tarp away after the fire started? Someone else must have come along. But who? Was it the same person who made the 911 call to report the woman was on fire? Dennis had no answers.

Arriving at the precinct for the second time in one day, he parked his car in his specially marked parking spot. He sat for a few minutes still thinking, and then finally exited the car, and walked through the automatic doors on the side entrance. He was heading toward his office, but was stopped before he'd crossed the lobby.

"Hey Cane!" Clyde Brown, an obese officer Dennis despised, yelled from the hallway leading to the open area where several cubicles were located. "The chief wants to see you. Now."

Dennis didn't bother to look at him. He just walked past him and down the hallway to the office of the police chief and knocked at the door. He didn't despise Clyde because of his obesity, but because he was an egotistical jerk.

"Come in," the chief said.

Ovoid Frame oozed, rather than sat on his chair. He was six feet four, and around four hundred pounds. To call him huge would have been kind. His beady eyes sat back in his head underneath thick and hooded eyebrows. His splotchy skin hung loosely from his chin, as he chomped on the unlit cigar he held between his fleshy lips. His head was beginning to bald, but he kept what hair he did have cut low.

"Who the hell sent you to Grady Hospital this morning?" Ovoid said.

"You the hell sent me," Dennis said. He was irritable but smiled inside at his quick wit.

"Don't get smart with me!"

"Not trying to get smart. A degree of smart is necessary to do my job so it behooves me to be smart rather than get smart." Dennis focused his eyes like laser beams, boring into the tiny beads that represented Ovoid's eyeballs. If someone walked in unexpectedly, it would be obvious that the chief and Dennis were on the verge of another spat. It was already rumored that the two couldn't get along.

"I'll ask you again. Slower this time. Who . . . the . . . hell . . . sent . . . you . . . to . . . Grady Hospital?"

"Okay, let me rephrase. You . . . did. Do you need me to speak slower?" Dennis asked.

"Enlighten me, Lt. Cane. Tell me how I sent you when this is the first time I've seen you today. And when I spoke to you this morning, I told you to tread lightly. That did not mean going to the hospital. We can control our news here, but we can't control what happens in the Atlanta papers."

Ovoid's face took on a purple hue as he tried to control his emotions, but breathing like an asthmatic pit bull gave the anger away.

"You gave me absolute authority when it comes to homicide. I have a copy of the contract we signed and I read it. Shall I get it and read it to you?"

"No, you don't have to read anything to me. You said the magic word—homicide. We have not had a homicide!"

"We had a homicide attempt. And the woman's not guaranteed to live, so if she dies we will have a homicide. A murder, in other words. Hopefully she can identify who did this to her and then we'll have a suspect. I've assigned an officer to stand guard at the hospital because she's not safe."

"Okay, that makes sense. But let's not toss the word murder around until we have to. If the woman makes it and can identify who did this to her, we will have a serious problem. Right now we don't have a serious problem. And with this major real estate development on the way, we can't afford to have bad press. Not yet. Nobody wants to live in a place where a murderer is on the loose."

"I understand. It doesn't matter that someone tried to kill her. I can't call it a murder unless she dies," Dennis said.

"You know the city fathers want to encourage people to move here. Their best selling point is no crime. I don't want to tarnish that image. And neither do you. It's my job to make sure we have our facts straight. They don't keep me around for looks. And you, you're here if anything major happens because you're a good detective who can wrap up an investigation. So you and I are going to keep a lid on this until time to lift it without all the crap boiling over. You got me?" Ovoid's face was a deep purple now, his breathing still loud and raspy as his lungs, weary from cumbersome fat, struggled to take in air, especially when he tried to talk at the same time.

Dennis, becoming impatient in the midst of this chastisement, refused to come to his own defense again. Ovoid was right. It was premature to talk about murder without a shred of proof. He needed his job, too. And he wanted to do it right. He took a deep breath before speaking.

"You were out of the building when I returned from the scene. I know that timing is important in cases like this, so I left to see if I could question the woman at the hospital. To try to get some information; to see if she could identify who attacked her." Dennis sat down. One good thing that he could say about the chief was that he was a neat freak. He had a fine cherry desk and credenza that he insisted stay shined and polished. The chairs around his desk were not even regular office issue.

The chief hoisted himself up from his chair, walked around his desk toward the door, giving Dennis the well-known silent signal to rise and follow. He continued to rant as he opened his door. Loud enough for everyone in the office to hear. Dennis applauded on the inside. The man was a great performer.

"We don't go to the burn unit. If a person goes in through the emergency room, that's a different story. We can go to the emergency room for questioning. This patient was admitted into the burn unit, with doctors, nurses, and attendants in the trauma area. And you come busting in with your badge and your superior attitude and interrupted all of that? What the hell were you thinking?"

"I didn't get into the trauma room. I wanted to, but they said no." Dennis stood and listened. All activity outside the chief's door had ceased. All ears now focused on the two of them, and they both knew it. There was nothing else for Dennis to say. Not unless the chief asked him some pertinent questions. He was not volunteering anything else. He had already gone too close to the edge.

"What are you not saying?" the chief asked. "What you're saying isn't making sense. I know you're hiding something from me. I see all those reports you've been requesting from IAFIS. But I don't really care about that. What I do care about is following procedure and the chain of command."

Dennis drew in a deep breath. This was not the time or the place for him to open up about his suspicions. He worked for Ovoid, but he didn't trust him. Not yet.

"Chief, if you don't mind, I'd like to get a cup of coffee and then I have some work to do."

The chief nodded and Dennis walked out of the door. He'd learned on the basketball court to keep his eyes on the ball, because the man he was guarding could fake him out. He wasn't talking to anyone in Peach Grove about his suspicions. Not until he had ironclad proof.

"By the way, your plants need watering," Dennis said over his shoulder. Every green plant in the chief's office—and there were many—was healthy, shiny, and well-watered. But the chief needed a return jab.

Twenty minutes later, cup of black coffee in hand, Dennis sat down at his desk. He logged onto his computer and pulled up a search engine. He typed the name *Winston Merlot Candy* and got several hits. He clicked on the first one and began to read. Merlot had established quite a reputation for himself and Dennis was impressed how successful his old friend had become. He was on the fourth site, completely engrossed in what he was reading, when the phone rang.

"Lt. Cane," he answered.

"Afternoon, Lieutenant," said a female voice. "This is Darcy Goodman, homicide detective in Wilder County. You came in a few months ago asking about that burned body we found and couldn't identify. Are you still interested?"

Dennis sat his coffee cup down. His heart skipped a few beats, and his hand trembled as he reached for a peppermint from his candy dish. Dennis used peppermints the way drinkers use alcohol and smokers use cigarettes—to calm his nerves.

"Yes I am," he replied as he popped the candy into his mouth.

"Our medical examiner was finally able to trace a knee

replacement from a serial number to a doctor overseas. We identified the victim over two weeks ago. Her name is Clementine Ments and her parents live right there in Peach Grove. I just thought maybe you'd like to know. I noticed in the news that you had a burn victim yourself this morning. Maybe you'll get lucky this time."

"Thanks, Darcy. I appreciate the intel. As far as my burn vic, I don't have a suspect either. But hey—we keep coming back for more. Take care."

"You too, Lieutenant. I want to catch the son of a bitch as badly as you do. Enjoy your day."

Dennis hung up the phone. And just like that, light flooded into his office as if God himself had come in person to give him a nudge. The first person he'd met when he moved into his new house was Ben Ments who was working in his yard when Dennis came out to take in another box.

"Hello, neighbor!" he had yelled over to Dennis. When Dennis waved his hand, it must have been an instant invitation to come closer because that's exactly what Ben did.

"I'm a good humor man," he said.

Dennis waited. Something else had to follow an opening

statement like that.

"A buzzard and a crow lived next to each other for years and never spoke. One day the crow noticed that he hadn't seen the buzzard for a few days. He went over to see if he was okay. The buzzard told him that he'd been under the weather but was much better. The next day the crow saw the buzzard leaving home with his bags packed. 'You going somewhere?' he cawed. 'I'm moving. You talk too much,' the buzzard answered."

Ben laughed so hard tears came from his eyes, and Dennis couldn't help but laugh too. He also couldn't miss the point of the little joke. He and Ben spoke when they saw each other, and a few times they'd made small talk about their work, the neighborhood, and the town. His wife had even baked a casserole for Dennis, but that was the extent of their relationship. It had certainly not been clouded by too much talk.

But today Dennis planned to make a neighborly visit. He recalled noticing a lot of cars over there a week or so, but hadn't really given any thought about why. He'd drop by and offer his condolences.

Same Day

Chapter Eighteen

Merlot Candy hesitated before entering the home of Mona Challis, Chanel Franco's best friend. His raincoat was wet and he did not want to create a mess in her home. Not to worry. If a prize existed for worst housekeeping combined with the nastiest smell in town, Mona would beat out all competitors. The living room was apparently used as a dining room and a closet. Merlot could tell the room would have taste if one could actually see it. The furniture was expensive and well made, withstanding all the pressure of stuff crowded on top—perfume bottles, makeup, empty Chinese food containers, empty paper plates, and a black patent leather pump. Mahogany legs supported the heavily laden tables. A Tiffany floor lamp stood in the corner, and two upholstered chairs with a teal-and-yellow geometric pattern sat at attention across from the sofa, piled high with clothes. The walls—bluish-green and pristine without a handprint or smudge in sight—belied the messy conditions of the rest of the room.

"Have a seat if you can find one," Mona said without making a move to help.

She was pretty in a well-put-together sort of way. Her makeup was flawless, her short black hair hung below ears adorned with five silver hoops of graduating size, and her curves screamed optimal gym workouts. Her murky lake-blue eyes scrutinized Merlot from head to toe as she extended her arm to welcome him. Mona was the last person to talk to Chanel before she disappeared.

"Don't mind if I do," Merlot said. He handed her his business card with one hand as he used the clipboard in his other hand to shovel the clothes from one armchair to the floor. "Like I said over the phone," Merlot began as he sat down, "I want to talk to you about Chanel Franco."

"Nothing to talk about. She was my friend. We hung out. End of story." Mona's voice cracked, revealing a softer side of the hard front she was pushing forward.

"You're saying was. Past tense. Do you know something I don't? Like maybe she's not coming back?" Merlot asked.

"She is my friend. All better now? I'm sorry. I didn't mean to imply that she won't show up sooner or later," Mona snapped.

"Where did the two of you hang out?"

Mona shrugged her shoulders and sat down on top of the clothes on the sofa, crossing her legs. "Bars, lounges, the occasional strip clubs."

Merlot pulled a pen from his inside pocket, crossed his legs and sat back, noticing how comfortable the chair was.

"Which strip clubs?"

"I'm kidding. I don't do strip clubs. I like men. You know you're kinda cute yourself," she said as she winked at him.

"I'm a serious guy. Serious enough to suggest to the police that you are withholding valuable information if you don't start acting like someone who cares that their best friend has not been seen for days." Merlot winked at her.

Mona's eyes flashed with anger. "Slow down, Mr. Lawman. I'm just on edge. And I care about my friend," she said. "Chanel fell for some guy from out of town and for all you and I know, she could be with him in his fair city having a good time. For her sake, I hope so."

Merlot's interest suddenly piqued. According to Louise, Chanel didn't date anyone seriously. She'd been online and going to singles events lately looking for a decent date.

"What guy?"

"That's none of your business. Chanel knows how to take care of herself. She'll call me soon to tell me all about it." Mona didn't sound at all convinced that what she was saying was true.

"You hope she does. But what if she doesn't? What if something is happening to her right now and you could help?"

"I don't know the guy, okay? All I know is that he's an artist and he lives in Macon. She usually drives halfway down there to meet him at a hotel. Chanel was getting serious. She bought one of his paintings at the arts festival last year. That's how they met." Mona folded her arms across her chest with a hint of finality.

Merlot decided that she was telling the truth as she stared back at him. If what she'd said was on point, he had a lead Louise had not known about. Most artists sign their work, so the guy could be found. Merlot remained silent, aware that his steady gaze was unsettling.

"I love Chanel. She's a good friend. And we talk to each other every day. I'm worried about her, too. This isn't like her at all. But I also have respect for her and however she wants to live her life. I wouldn't want her telling a strange man about my love life."

"You're not missing, are you?" Merlot asked.

Mona stood and walked over to an end table. She pulled open a drawer and came up with a business card that she gave to Merlot.

"That's all I got. That's his name, email, and phone number. And Chanel and I planned to meet up at Club Everywhere on Friday for happy hour, but when I got there she was gone. She left a message with the bartender saying she'd see me later. Don't say I didn't do everything I could to help you." She sat back down on top of her clothes on the sofa, shooting a defiant look at Merlot as tears filled her eyes.

Merlot studied the card. “Thank you, Mona,” he began. “I hope he leads me to Chanel. Her sister is worried about her.” He stood as Mona hopped up and threw her arms around him.

“Please find her. I’m worried about her too,” she whispered.

Same Day

Chapter Nineteen

The sound of her Aunt Connie's heavy breathing woke Missy Kinner. As she opened one eye, she saw her only living relative on her mother's side gathering clothes off the floor. Before Missy could close her eye, Aunt Connie looked right at her.

"Good afternoon, Missy. You think you'll be getting out of bed today?"

Missy wanted to curse. She wanted to say as many hateful words as she could to make this old person stop caring about her. But she knew it would do no good. No matter what she did, Connie treated her like a debutante. And it made Missy sick with guilt. She'd shown up and completely destroyed the life Connie had made for herself, losing friends and her reputation. All except Miss Etta—a nosy old woman, but a true friend.

"What time is it, Aunt Connie?" Missy asked. Her mouth tasted so nasty she could hardly bear it.

"It's 2:45 p.m. I got dinner on the stove, but if you're hungry I can make you a sandwich."

"No thank you. I'll get up and brush my teeth, take a shower, and see how I feel. I may not be hungry," Missy grumbled. Having her aunt offer to feed her only intensified her guilt and added on to the mountain she already carried—an uncivil divorce, a knock-out custody battle, the total annihilation of her self-respect, and the fact that she'd never see her only child again. But she wouldn't think about that now. She'd think about gargling mouthwash; showering; shampooing, blow-drying, and styling her hair. Ibuprofen would get rid of the pain that had taken up residence inside her head. Maybe some steamy hot water would help clear out the cobwebs, and help her think of something nice to do for Connie.

"Aunt Connie, leave all that stuff alone. I'll get it. I'm a grown woman. I can pick up my own clothes," Missy said, simultaneously realizing she'd sat up too fast. The room was spinning and she felt like she was going to throw up.

"Don't worry about it. I looked in on you and noticed that your clothes are soaking wet. I'm not going to leave them here long enough to mildew the carpet. I'll wash these things. You can wash your own underwear," Connie said as she closed the door behind her.

Missy, feeling naked down below, looked underneath the covers. Her cookie box was all exposed. Her underwear was missing. How did Connie know that? Was she trying to make a point? *Now where in the world are my panties?* Missy wondered as she got out of bed and stumbled to the bathroom. And then a wave of guilt rushed over her. When was she going to stop waking up knowing that she'd shared her body with someone without a clue as to who the someone was? A feeling of revulsion joined the guilt. The nights may have been fun, but the mornings after were never great. And the idea that sleeping with enough men would help her leap over the ache in her heart created by losing the one man she'd allowed herself to love was not working out.

Her hangover was pretty bad. She would usually get dressed and get out of the house. She was not one to spend much time at home with nothing to do but watch television or play dominoes with Aunt Connie. Missy had been on a four-day binge and it finally caught up with her. Her only child, a daughter, had turned six four days ago and she'd missed the party. Custody laws mandated that she miss all the birthdays for years to come. She opened the cabinet, found the ibuprofen and plopped five into her hand, turned on the water, and cupped a hand full of water to her mouth to swallow the pills. She looked at herself in the mirror and shuddered. Maybe she'd shower later—after this awful headache died down. A nice game of dominoes and an early bedtime appealed to her in more ways than one at the moment because getting drunk again today would only erase the pain for a while. Sleep could bring a night filled with dreams of her little girl blowing out the candles on her birthday cake.

Blackout drinker that she was, she had no remembrance of the night before. Not the apparition driving the car, not the woman on fire with the glow-in-the-dark nails, not the waist pouch that she'd shoved far underneath the bed to keep her aunt from finding it. Without a clue that she'd made a phone call to a 911 operator to report the burning body, she went back to bed and pulled the covers over her head.

Chapter Twenty

Dennis rang his neighbor's doorbell and waited. Mary Ments—a petite woman with a head of ash-blonde hair and graying temples—opened the door and looked out with a sad face and clear blue, reddened eyes. Her whole demeanor changed when she recognized her caller. She invited him in, led him to the kitchen, and offered him a cup of coffee. While she prepared it, he focused his eyes on the knickknacks on shelves, pot holders with exotic scenes hanging on cabinet doorknobs, souvenir magnets covering the refrigerator—all from various cities and countries of the world.

She placed a china cup and saucer in front of him, one no doubt reserved for holidays and special guests, and poured the steaming coffee. He didn't feel like a special guest. He felt like the worst kind of intruder, but if they knew something or remembered something that could help lead him to their daughter's killer, it was worth the discomfort. She placed a container of cream and sugar on the table and then called her husband in from the back. When they both stood looking at him, he took a sip of coffee and decided to plunge right in.

"I just heard the news about your daughter and I wanted to offer my condolences," Dennis began.

"Thanks, Dennis. It's been pretty rough for us. You never want to face the fact that your only child dies before you do. We kept expecting to hear from her ever since last June. That maybe she'd run off and married and wanted some time to pass before she broke the news," Ben said, remaining by Mary's side as she leaned against the kitchen counter beside him.

Dennis cleared his throat. "I'm your neighbor, Ben. I care about what has happened here. I don't know if you've heard, but someone tried to burn a woman to death here in Peach Grove early this morning. The rain saved her life. I don't know who she is yet, but I believe that the same person who murdered your daughter is responsible. If she survives she may be able to help us find him. I’m hoping maybe you and Mary can shed some light on what happened with your daughter.”

Mary shook her head from side to side, tears running down her face, as her head went back and she cried out loud. Dennis could hardly bear her anguish, but he had come with a mission. Although now entrenched in their grief, he had to find out about the last time they saw their daughter.

“Please understand that I’m not here in an official capacity, but as your neighbor and friend I’m here because I want to bring this perpetrator to justice.”

Mary sobbed aloud again, moving away from the counters to a wall lined with family photos. With her back to Dennis and Ben, she began to beat her fists against the wall as photos toppled to the floor. Dennis waited for calm. Ben moved toward his wife, who inhaled sharply, grasped her heart, turned her face to her husband’s chest, and sobbed with abandon. From his vantage point Dennis could see Ben shaking, his jawline quaking as he swallowed audibly over and over again in an effort to control his emotions.

Dennis looked down at his shoes; the floor; the molding along the bottom of the cabinets, noticing a spot that had been missed underneath the dishwasher. Perhaps it was done intentionally to make it easy to slide the dishwasher in and out. He'd have to check out his setup at home. He'd never really stared at his own floor this long.

"How can we help? The police from Wilder County notified us. They told us they were handling this whole thing," Ben said.

Dennis cleared his throat again. "I'm not interfering with their investigation. As I said, I'm here as your neighbor. I know you sort of established your viewpoint of neighbors the first day I moved in and I've respected that. But the way to get answers is to ask questions. Do you understand what I'm saying, Ben?"

Ben released his wife, took her by the hand and both walked to the table. He pulled out a chair for Mary to sit down. Then he took tissues from the counter and gave them to her to dry her face.

"I remember that joke I told you when we first met," Ben said with a chuckle, and then his expression returned to serious as he sat beside his wife. "I just wanted to let you know that we minded our own business over here. I knew you were with the police department—we all did—and I didn't want you thinking I was looking for special treatment. I tend to have a heavy foot on the gas pedal sometimes. I feel like I need to apologize for giving you the impression that we didn't want to be bothered."

"No, you don't owe me an apology. I like to mind my own business, too. But crime is my business. And a grievous crime has been committed against your daughter."

Ben sighed as Mary got up and grabbed more tissues. She picked up the coffee pot and poured more coffee into Dennis's cup. In spite of her pain she remained the perfect hostess. She placed a cake plate on the table, removed the cover to reveal a half-eaten pound cake, and sliced three sections.

"We're angry, too," she said as she opened a cabinet and took out three china dessert dishes that matched the cups. "I've been asking myself over and over who would do such a thing to my Clemmie ever since the police came to tell us they'd identified her."

"When did they notify you?"

Mary hesitated. "Two weeks ago." She glanced at Ben as she placed three forks on the table and then served the pieces of cake, one for Dennis and one for her husband, nodding toward him as if giving him permission to speak. She poured coffee for him and then sat down with a slice of cake in front of her.

"It was a shock," Ben said. "But we're trying to move on. We don't know what you want us to tell you. Clemmie lived in Atlanta. She usually came up on the weekend. The last time we saw her was on a Sunday evening." Ben's hands shook as he lifted the cup to his lips and took a sip of coffee.

"Clemmie was a good girl. She went to work and to church. She minded her own business," Mary added. She stood and walked over to pick up a photo of Clementine from the floor, and then brought it to Dennis. Dropping into her chair, she wiped her eyes as she struggled to control herself. She took a bite of the cake, her hands trembling. She chewed slowly, swallowed, and then looked at Dennis. Ben didn't touch his cake.

Dennis studied the photo. Clementine Ments had worn her hair cut asymmetrically, and was a natural blonde. Her eyes were clear blue, like her mother's. She smiled from the photo that had been taken in the living room of this same house.

"Can you tell me a little about your daughter? Her

habits, her friends, anything you can think of, no matter how insignificant you feel it is?" Dennis put the photo on the table facedown.

"On the fifteenth of June, last year, she called me on her way home from work like she always did. She said she had some kind of church meeting that night. That's the last time I talked to her." She began to cry again.

Ben rubbed his forehead. "It seems to me that it took an awful long time for the police to finally identify her. They gave us some cockamamy story about not being able to track down matching records of her knee replacement. We tried to tell them that she didn't have the surgery in the United States. We did everything we could to find her. Like I said, we kept waiting for her to call or come through the door." He stopped abruptly and looked at his wife and then down at his hands, seeming unsure as to what to do with them.

Dennis looked at his own hands. How could he tell these people he thought a serial killer was responsible? They wouldn't know how to handle that information. But he wanted to be honest with them.

"Did she have any enemies? Anybody who wished her ill?"

“Not a soul. Everybody liked her. Like Mary said before, she was a hard worker, she went to church, she was a good girl,” Ben said.

“Did she sound unusually stressed or worried when you spoke to her the last time?” Dennis turned toward Mary.

“No. She was happy. And Ben’s right. She didn’t have any enemies or at least none that we knew about.” Mary got up to get the pot and poured more coffee into Dennis’s cup. He’d only finished a third of what she’d given him the first time.

“Like Ben told you, she didn’t live with us,” Mary said. “The last time we saw her was the Sunday before. She came by, ate, talked about her job, helped me repot some plants, watched a movie with her father, and then went home. That Friday she told me there was something going on at the church.

“On a regular day, she was home by six. Days with errands and church, she’d be ten or eleven getting home. When I didn’t hear from her by Sunday evening, I got worried. I called her over and over and got her voicemail. Finally Ben went over to her place. Her car wasn’t there. We called Gail, her best friend, and she hadn’t heard from her either. We called the police and reported her missing. We put up fliers. Our friends and church members formed search parties, but nobody found her. Nobody thought of looking in Wilder County. I called the police almost every week. Nothing!" Mary's whole body began to shake as she started to cry again. Dennis knew that it was time to go. He stood.

"Thank you, Ben and Mary. I'm going to give the both of you some privacy. I'm certain the Wilder County detectives have been to her place and looked around. Please believe me when I tell you that I am going to do everything in my power to bring this person to justice." Dennis turned to go as the couple stood and followed him to the front door. He walked out without looking back, but was stopped in his tracks when Ben spoke up again.

"We thought maybe she'd met up with Mike somewhere. Mike's her ex. They were on again off again, always having a falling out. We hoped that maybe they'd made up with each other for good and ran off somewhere to set up house without telling us. I didn't like Mike and Clemmie knew it."

"And this Mike, he hadn't seen her?" Dennis asked, turning to face them again.

"No, he was in Texas all last summer. We didn't even know how to contact him. He came around asking about her, and we told him about it and how we'd filed the missing person's report. He wanted to gather another search party, but of course we had to tell him we'd already done that and had no luck finding her."

Dennis had never seen a man shrink before his eyes before. Ben Ments had gone from tall with his shoulders erect to completely broken with stooped shoulders and tear-filled eyes.

"And if you don't mind my asking, what's the name of the church that Clementine attended?" Dennis asked, pulling out his notepad.

"Peach Grove Praying Hands Non-Denominational Church. Over on Smithstone Boulevard. She liked going to that speed-dating event they have once a month."

"And how do I find Mike? What's his last name?"

"Mike Alpine. He drives an eighteen–wheeler. And when he's in town stays in an apartment in Atlanta on Memorial Drive. We found that out after Clemmie went missing."

"Thank you, Ben, and you, too, Mary. Again, I'm very sorry for your loss."

Dennis left them alone with the grief his presence had stirred up. But he was not entirely to blame. A murdering psychopath was responsible for their loss. Dennis had to stop him.

Same Day

Chapter Twenty-One

Merlot sat in his Mercedes in the parking lot directly across the street from Club Everywhere. The club was located just off Highland Avenue in the Old Fourth Ward area on the fringe of Inman Park and Edgewood Avenue. Only a few seconds east of downtown Atlanta—a city of multiple neighborhoods inhabited by all kinds of people, activities, and lifestyles. This new dance spot was another addition to the trendy area that was teeming with restaurants, bars, and other businesses that attracted a young crowd. Opened in early 2006, the club was already making a name for itself. The new owners had converted the old warehouse into a two-story, 36,000-square-foot space with good sound and the best DJs and live music around town.

Glenn had come up with the names of the owners, who

turned out to be friends of an old client of Merlot's. Through him, Merlot had arranged to meet with the bartender before happy hour. A glance at his watch let him know that by the time he crossed the street and entered the club, he'd arrive five minutes earlier than their agreed upon time—something he liked very much.

The place was well lit this time of day allowing Merlot to appreciate the décor. Mostly dark wood tables and chairs with light-beige padded seats were sprinkled around the dance floor. The bar was shaped like a horseshoe and took up the back of the room. A lot of money had been invested in the light fixtures that hung over the area. Directly to the left on the second level overlooking the bar was the VIP area. White leather couches, colorful table lamps, low glass tables—all made an invitation to spend money. The bartender was there, waiting with arms outstretched and palms down on the bar.

"Mr. Candy?" he said, his eyes inspecting Merlot's green suit, his shirt that softened the suit color, and the matching tie and kerchief with its green set against muted tones of pink. Merlot smiled to himself when the guy's eyebrows lifted a notch in open admiration for the statement made by the bold colors.

"That's me," Merlot responded, extending his arm to shake hands with the young man who was mid to late thirties, with tattoos peeking from beneath his rolled-up shirt sleeves. He beamed a crooked smile.

"Naim Boudrot," he said, clasping Merlot's hand with a firm handshake.

"I understand you work here most nights. I'm looking for a young lady." Merlot produced a photo of Chanel and handed it to the bartender. The young man stared at the photo, nodded his head, and gave it back to Merlot.

"I've seen her before, and her friend, Mona," he said.

"Did you see her this past Friday?"

The young man leaned back on his heels, looked straight ahead for a few minutes, and then returned his gaze to Merlot. "That's my recall method. I think back to the night, then I get the DJ, and then I see the crowd. Yes, she was here. She sat down on that end, had a beer, texted for a few minutes, ran two guys off, and left. I'd say just before ten, because the band starts at that time and they began banging out the funk a few minutes after she left. The chick that took her seat was the dancing-in-her-seat kind."

"Good observation. Did she leave alone?" Merlot asked.

"As far as I could tell. My peripheral vision takes in all the area around this bar and I take in the door from time to time. When she walked away from the bar she was alone, and as you can see, even with a crowd, it's a straight shot to that front exit."

"The two guys she ran off, did they seem offended? Like the kind of guys who might follow her out and try to convince her that they were fun once she got to know them?"

"No, each one of them took it like a man. They moved on to the next chick. Did something happen to her?"

"That's what I'm trying to find out. No one's seen her since Friday."

"Wow, that's a bummer. I wish I had more information, but that's all I know. She was here. She left. And then her friend came, stayed awhile, and left alone, too."

Merlot reached inside his jacket pocket and pulled out one of his business cards and handed it to Naim.

"Thanks a lot, Mr. Boudrot. If you think of anything else, give me a call."

"I will. Sorry I couldn't be of more help."

"You've been a great help. You told me she was here. You told me she left. You also told me she was texting, which leads me to believe that she was in contact with someone and that maybe she went someplace else to meet the person sending the texts. So I know I've still got work to do. Thanks again. Nice setup you've got here."

"It's a fun place. Come back at night and party with us."

"Thanks, I just might do that." Merlot left the building, thinking a mile a minute. Then he pulled out his phone and dialed Glenn's direct number. He picked up on the first ring.

"Boss. What's up?"

"I need you to check out Chanel's cell phone activity for last Friday night to see if you can pinpoint cell towers where her texts could have generated from between nine and ten."

"Will do, boss." Glenn disconnected.

Heading toward downtown, Merlot could see Grady Hospital in the distance, and it occurred to him that he had not spoken directly to anyone in the hospital. And that was not how he did things. He liked to engage people himself. Actions, facial expressions, nervous tics or the lack thereof said a lot. He'd taken Dennis's word about the doctor not allowing visitors. Dennis could be trusted, but Merlot was a different guy with a smooth approach. He knew that Chanel had a birthmark that resembled a four leaf clover just above her right breast. If the Jane Doe had such a mark, his job could be finished. Merlot was used to getting around rules and naysayers. But he'd never talked to anyone who worked in the burn unit at Grady. He'd only heard from reliable sources that the medical staff protected their patients from all enemies, both foreign and domestic.

Same day

Chapter Twenty-Two

Mira Dream—fifty-nine years old, African-American, and known as the best nurse on the burn unit—like most of the nurses, avoided the reception desk because her patient duties were vast and time was precious. Too precious to spend explaining to visitors why they could not see a patient. The girl who worked the desk had been on the job for two weeks and Mira was certain she would not be around much longer. She left the desk unmanned too many times. Like now. Mira had come up to check Dr. Salada's chart for instructions for her patients' care and found the area deserted.

The new girl's only redeeming quality was neatness. The area was in order, all the notebooks alphabetized and on the shelves. The fax machine was cleared, and no written messages were scattered about waiting for the intended person. Mira sighed. Perhaps the girl had gone to hand deliver another message. Mira selected the binder that contained a printout of details from the doctors on the floor. With her fingertip she scrolled down to Dr. Salada's name. At that moment the buzzer sounded. Mira's first instinct was to ignore it and leave the area, but she hadn't read her instructions yet. The entrance to the burn unit was kept locked. Automatic metal doors opened by a button at the reception area to permit entrance. But first, visitors had to be cleared to proceed down the hallowed hallway. Mira pressed the call button to answer.

"Burn unit. May I help you?" she asked as cheerfully as she could in her present state of annoyance.

"I'm here to see my friend," a pleasant, well-articulated voice responded.

Mira shook her head in agitation. "Your friend's name?" she asked.

"Chanel Franco," the voice answered.

Mira was familiar with the names of all the patients, but not that name.

"No, we don't have anyone by that name," she replied. "Check with the information desk on the main floor."

Mira turned back to the printout, satisfied that the person would move away and go back to the first floor. Occasionally visitors were able to slip into the unit when the doors opened to allow someone to leave. And then of course both doctors and nurses had to sternly redirect the intruders because unwanted germs, traveling with each and every human being, could spell death to some of their more severely burned patients. If this person showed up, Mira was ready for them. Her aggravation reached a new level when the buzzer sounded again.

"Burn unit," Mira snapped.

"I'm still here. Sorry to bother you, but my friend may have come in early this morning with no identification. She smokes and we're always afraid that she might set herself on fire and no one's seen her since last night. And that's not like her. I watched the news this morning, and I heard about that woman that you found. I just wanted to make sure . . ." the voice trailed off.

Mira took a moment to consider the person's request.

"I'm sorry. The only new patient that we have is comatose and is not here because of smoking a cigarette. Check the information desk. Please," Mira urged.

"Thank you so much. I'm glad to know that she's not here."

Silence.

Mira waited a beat. No one came around the corner. She fled the reception area. It was time to get to her patients.

Same Day

Chapter Twenty-Three

The elevator outside the burn unit on the third floor opened. A doctor and an intern emerged, and walked by the person waiting to go down without so much as a glance. Michael smiled at them and stepped inside the elevator where seconds later the door closed.

She's in a coma and they don't know her name.

He took a deep breath. A coma was probably induced to keep her body still and to keep her from experiencing the horrible, horrible pain. The coma could last for weeks. One week was all that was necessary to figure out a way to get inside the room and place a pillow over her face or to inject insulin into the obligatory IV line that would silence her forever.

The elevator doors opened on the first floor. A loud woman pushed three children onto the elevator, fussing a mile a minute. She didn't look at Michael.

That's good. Carry on as if I'm invisible. I'm safe that way.

Outside in the sunlight, he looked up and bemoaned the brightness that bathed the earth after the downpour earlier that ruined a perfectly planned and excellently executed rite of vengeance. Eight more days and it would all be over. Confident and immaculately dressed in a tailored black suit, Michael turned to walk down the sidewalk, passing close to a tall, handsome man dressed to kill in a green suit with matching tie and kerchief.

Same day

Chapter Twenty-Four

The metal double doors to the burn unit opened just as Merlot was about to push the buzzer for permission to enter. A young woman exited, her mind clearly elsewhere, allowing Merlot to move through the doors before they closed and barred entry pending approval from the doorkeeper. Moving forward with caution, Merlot first saw a nurse with her back to the hallway in a room for physical therapy as she helped her patient from a wheelchair onto a long table. He walked with purpose as if he belonged there in case she glanced his way. Next he passed a small office and surmised it was probably for consultations with family members. He turned the corner and found the reception desk unmanned. He continued, expecting a doctor or nurse to halt his progress at any moment. Sure enough, a serious nurse came rushing down the hallway and nearly collided with him.

“May I help you?” she asked, enunciating every word sharply.

Merlot read the name Mira Dream on the nurse’s badge. She was very attractive and her body language spoke volumes. Strength, determination, impatience, and aggravation—all behind a forced smile.

“I hope so,” he answered. Over her shoulder he noticed a police officer sitting in a chair beside a doorway of a room down the hall. Mira Dream, who was trying hard to hold her true emotions in check, had just come from that direction. The emotions that she allowed herself to show ranged from tolerance to anger. His best bet was to be brief and concise.

“I’m looking for a missing woman,” he said as he pulled out his card and handed it to her. “I understand from a news report that you have an unidentified woman who came in early this morning. I just wanted to see if she’s the young lady I’m looking for.” He smiled his most charming smile.

“The patient that came in this morning is in critical condition. We had to heavily sedate her, and right now it’s time to change her dressings. You may not know this, but changing dressings takes time and I don’t have any to spare. Now if you’ll excuse me, I’ve got to get to that supply room right behind you to get some more gauze wrapping. You shouldn't be back here. Please leave."

Mira sidestepped Merlot, heading toward the supply room, and completely ignored his card. Thinking fast, he followed, extending a photo of Chanel to her in hopes that she would at least glance at it. She moved so fast, and he not fast enough. The photo fell to the floor and he stooped to pick it up.

"If you have time later, please take a look at that photo. Her name is Chanel Franco and she has a sister who's worried sick about her. I'll just leave my card and her photo there on the counter," he called after her.

Merlot turned to go back the way he'd come. He passed the reception area where a twentysomething, nervous, dark-haired young woman was busy writing down a message from whomever she was talking to on the phone. Merlot placed his business card and Chanel's photo facedown on the counter and continued past her without another word.

Same Day

Chapter Twenty-Five

Mira carefully rolled her patient over onto her back. Finished at last, she took a deep breath as beads of sweat dropped onto the plastic pinafore that she wore. The room temperature was hot because she had just finished exposing her patient's naked body to the air. She began the arduous task of placing scissors, clamps, forceps, and other instruments into a wash basin to be sterilized for the next dressing change. The patient was stable. The most important thing now was to keep down infection.

Mira shook her head as she gazed at all the tubes feeding into the body. She sighed as she considered how little the lay person really knew about burns—how it never occurred to them that the skin was the body's largest organ. Any type of burn sent alarm signals throughout the body, looking for help to fight the chaos created by combustion.

Mira placed the basin, the remaining gauze wrapping, the stretchy fabric that holds the gauze in place, the gauze sponges, the silicon, hydrogel, foam pads, and the remaining sterile water onto her cart. Taking one last look at the patient she emerged from the tent-like structure surrounding the area around the bed, removed all of her protective clothing, and sat down in the comfortable chair to rest her feet. Knocking on sixty's door, there were some days, like today, when Mira felt much older. Many days she asked herself how much longer she could continue to do this job, but the answer stared in her face—until her two granddaughters were prepared to take care of themselves. That meant a college degree for both of them. The oldest was a senior at Georgia State University and the youngest a sophomore at Kennesaw State University. With no time for sitting and thinking about how tired she was, she got up to check on her next patient, a thirteen-year-old boy who would soon be released. And then she was going home. She walked past the young police officer.

“Don’t fall asleep out here. I hope they send someone to relieve you soon,” she said.

“Good night, ma’am,” the officer replied. Mira smiled. He was so polite. She shook her head thinking about the patient he was guarding. Her condition upon arrival to the burn unit had been bleak. Now it looked as if she might make it. She had a long, rough road ahead, but she’d be alive. It was a shame what someone had done to her.

“Nurse Dream, do you want this business card and the picture that the man left here for you?” the receptionist called out from her post as Mira walked by.

“What is your name, sweetie?” Mira stopped and turned toward her.

“Claire Journey, ma’am.”

“Here’s some free advice, Claire. If you want to keep this job, it would be wise for you to stay put behind that desk. That man had no business getting as far as he did. And no. I don’t want anything that he left here, Ms. Journey. I want you to be in that same spot the next time I come back this way. You don’t have to hand deliver messages. Doctors can pick up their messages right there in those boxes with their names on them. You see them?” Mira pointed to a stack of alphabetized cubbyholes with names on them. By this time Mira couldn't even remember the man or what he wanted. Care of her patients was always foremost in her mind.

"Yes, ma'am," Claire answered with her head down. Mira went on her way, never noticing that Claire studied the smiling face of the woman in the photo.

Claire Journey was twenty-six years old and had dreamed of working in a hospital ever since she was a child. She was one of those children who asked for Operation—a game that taught her the major organs in the body—every year for Christmas. She wasn't smart enough for college or medical school, but she had plenty of common sense and keen observation skills. She knew that she didn't have to hand deliver messages, but as she did so, she was getting to know the doctors.

Aware of the high turnover of her new position, she wanted to understand why. The main reason was, they didn't tell you anything. They left you alone to make mistakes. But Claire wasn't a screw up. She intended to do a good job. Knowledge was the key that unlocked the door of ignorance, and where this burn unit was concerned, she wanted no part of ignorance. If no one would tell her things, she'd find them out for herself. And if she got fired, so be it.

Claire had done a lot of exploring since she arrived on the unit, and seen things that she's certain she should not have seen. But she'd always been curious. When everybody was busy elsewhere, she put on a head covering, a paper coat that tied behind her back, a mask for her nose and mouth, and plastic gloves and gone inside that tent to have a close look at a badly burned patient who'd arrived reeking of gasoline. And it was good that she took the opportunity before that police officer arrived.

She tucked the photo inside the desk drawer. She was certain that the woman in the photo was Jane Doe. Maybe Dr. Salada would be interested in knowing this information even if the reigning queen, Mira Dream, did not. Claire was in hearing distance when the handsome man said that her name was Chanel—like number five, the cologne that Claire got herself for Christmas. Chanel Franco.

Same Day

Chapter Twenty-Six

Vincent Salada had been a precocious child whose constant curiosity never exhausted his parents. They welcomed his questions with encouragement, wanting their only offspring to succeed in life as they had never done. His father was a plumber and his mother a homemaker who loved to read. It was Vincent's mother who gave him his first book about a doctor: Dr. Appleby Goes Home. Dr. Vincent loved how his mother changed her voice to sound like a man as she read Dr. Appleby's motto: "A doctor is only as good as his desire to save his patient!"

Vincent considered himself a good doctor, with a few character flaws. One of them being a perfectionist. He stood at the counter looking at the chart generated by the computer overnight, knowing he would change whatever tasks had been added to his day. His one concern now was Jane Doe. From the looks of the right side of her face, the young woman had been very attractive. Without an ample supply of skin, there was no way to avoid hideous scarring. A sizable amount had already been removed from the right side of her back to cover her left arm. Not enough healthy skin remained and harvesting what they needed doubled the risk of infection. To make matters worse, she had no known next of kin and no known insurance or finances to cover the medical expenses involved in her care. That could create problems for the hospital board, causing a delay in treatment.

She'd get the treatment eventually because of a program they had for indigent patients. But she needed help now. The time it took to cut through the red tape could be used to care for her. At medical school he remembered the one class in which the professor had discussed burn victims at length, describing how the first twenty-four hours were the most critical, especially for a patient with third- and fourth-degree burns. It would take time and it would take resourcefulness, but he had both and was willing to do everything gratis.

He scanned her chart, deciding to meet with his team to discuss the next steps as Claire Journey returned to her station. He'd noticed that she did not stay in place to receive visitors as she should, but when a need arose to locate a nurse or supplies or a vendor's number or just an extra hand, she always magically appeared with the knowledge of how to get whatever was needed, including running down a nurse and getting her to a patient's room.

"Good evening, Claire. How many ways will you be of service to me before the night is over, I wonder." Dr. Salada smiled at her. She was a pretty young lady, ambitious and smart, and she had a delightful sense of humor.

"Wonder no longer, Dr. Salada. I believe that I know our Jane Doe's real name. And didn't you say that it would be a miracle if family could be located?" Claire reached into the desk drawer and pulled out the card the detective had tried to give Mira. She presented both to Dr. Salada with a pleased expression on her face.

"A private detective came looking for a missing woman today, said her name is Chanel Franco. I believe in miracles, Dr. Salada, and I also do not believe in coincidences. Like my grandmother used to say—and I had no idea what she meant—but she'd say, 'A stitch in time saves nine.' And a call to this gentleman wouldn't hurt a thing because he's probably got a good description of her, right down to that little birthmark on her right breast." Claire stood there.

Dr. Salada considered her unabashed gall and decided to make the phone call as he walked away to find the nearest telephone.

Same day

Chapter Twenty-Seven

Merlot Candy was just turning over his ignition when his cell phone rang. He let it ring twice before answering; never having appreciated giving the appearance that he was sitting by the phone waiting—plus it was after business hours. But he'd left his card with three people who could be calling with news about Chanel Franco.

"Merlot Candy," he answered.

"Mr. Candy, my name is Dr. Vincent Salada, and I understand that you were here at the burn unit at Grady looking for a missing woman. Is that correct?"

Merlot loosened his tie. He had a tendency to feel choked when he was excited.

"Yes, I did." He waited, listening in the background at the sound of keys clicking on a computer keyboard.

"Does the young woman that you're looking for happen to have a birthmark on her body?"

"She has a spot that looks like a four leaf clover on her right breast," he said, flexing his left hand as if he held onto a stress ball.

"I believe our Jane Doe is the woman you're looking for. What I need right now is to talk to a close family member. Did a member of her family hire you to find her?"

"Yes." Merlot remained quiet. Silence never failed to get the other person to continue talking.

"I don't want to alarm anyone unnecessarily," Dr. Salada said. "You are a professional and you know how to contact her family. If I can help you at all within my limited realm of patient privacy, I will do so."

From the sound of it, computer keys clicking, Merlot figured the good doctor was looking at his website where he'd find testimonials and recommendations galore. His business cards, designed to make an impression, used heavy stock with embossed printing. Of course he was professional.

"I'll get a family member there immediately. And thank you for your call." Merlot looked out into the parking area that was a multileveled parking deck filled with cars in dim light. He could almost see the sun shining above his head.

"You're welcome. I look forward to meeting someone from her family soon. I cannot stress enough the importance of haste. Goodbye, Mr. Candy."

Merlot stared at his phone for a second. "Haste?" he said aloud as he dialed the number Louise Canola had given him. "Haste is one of my middle names." He listened as the phone began to ring. He wasn't looking forward to this conversation. It was not going to be easy, but then what was?

Same Day

Chapter Twenty-Eight

Louise Canola had just stepped out of the shower when the phone rang. Since Chanel had been missing, she kept her phone near her at all times. The phone was on the vanity. She nearly slipped and fell as she lunged forward to answer on the first ring.

"Hello," she said as she snatched a towel from the rack and began to dry herself off.

"Louise, this is Merlot. I believe I've located Chanel. If I'm right she's a patient in the burn unit at Grady," he said.

"A patient? In the burn unit? But what does that mean?" Louise dropped the towel to the floor. She suddenly felt dizzy and her breathing began to vacillate. Knowing this was the kind of thing that could cause her to hyperventilate, she grabbed the dropped towel, wrapped it around her body and knotted it, and then headed toward the kitchen where she kept a supply of brown paper bags.

“It means she’s been burned. Badly. You need to get to the hospital as soon as possible to positively identify her and to authorize further treatment,” Merlot said.

By that time Louise had reached the kitchen. She fell onto the granite countertop gasping for breath, inhaling raggedly. She opened a drawer and pulled out a bag.

“Ho . . . ho . . .lld . . . on.” She placed the phone on speaker and dropped it onto the counter. She bent over from the waist, and held the bag in place over her mouth and nose.

Merlot waited. The room was silent except for Louise’s loud grunts. She took a deep breath, and put the bag down, sobbing.

“How did she get burned?” she asked, still breathing unevenly.

“I’m not certain. I’m about ten minutes from your house. Can you meet me outside?”

“I’ll be outside in five!” Louise rasped. She dropped the towel to the floor, raced to her bedroom, opened underwear drawers, and snatched up the necessary garments. A pair of jeans and a top lay on the bed. She pulled on the jeans, snatched up the top and pulled it over her head, and stuck her feet into a pair of sneakers. She ran her fingers through her hair, grabbed her purse and her keys, rushed to the door, threw it open, and stopped. She raced back to the kitchen, snatched up the brown paper bag, ran back through the front door and locked it behind her.

She spotted Merlot's Mercedes rolling toward her. When the passenger side of the car was abreast of her, the vehicle stopped and the door opened as Merlot leaned toward her.

"Get in," he said. Louise got in and slammed the door, still visibly upset.

"What happened, Merlot? How did something so terrible happen to her? Was she in an accident?" Louise sounded hysterical.

Merlot maneuvered his car away from the curb and up to the main street. He made a right turn and merged onto I-75 North. Louise waited for his answer, hoping he'd be direct.

"Someone tried to kill her," he responded.

“What?!” Louise screamed. “Kill her? Who? And why? I don’t understand,” Louise’s hands shook as she rocked back and forth on the seat, her eyes ordering Merlot to tell everything he knew. She pulled the paper bag up to her nose and mouth and bent over.

“Nobody knows. She’s sedated and unable to communicate. She was found without any identification.”

Louise removed the bag. “Why didn’t the police notify me? Or the hospital?” She sat up straight.

“They didn’t know who she was.”

Louise sucked in her breath with one hand to her stomach, the other holding her mouth as it widened in shock. She stared unbelievingly at Merlot.

“I can hardly believe what you’re saying to me,” she said.

“It’s true. She’s in critical condition.”

“Critical condition? She’s dying? Oh God!” She began to gasp for breath again. She pulled the bag up and covered her nose and mouth and forced herself to bend over again and go through the routine she’d gone through so many times to regain control of her breathing.

“The heavy sedation spares her pain from her burns.

And I didn't say she's dying. She's being cared for and the doctor seems to think she'll recover," he said in a calm voice.

"You said someone tried to kill her? How did she get burned? What does that even mean?"

"Someone poured gasoline over her and lit a match. That's all that I know." Merlot's speed increased as he shifted from lane to lane.

"Chanel? You're sure it's Chanel?" Louise said, beginning to breathe crazily again.

"She has a birthmark on her right breast that looks like a four leaf clover. That's pretty unique. At this time you're the only person who can definitely identify her and give the doctors permission to proceed with her care. I know this sounds bad, but let's not get too upset until we're sure that it's Chanel. Can you do that for me, Louise? Pull yourself together long enough to verify that it's your sister?"

Louise nodded her head but looked at Merlot like he was crazy. All sorts of questions were running through her head. *Who would want to kill Chanel ? What happened? Why did it happen? How could she not have any identification? She always carried a purse. Why? Why?* That question screamed inside her head as she breathed in and breathed out, counting down from ten. She began to repeat the silly rhyme that her mother had taught her when she'd been out playing with friends next door:

Breathing's not that hard, if you stay in your own yard. If you keep your mind free, and your eyes so you can see, my face so full with love for my angel from above. Now go to your happy place.

She closed her eyes and saw her mother's face and slowly her breathing returned to normal. Soon her mother and father would be here, and maybe it wasn't Chanel in the hospital burn unit after all. It had to be someone else. Nobody would try to kill Chanel. Everybody loved her. It was a mistake. A terrible, horrible, awful mistake.

Same Day

Chapter Twenty-Nine

Once they arrived and were introduced, Dr. Salada promptly led Louise past the officer on guard at the door into the outer room of the BCNU where she was given protective coverings for her head all the way to her feet. She was nervous as she approached the tent surrounding the bed that contained the patient known as Jane Doe. She grabbed the doctor's hand—he, too, was now covered from head to toe—and took deep breaths as he pulled back the plastic and allowed her to enter first. She almost fainted because of the smell and what she saw, but she immediately knew it was her baby sister. In spite of the swelling and contorted shape of parts of her face not covered with bandages, Louise recognized Chanel.

The hair color was also a giveaway. Louise began to cry

as she saw the singed hair that remained. Chanel lay on her back. Her left arm stretched straight out from her body and her left leg at an odd angle. The head of the bed was raised, elevating her head and shoulders. The doctor explained that it was to keep fluid from accumulating in her lungs. Tubes running from her mouth, her nose, and from her arm underneath all of the darkened bandages made her look like a half-mummy. She looked like she'd gained one hundred pounds or more since the last time Louise saw her. Her right side wasn't as bad, but it didn't look normal. Thank God her face was damaged on only one side. But all that beautiful hair. A bag containing her urine hung by the side of the bed with a tube running under the covers, while a machine in the corner was beeping. *Beep, beep, beep.* Her eyes were closed. Louse stared at her chest until she could finally see that it rose and fell from her breathing, due to the respirator that she was attached to. Louise couldn't stop the tears as she looked at Dr. Salada.

He took her arm and led her closer to the bed. He pulled back the swath of fabric that lay over the upper-chest area. Just above her right breast, Louise saw a four leaf clover, stretched to such an extent that it was larger than ever. The nails on her right hand were polished with Chanel's signature glow-in-the-dark purple. Tears continued to stream down Louise's cheeks.

"That is my sister, Chanel Franco," she whispered.

The doctor exhaled with relief and led her out of the tent. He watched as she mimicked him in removing the protective clothing and placing them in the disposal bin. He visibly relaxed, a mixture of gratitude and solace showing on his face. Now he could proceed. A nurse, emerging from a tent on the other side of the area, approached them as she pulled away her mask and head covering.

"Evening, Dr. Salada. Is this lady related to our Jane?"

Louise winced at the sound of the name *Jane.* She snapped her head around and looked at the nurse who smiled kindly at her.

"I'm Sally and I'm one of the nurses for the patient. We'll take good care of her," she said as she turned toward Dr. Salada. He nodded his head and then took Louise by the elbow and guided her out of the room.

By the time Louise returned to the family waiting room, she was unable to breathe. She gasped for air as she pulled the brown paper bag from her purse. She fell into one of the chairs and went through her routine. It took several minutes for her to pull herself together and breathe normally.

"Are you alright?" Dr. Salada asked.

"Yes. I've done this all of my life. Please go on with what you need to say."

He explained the treatment that Chanel had already received. It sounded gruesome and the more Louise heard the more she wanted to scream. But she couldn't. She had to remain calm and steady. As the doctor talked he placed so much paperwork in front of her that her eyes began to blur. She began to cry.

"Your sister looks a lot worse than she really is," Dr. Salada said with a smile. "She has no damage to her lungs, and so far there's no fever which means no infection yet. The respirator is there for precautionary measures. Burns are not simple. They're more like a very complex disease, which is why we call our patients sick. The tubes are there to keep pumping fluids, because as her body fights she's losing vital fluids, especially blood plasma. I know this all sounds crazy, but you need to understand that her body is undergoing warfare with heavy arsenal. The edema, the swelling, is normal. It's water weight. After twenty-four hours it will begin to dissipate."

He paused for a minute and Louise tried to gather all the thoughts running through her head. She was not really hearing what he was saying. The important thing was to keep signing papers. He pulled the ones she'd already signed toward him and slid the remainders in front of her.

"I understand this is hard for you," he said. "If you'd like we can wait until your parents arrive to go over the next steps. You've taken care of most of the preliminary authorizations." He glanced over at Merlot Candy who'd joined them in the family room but remained silent throughout the doctor's explanations to Louise.

"That's fine. I don't want to delay anything," Louise responded as she moved the pen from one line with an X beside it to another.

"Now would be a good time for me to say how relieved I am to see you," Dr. Salada said. "After the rain, this is the second most fortuitous circumstance for your sister." He seemed almost gleeful.

"How is anything 'fortuitous' for her?" Louise asked, pausing to look up, her eyebrows raised.

"The fact that the two of you are twins! It means that we don't have to worry about a shortage of skin for all the grafts she will need. Your skin will match perfectly," he said.

"Really?" Louise asked. "I've been so focused on the agonizing pain my sister must have suffered that skin grafts never crossed my mind. No matter how much pain and healing that means for me, it doesn't compare to all she's been through. I'm so thankful to know that I will be able to help.

"By the way," Louise continued, "I can't tell you how relieved I was that you didn't offer one of those lame questions that we hear so much. You know like 'Has anyone ever told you that you two could pass for twins?' That one is the worst," she smiled as she looked over knowingly at Merlot, who sat in a chair across from her.

"You didn't say you were twins," Merlot said. "You were upset, she was smiling. She's strawberry blonde and you're brunette. Her name is Chanel. Your name is Louise. Don't twins usually have names that rhyme?" Merlot smiled back at her.

"My full name is Jhanel Louise. Our names rhyme, okay?"

Same Day

Chapter Thirty

After Louise met her parents at the airport, they went directly to the hospital. Lausanne and Theo Canola were physically exhausted from the long flight even though they sat in first class. Tiredness combined with age made for a touchy state of mind and Louise did not want any more complications. They knew that Chanel had been burned. They didn't yet know that it had been deliberate—that someone had tried to kill her. Nor did they know the police had warned she could still be in danger.

Now Louise glanced over at her mother, who sat in the passenger seat across from her. Lausanne had a habit of biting her nails when she was upset. She sat now, gnawing away.

"Mom, the doctor says it's going to take time, but Chanel is going to come through all of this," Louise said.

"And you're telling us that you have to have surgery as well?" her father asked from the back seat.

"Yes, but I'll be fine. Twins make the best donor matches. Otherwise, they'd have to use cadaver skin or some of these new artificial skin replacements. With my skin and a good plastic surgeon, even her face can look good. She may never look the same, but she won't be all scarred up," Louise said, unable to hold back a few tears. She wiped them away and concentrated on the road, trying not to think about how much she'd tried to look different from Chanel when they were growing up in Paris. Chanel had a bubbly personality and people were always disappointed when they learned that it was Louise they were talking to instead of Chanel. This inspired Louise to drop her first name and cut her hair off and dye it purple. And then she left home. She wanted to get out from under her younger sister's shadow. Chanel had made all of the mistakes and still she was everybody's favorite. Today those feelings of resentment slipped away and were replaced by deep sadness. There was no denying that Chanel had suffered and would suffer more before this was all over.

"So someone has tried to kill one of my daughters, and now you will have to suffer pain, too. Have the police found out who is responsible?" her father asked.

"What makes you think someone tried to kill her?" Louise momentarily swerved from her lane. *How did he know that?*

"We may live a thousand miles away, but I have friends that can be reached by phone in minutes. You know I don't walk into traps," her father said.

"Who said anything about traps, Daddy?" Louise glanced sideways at her mother, realizing her lack of response in the face of her father's outbursts meant she already knew. They'd merely played along with Louise's account of what happened.

"Again, have the police found out who did this?"

"No, Daddy. I've only seen one police officer, and he's sitting outside of Chanel's room to protect her," Louise answered as she pulled into the parking deck.

"Well for his sake, I hope he's armed and extremely dangerous," her father said.

Minutes later they exited the elevator on the third floor, walked toward the double doors that led to the burn unit, and stopped while Louise pressed the buzzer.

"May I help you?" a female voice asked.

"We are the family of Chanel Franco and we have come to see her," Theo Canola said in his perfectly accented don't-jerk-me-around English.

The doors swung open. Louise led the way as her father took her mother's hand. They walked side by side, trying their best to present a brave front. Louise knew that it would not be easy for them to see their daughter. She dreaded having to witness her sister again in that condition as well. The good thing was that she was safe.

Same Day

Chapter Thirty-One

Louise and her parents rounded the corner and walked toward the vacant receptionist's area. Straight ahead, down the hallway, a tall man walked out of Chanel's room, past the police officer seated by the door who never looked up, and headed toward them. The man was covered from head to foot with the protective clothing. Louise's heart began to race. She looked over at her parents. They were both stopped at the receptionist's counter and had not noticed. Louise moved forward to stop the man in his tracks.

"Pierre! I thought you'd wait for us," Louise said as she embraced her brother. She pulled his mask and plastic head cover away to reveal tousled sun-bleached hair and a handsome face with smoky brown eyes filled with tears. He kissed Louise on the cheek.

"I couldn't. I wanted to see her. Man, she's a mess. When they catch whoever did this to her I want to light his ass on fire."

"You sound like your father," Louise whispered. "I feel so sad for her. She looks so pitiful, all swollen, head huge. She'd die if she could see herself right now," she said in a somber voice. "But she's alive and she's going to be okay, although it'll take time. I trust her doctor. He seems confident about her outcome."

Pierre and Louise approached the counter where their parents now conversed with the receptionist. Lausanne's face lit up when she turned and saw her only son. Pierre embraced her and then his father. He stood back and looked at both of them. Anyone at first glance could see that Lausanne was his mother. He had her brown eyes, facial features, and her smile. His height and build he'd inherited from Theo.

"Mom, Dad, she's not talking. They've got her sedated very heavily. And she looks nothing like herself, but these good people tell me that she's going to get better." Pierre wiped away his tears, and then took his mother's hands as he led the way toward the intensive care unit where Chanel lay in a silent fight for her life. When they arrived at the outer room, Dr. Salada and the nurse were waiting for them.

"Come in, come in. I'm Mira Dream," she said to the parents. "The young Mr. Canola and I have met already, but you will have to put on fresh protective clothing," Mira said to Pierre. "You got germs on those in the hallway." With a huge smile on her face, she handed a package to Pierre first and then proceeded to Theo, Lausanne, and finally Louise, chatting away the whole time.

"I'm the day nurse assigned to take care of Miss Jane," she said, pausing in front of Lausanne who visibly winced at the name Jane. "I'm so sorry. I'm a mother too, you know. It's a hard thing to see your child this way, but have faith and trust us. She's going to be okay. She's come through the most dangerous period with flying colors."

"Who is Miss Jane?" Lausanne asked.

"Oh my goodness, forgive me, ma'am. We called her Jane Doe when she first got here. I mean your daughter Chanel," Mira said.

Dr. Salada moved to Theo and extended his hand.

"I'm Dr. Salada. When we don't have identification for a patient, the females are called Jane Doe, and then males of course are called John Doe. Mira meant no offense."

"Of course," said Theo as he shook the doctor's hand. "I'm Theo Canola, Chanel's father. This is my wife, Lausanne, and it appears that you have met all of our children."

"I know you'll have questions after you see her. I will address any of your concerns," Dr. Salada said.

Once they were all prepared, Mira patted Lausanne's hand to reassure her, and then led the family over to Chanel's tent and pulled back the plastic drapery. Lausanne began to cry aloud when she saw the bandaged, swollen body of her baby girl.

"Oh *mon dieu*! How can you tell that it is Chanel?" Lausanne whispered.

Louise saw tears fall from her father's eyes. She'd never seen him cry. Pierre was the sole family member with dry eyes. He looked at Chanel and then left the tent. Theo's eyes traveled from Chanel's swollen head, down to the left arm heavily padded and wrapped in gauze and bandages extending straight out from her body, and then all the way down to her swollen feet, the left one heavily bandaged. Mira checked one of the lines leading to the catheter protruding from Chanel's right arm.

"Okay, everybody, let's leave her to rest now," Mira said softly.

Same Day

Chapter Thirty-Two

Minutes later they all sat in the family waiting room while Dr. Salada explained the treatment scheduled for Chanel. Louise, glancing at her parents from time to time, imagined they were in the same fog she was in after she first saw her sister. The doctor did his best to give the family hope for Chanel's recovery and answered every question her father fired at him. After what seemed like an eternity, Dr. Salada leaned back in his chair and took a deep breath. When he spoke again he was looking directly at Theo.

"Chanel is not out of the woods yet, but she has made remarkable progress so far. From now on you will only be allowed to go inside the tent one at a time. And later, if you want, one of you may remain with her during the bandage changing. Many patients like to see that their loved ones are actually healing, and the best evidence of that is seeing when the bandages come off," Dr. Salada said.

"I must tell you that I considered moving my daughter from your facility," Theo said. "But I have a very good friend who spoke with your hospital administrator. You were the doctor that he recommended."

"Thank you for sharing that," Dr. Salada said, his eyebrows lifting. "I'm very happy that you've changed your mind. Moving her now would certainly not be good."

"My family has a bad history with the medical profession. In fact I've got a long list of professional people that send me running for cover. But you've been very straightforward. I feel like you have a firm grasp on this situation."

"I appreciate that, Mr. Canola. My first concern is the health and welfare of my patients."

"My concern is for both my daughters. We are a very close family, you understand. My family roots go all the way to Pisa, Italy."

Dr. Salada's expression changed. For the first time he smiled. "Your family is from Pisa? My grandfather was born there. I've only been there once and was devastated because

I could not go into the leaning tower. Our world just got smaller."

"Indeed. You'll have to come again to visit. Perhaps when you've gotten both my daughters back on their feet, a little vacation could be in order," Theo's expression had gone from one of doubt to respect. "It would be my pleasure to arrange such a trip for you."

"Please, Mr. Canola. That is not necessary, but it is very kind of you. But back to your daughters. You cannot imagine the fortuity of having twins. I am so relieved to know that we will have enough matching skin to work with. Your daughters will be fine. It will take time, but Chanel will be a beautiful woman again."

Louise felt relief. She knew her father was strong willed and Dr. Salada had passed the test. She believed he was perfect for the task ahead. Early Thursday morning she would be admitted to the hospital. Skin grafting would begin for Chanel Thursday afternoon.

June 17, 2008

Tuesday

Chapter Thirty-Three

Etta Wasp stirred the batter for waffles, having changed her mind about oatmeal. She felt like something fun this morning. A body could use some fun, no matter the age or condition of said body. She'd enjoy these waffles and walk an extra lap around the block to keep her blood sugar in check. Or else she'd go over to Connie's house and talk her into participating in their favorite activity to drop pounds and cholesterol—a blight on Connie's health—and guilt brought on by overindulging. She dropped a dollop on the waffle iron to test its readiness. It was hot enough. She poured out two waffles and closed the lid so the little machine could work its magic.

Minutes later, Etta removed the waffles and placed them

on her plate. Good thing Pearl was still sleeping; if she was awake she'd be busy chastising. "You know that those waffles have too many carbs for your body. You have to keep your blood sugar under control!" Etta could hear her as if she was standing right in the kitchen. *Control-shemol,* Etta thought to herself. She was so tired of this accursed disease. It was a good thing Pearl was still in bed. Etta added her preferred toppings and sat down at the dining room table to enjoy her waffles. They were a delicious sight to see with melted butter, sliced strawberries, a sprinkling of juicy raspberries and blueberries, blueberry syrup, and mounds of whipped cream. *Yum!*

Looking out of her kitchen window as she savored her first bite, she spotted a squirrel scurrying across the back yard. Directly behind him came a big crow. The squirrel would make a move and stop; the crow would make a move and stop. This continued as the squirrel crossed the yard. She couldn't help but laugh aloud, almost choking, as the crow stalked the squirrel all the way into the shrubs and trees at the edge of her property. The squirrel obviously had something that the crow wanted. Over the shrubbery Etta could see Connie's house. Her yard was the only one that

Etta competed with. Some people have green thumbs. Her friend, Connie, had a green hand.

After the last bite she began the clean-up. Afterwards she decided to walk over to Connie's and skip the walk around the block. Besides, her friend always displayed a burst of good spirits when Etta showed up a morning or two after Missy had stayed out all night. Now was the perfect time to schedule one of their private exercise sessions anyway. Etta smiled, thinking about the secret she shared with Connie. To keep fit, Connie liked to dance. For sure a good dance session lowered Etta's blood sugar.

Etta left the kitchen and went back to her bedroom to change out of her night clothes. She put on a pair of shorts and a red T-shirt, pulled her hair back in a ponytail and tiptoed past Pearl's bedroom door. Pearl enjoyed sleeping her mornings away. Closing the front door behind her, Etta stopped for a moment to smell the roses in her garden bordering her front yard. She looked toward Connie's house and sighed, thinking about her. And Missy, who had shown up out of nowhere and set the whole neighborhood on its heels.

Connie was originally from New Orleans. She'd come

to Georgia to study at Emory, graduated and remained in Atlanta to live and work as a social worker until she retired almost ten years ago. Connie was not only tall and pretty but also cultured and sophisticated. It was odd that the two of them had become friends because the only thing they seemed to have in common at first was a love for flowers. She and Connie attended the same church, were members of the same garden club, and belonged to the same bridge club. Until Missy showed up.

Missy with her smooth complexion and worldly ways was Connie's sister's child. She'd shown up unannounced on Connie's doorstep a year ago and Connie didn't turn her away. At the time Connie had a secret that Missy didn't know about until she arrived. Unfortunately, Missy let the cat out of the bag at the wrong time. The same day Missy arrived was Connie's date to host the Friday night bridge club. Connie's basement had been converted to a theater and a game room with a fully equipped bar, and it was there that sixteen of Connie's and Etta's closest friends were congregated to enjoy the evening. And enjoy they did. Until Missy, completely unsuspecting, stumbled down the stairs with an empty cocktail glass, intent on refilling it. Realizing that Missy was intoxicated, Connie sprang up to help her up the stairs to the main part of the house. And that's when all hell broke loose, so to speak.

"Uncle Conrad, you don't have to help me. Go back to your guests," Missy said in a loud voice.

At first Etta thought she heard wrong or that Missy misspoke. But Missy continued as Connie took her by the arm to turn her around.

"Let me go, Uncle—I mean Aunt Conrad! Aunt Connie or whatever!"

The intake of breath by sixteen startled women is deafening. Connie released Missy, held up her hands in surrender, and then returned to the card table. She picked up her hand and looked at her cards.

"Where are we?" she asked. No one said a word.

As Missy staggered back up the stairs, Connie's eyes moved from one woman's face to the next until she'd scanned every one of them, stopping at Etta. The only thought that came to Etta's mind at the time was, *That's why her hands are so big*! To say the moments that followed were awkward would be putting it lightly. The tension in the air was thick as gravy. Finally, Connie cleared her throat, still looking directly at Etta.

"I guess I'm out of the closet now. Ladies, my birth certificate reads Conrad Dillon Henderson," she said. "All of this is who I was meant to be." Connie spread her arms wide and moved her hands down her body. Connie, a refined southern belle, had started life as a bouncing baby boy. In plain English, she—or he at the time—had undergone a sex change. The thing to have done was explain to Missy that no one knew. Or else sent her packing but Connie did neither. Etta knew Connie focused on her to gauge her reaction, because she was the only woman in the room Connie considered a real friend. The news flabbergasted Etta, but she managed not to wither under Connie's scrutiny.

"Close your mouth, Etta," Connie said.

Etta didn't realize that her lips were agape. She followed Connie's command and shut her mouth. And then opened it again, saying "Whose bid is it?" That question put everyone's mind back on the game. That was the shortest bridge night they'd ever had. One by one, the ladies made an excuse to leave early. Leaving Etta as the last guest.

Etta couldn't help but think about all of the times they'd

been in different social settings and someone made a slur about homosexuals or told one of those nasty jokes. Poor Connie—she'd kept a stiff upper lip about the whole thing, even though she refused to laugh at the jokes. She even got into several disagreements over human rights and the fact that everyone had the right to live their lives anyway they wanted. Everybody just called her a liberal and laughed it off. Etta was certain she'd never made any slurs or negative comments. But she had voiced that she had a hard time believing people were born that way.

"Who would choose to be gay?" Connie asked.

"I think anyone who feels like they don't fit in will opt for any lifestyle where they are accepted. It seems to me that all people want to have friends and belong. Sometimes they make the wrong choices is all I'm saying."

Etta's response had almost started an argument between the two of them. Connie had disagreed, and Etta understood for the first time that night why her friend had been upset when they'd argued. From Etta's perspective, knowing the truth did nothing to change her feelings about Connie. It was also on that same evening, during those same few moments, that Etta wanted to ask Connie why she had never told her she used to be a man, but then she reconsidered. Of course Connie didn't tell her! Why would she? It's not like Etta wanted to date her and therefore things like that would be important to know. All she'd ever wanted to be was Connie's friend and nothing could change that.

Not so with the rest of the women. One by one they'd dropped Connie from their petty social registers. They no longer invited her to bake sales, the garden club held unannounced meetings, and the bridge club collapsed. The members of Peach Grove Praying Hands Non-Denominational Church, where Connie and Etta attended, were not judgmental at all. With everything out in the open Connie joined the Alternative Lifestyles ministry and Etta volunteered to help with the Singles ministry. Both women were active.

Etta's duty with the Singles ministry required attending the bimonthly meetings—or rather, being present on the campus during activities for singles. Etta alternated between the sanctuary, the nursery, and the senior citizens' library where she'd select a book to read during those nights. Technically she was single herself, but most of the men attending were much too young for Etta's comfort. Plus she was not looking for another husband. She'd had one. All first-time visitors were given cards to supply their names, addresses, and phone numbers. Etta would collect them all after the meeting—it was important to the pastor that it be immediately after the meeting—in order to have a welcome packet go out in the morning mail. The packet always contained a thank-you note from the pastor and his wife, notices of upcoming events, and an invitation to return.

Connie's duties with the Alternative Lifestyle group consisted of sharing her experience, strength, and hope. She also taught lessons for living once a month. Their duties took them to the church on different weeknights, but both sat together in the sanctuary on Sunday morning. As Etta walked the short distance to Connie's house, she felt her heart swell with gratitude. In this world, Etta knew, a real friend was hard to find.

Same Day

Chapter Thirty-Four

Dennis Cane sat in one of the huge leather chairs that flanked Merlot's desk. He whistled softly as he took in the furnishings and wall art that gave the office a flair equal to its owner. Merlot sat behind the desk dressed in a deep-purple suit, so deep that Dennis at first mistook it for dark gray. But the lavender shirt and matching tie left no doubts as to its true hue. While Dennis looked around, Merlot held in his hand several papers attached with a paper clip, flipping each page over as he went along.

"Man, this is what I call living the dream. You always had good taste, but now you've got class. And you dress like a rock star, but different," Dennis said.

"'Class' is one of my middle names. 'Sensible' is yours, as in your shoes and your shirt and your khaki pants, whereas

I only dress sensible on my working days," Merlot said making the quotation mark signal with his fingers on the last two words.

"Merlot is your middle name. What do you mean working days?" Dennis imitated the quotation marks.

"Days when I get into it, man. When I'm looking for someone, I have to change who I am so I can move among the people undetected. On those days I might have to be a plumber, a pizza delivery guy, a cable guy—days when I wear T-shirts, jeans, khakis, and work shirts. No offense to you, of course."

"And none taken. My clothes are comfortable, dude. I have to get down on my knees sometimes and get dirty which, by the way, is one reason I'm happy to see you today."

"I don't get down like that, man. No dirty stuff for me unless it's with a woman," Merlot winked.

"So you called to tell me you saw the light? Is that the good news you have for me?" Dennis laughed. He'd been told by one of the secretaries at the precinct that Merlot had called and left a message saying he needed to talk to him ASAP. Since Dennis was in his car at the time, he decided to drive into the city and visit Merlot at his office.

"I found my missing lady. I also identified the woman you wanted to talk to at the burn unit yesterday morning. They are one and the same. Her name is Chanel Franco. She's heavily sedated so you still can't talk to her. Her own family can't talk to her. But there you go. Mystery solved," Merlot announced, his hands spread apart and a big smile on his face.

"Are you serious? It sucks that I can't talk to her. I got a report from my officer on duty informing me that she's going to survive and her family was contacted. So eventually I will talk to her. Good job, man! It doesn't take you three years to track down someone."

"That's a true story. I aim to please," Merlot said. Both men laughed.

"Thank you for letting me know that you identified the woman," Dennis said in a serious tone. This news puts a platinum stamp on the omen!"

"Omen? Isn't that for bad things? This is good info for you," Merlot said.

"It's a good omen! I need help, dude. I've had my sights on this killer for three years and I've got to find him this time, or I'm going to witness two other women dying a horrific death at his hands this time next year. I've got to change something, do something different like he has. You're different! It's a sign. Go with me on this," Dennis said. "Maybe you can help me, give me a few tips . . . something . . .anything."

"Yes, I do know how to track people down. And that's what I'm going to continue doing. It helps to know the name of the person I'm looking for and to have a general description of them or an image. But, and this is important, I don't look for killers. I think I told you that."

"Remember that criminology course we had together in high school just for a hoot? We took it because some college made an offer the school superintendent couldn't refuse?"

"Yes."

"Remember how the professor told us that there are two types of homicides, and we looked at each other like he was crazy? Remember? You passed me a note that said, 'What? Homicide and murder? Those two types?' Do you remember that?"

"Yes, I remember." Merlot sighed. "Those that are solved with ease and those that are mysteries. He's the reason I started reading murder mysteries. Do you remember that? I was the only dude reading novels. I tried to keep that under wraps until stupid Josh found it and I had to put a spotlight on him after he couldn't say the word nemesis."

Dennis laughed. Deep, belly-shaking laughter.

"Dictionary Josh! You shut his mouth forever when you asked him to define the word."

Merlot joined in and the two laughed together for several minutes, each conjuring up his own image of a flustered, embarrassed Josh standing in the locker room with all the other guys laughing at him. As it turned out, that was a good thing for the kid. He started carrying around a dictionary after that and earned the nickname that stayed with him.

"So. You remember that mysteries, by definition, need widespread, all-inclusive, careful investigation to solve them. I have a mystery on my hands. This killer is selectively abducting young women and setting them on fire. Look at how quickly you found Chanel. I'm telling you, man, we can do this. We can stop this killer! Doesn't it bother you that he may come back to finish the job? You saw his intended victim." Dennis was on his feet now with his hands spread wide on Merlot's desk, as he moved in close enough to almost touch noses.

Merlot pushed back in his chair. "You know that I am not easily coerced. Yes, it bothers me. But I trust that you will do your job to protect her. Don't you have some kind of protective detail on her now? I don't chase killers! Can't you get that through your skull?"

"Well, if she hadn't lived, you would have been looking for a dead woman. And since she was unidentified, you wouldn't have known it for what? Years maybe? This killer could have spoiled your perfect record. Now that has to get under your skin, doesn't it?" Dennis had always known that Merlot was never a dumb jock counting on a scholarship to get to the professional level of a sport. He used his brains. And Dennis needed brain power. He moved over to the windows to stall by taking in the awesome view

"No, it doesn't. Because I found her and he didn't kill her. I completed the job. And by the way, how do you know about my perfect record?" Merlot stood and joined Dennis by the window. Both men peered down at Woodruff Park. People were sitting on benches, the chess players performing with an audience, and the early lunch crowd milling about.

“I did some research. You’re a good detective. Check yourself out on the Internet sometime,” Dennis turned to face Merlot.

“Thanks, Dennis. Good to know. But I never have nor will I ever look for serial killers.” Merlot replied as both men began to gesture with their hands. Anyone seeing them from any window across the way would swear that they were having a heated argument instead of one man begging the other to change his mind.

“But you search for people. That takes skill. And you’ve got resources! Resources that I don’t have because no one in my department wants to believe a murder almost happened this morning. They want to keep that news on the down low!” Dennis raised his hands in helplessness.

“And who coined the phrase *serial killer*? Didn’t we used to call them murderers? They didn’t call Jack the Ripper a serial killer. Serial killer is a new-age term. It makes the killer look smarter than he is. Or rarer. Plenty of killers have killed more than once. For years. Anyway, I’m done. I was hired to find Chanel Franco. I found her. I’ve been paid. Case closed!”

Dennis moved away from the window as he reached

Inside his jacket pocket, pulled out a peppermint, and popped it into his mouth. "You just saw several young women in the park. Any one of them could be next unless we stop this maniac." He turned back to Merlot with a pitiful, pained expression on his face and then plopped down in one of the leather chairs. He raised his arms toward the ceiling. "God help me!"

Merlot came back to his desk and sat down to face Dennis, while tapping a pen on the desk. He seemed to be in deep thought. He pressed his intercom buzzer.

"What's up, boss man?" Glenn answered.

"Glenn, come in for a minute. I want you to meet a living pest!" Merlot winked at Dennis.

"Will do," Glenn responded.

"Glenn is my investigator. He helps me do what I do so efficiently. You tell him everything you've told me. If there's a suspect to be found and he's left any type of trail, he'll find out something about him for you."

Dennis stood and came around the desk to hug Merlot's shoulders. They were like that, facing the door, when Glenn entered. His face showed no emotion as he looked at the two men.

"Glenn Bausch, meet Dennis Cane. I went to high school with this guy. We played on the same basketball team for four years. Best point guard I've ever seen. Just not tall enough!" Merlot explained coming from behind the desk.

Glenn stepped forward and shook hands with Dennis.

"Nice to meet you."

"Good to meet you too, Glenn."

"Dennis has a story to tell you. If you can help him, by all means do so. Take him with you to your office and do what you do. He's not a client. We're not involved. Just see if what he says makes sense to you . . . if you can make heads, tails, or a serial killer out of it," Merlot said.

"I'll do what I can, boss." Glenn turned to Dennis. "If you'll come with me, Dennis, my office is across the way."

"Thank you, Merlot. You don't know what this means to me," Dennis said as he followed Glenn out of the office.

Once the door was closed, Merlot stared at the abstract painting of a woman on his wall, thinking about the kind of nerve it took to douse someone with gasoline and set them on fire. And then his mind moved to motive. Crazy. Sick. Twisted. Hater. And then he decided to think about something else.

Same Day

Chapter Thirty-Five

Today Mira Dream arrived at work thirty minutes early. She knew her day was going to be filled, and she didn't want to be rushed. She had two patients to tend to—one was Jane Doe. She would have to scrutinize every inch of that poor girl's body. She thanked God that only half of the young lady's body had been burned. Months of rehabilitation might lead to an almost normal life. It was evident she'd been gorgeous before, and Dr. Salada and his team would work wonders to keep her from being an outcast because of her appearance. The arrival of her twin sister had dissolved any serious worries about adequate skin for grafting.

Mira sighed as she prepared herself for the task that lay ahead. She would repeat the debridement process, which involved the removal of damaged, dead, or infected tissue so that healthy tissue could heal.

She made a mental note of having seen Claire at her post two hours early. To Mira's surprise, most of the doctors were pleased with Claire's performance, especially since she'd helped to identify Mira's patient. Mira had no idea that she'd been handed the proof. If she hadn't been so busy, she could be having the celebrity Claire was now enjoying. But Mira's reputation was already well established, and she really didn't need extra attention. She cared about the health of her patients. Names meant nothing. And even though she knew her patient's name was Chanel, the patient would always be Jane Doe to Mira. She had asked God to heal Jane, "that poor burned child."

She entered the room just beyond the tent, stopped, put on the visor, making certain it covered her brow; put on a fresh plastic apron as she liked to call it, dipped her arms inside the huge protective arm coverings and a pair of latex gloves. She'd already checked the temperature, so she knew the inner sanctum was warm enough. She entered, armed with her battle weapons loaded on a cart. She pulled out a movable shelf attached to the bed and arranged her supplies—sterile instruments and a stainless steel bowl that held several pairs of sterile scissors—as well as the wash basin, three warmed bottles of sterile water, and a bottle of silver nitrate solution. She had plenty of gauze and tape. It was time to begin.

When Mira looked at the clock again, almost two hours had passed. She knew that she had done a thorough job, which is why she liked to work alone. Jane's family was all upset, understandably. Mira promised them she would take good care of this poor child. For the morning she'd done her duty. This had to be done twice a day, but when Miss Louise and her parents returned, they would see fresh bandages and bed linen, too.

Mira looked up as the tech who generally helped out with bandage changes walked past. The tech glanced in and went on her way. Everyone knew Mira was a one-woman bandage-changing show.

Same Day

Chapter Thirty-Six

Michael stepped off the elevator onto the third floor of Grady Hospital, and walked toward the burn unit. He stopped short when the police officers came into view through the glass windows of the double metal doors. So as not to appear suspicious, he proceeded to the buzzer and pressed it.

"May I help you?" asked a male voice.

"I'm here to see John McNamara."

A momentary pause. And then "Please check with the information desk. We have no patient by that name."

Of course you don't, Michael mused, taking long deliberate strides back to the elevators.

Now things were getting complicated. There was no way a strange visitor with no destination could walk past police officers without being noticed, and today was not a good day for any undue attention.

So what next?

Chanel Franco's room had already been located. Or was the proper term tent? It was amazing how easy it was to get into the burn unit coming into it on the other side because one never had to pass the receptionist. A casual late-night stroll down the hall had been productive. Injecting a high dosage of insulin into the IV was the way to silence her, but it could hardly be done while lawmen were on patrol. Or the round-the-clock nurses. One almost needed to be invisible. While waiting for the elevator to arrive, a friendly woman pushing a teenage girl seated in a wheelchair with both legs stretched straight and swathed in bandages passed by. The woman was dressed in jeans and one of those scrub tops. She had to be a nurse. She wore white orthopedic shoes and a lanyard with her employee ID badge.

"Hello," she said with a big smile.

"Hello," replied Michael, taking careful notice of the color, the design, and the cut of the top. It could be specially ordered or perhaps purchased from a hospital supply store or one of those uniform shops. Ordering would delay everything, and requesting next day delivery would surely be memorable. Oh, what to do? Certainly there was a room, a stockroom, somewhere in this very hospital where an employee could get things like that. Did the male nurses wear the same uniform or did they vary according to specialty? It was going to take a little more exploration in order to know exactly. Observing all nurses was priority one. And priority two was simple. What did every employee in this place have in common? Their ID badges, worn on a lanyard or clipped to some part of their clothing. How hard would it be to bump into one of those casual employees who clipped their badges, remove it, and continue on one's way? It couldn't be that hard. The only way to tell was to try it. The elevator finally arrived. It was going up, and someone had already pushed the button for the fourth floor.

Thirty minutes later, the elevator going down stopped on the fourth floor and A. D. Huff got on the elevator. It stopped on the third floor, where Charles Aver, and M. S. Leeds got on. At the second floor, Garcella Mack got on and started to talk, chatting all the way to level G where the supply room, stocked with supplies and employee uniforms, was located.

"As a matter of fact, I'm going that way. I'll show you, honey. You will find that you can't listen to nothing these people tell you. You have to find out for yourself! I've been here two years and just found out that there's a different way to get to the cafeteria besides walking for days and following the signs. Come with me, sugar. I'll get you fixed right up."

True to her word, Garcella opened the door to the stockroom, allowing A. D. Huff full access to all nurses' uniforms. She waited, nodding her head when the proper size top and pants were chosen.

"You'll have to go to see Loretta on the second floor of the North Tower to get your shoes ordered. I'm so sorry you got the wrong information. But, honey, you aren't the first one and you definitely won't be the last. At least you got your badge!"

A. D. and Garcella left the stockroom together, rode the elevator to the main level where Garcella gave instructions to get to the proper bank of elevators to get to the North Tower.

"Just follow those red tiles, sweetheart. It was a real pleasure meeting you, and I hope you'll stay a while with us."

A. D. thanked Garcella again and walked away. Arriving at the first open hallway, A. D. turned left to follow the signs to the exit. Finding white orthopedic shoes was not an issue. Getting out of the hospital without incident was Mission Important. A quick glance at the clock on the wall revealed plenty of time before rush hour. Michael felt no need to be in a hurry, but it was necessary to pocket the telltale ID badge until D-day.

Same Day

Chapter Thirty-Seven

Anissa Strickland took one last look in the mirror and fluffed her blonde hair. Satisfied, she grabbed a silver mesh shawl and walked from her bedroom to her living room where Merlot Candy waited. She always felt warm inside when she looked at him. From the day they'd met, she'd liked everything about him. But once she escaped her abusive husband and felt freedom, she knew she'd never permit herself to become easily entangled with a man again. Merlot had been hired by her husband to find her and he did. But he kept the information to himself, and instead made every effort to warn her so that she could stay free. Merlot had become her knight in loud-color suits, her magical Merlin.

Kathy Stockton, a friend who lived in a suburb of

Atlanta, convinced Anissa to move back to the South. She had lived in the Atlanta area for a brief period when she was on the run from her spouse. She was happy to call the capital of Georgia home again. It was a beautiful city, with trees, seasons, all kinds of people from all kinds of places, and activities galore. She had a nice apartment she wouldn't trade for anything. And she lived only a fifteen-minute drive from Merlot's place.

"I'm ready," she said, stopping in front of the armchair where he sat thumbing through a magazine. She smiled and naturally he smiled back.

"You look beautiful, as usual," he said as he rose to meet her. Merlot whistled softly. He always did that. He said she was his Helen of Troy and his Achilles' heel all wrapped up in one adorable package. He always complimented her, no matter the time of day or what she wore. His brown eyes turned green, a common occurrence, as he admired the orange dress that was a bit shorter than she normally wore.

"Why thank you, kind sir. You look good enough to eat yourself," she said. Flirting was not a good practice, she knew, but sometimes she couldn't help herself. He was all male with all the animal attraction. He looked so handsome, especially when he smiled. Perfect teeth and lips that begged to be kissed.

“Maybe we look too good to go out. I can think of several things we could do here and still look good and feel good,” he said as he looked directly into her eyes. She blushed.

“Shall we go, Merlin? Your magic is getting hard to resist.” As she stepped back, he leaned his head to the right and raised his hands in submission.

“Okay, but you don’t know what you’re missing,” he said. Anissa’s pulse rate jumped.

They both turned toward the door, with Merlot slightly in front so that he could be the first one out. She locked the door, and then led the way to the car thinking that he was beside himself tonight with his unveiled suggestions. It was hard to ignore them. She didn’t know exactly what she was missing by not having slept with him—like all his moves and rhythms—but she had a pretty good idea. He had big hands. If that was a true indicator, she was indeed passing up pure ecstasy.

“Now what’s this dinner about?” he asked as he came up close behind her and grabbed her hand.

Unable to help herself, she caught her breath. *Calm down, Anissa.* She remembered her mom telling her once that holding hands was the most romantic and tender thing a man could do for a woman. And Anissa needed tenderness for the rest of her life.

"We're having dinner with Louise and her parents. Her brother may or may not join us, depending on his playing schedule tonight. He's in some kind of band. I hear he's pretty good," she replied, silently willing herself to become indifferent.

"And why are we dining with these people tonight when the Boston Celtics just might win the NBA championship? We can watch the game here. It'll be fun," he said.

"We're dining with them because Mr. and Mrs. Canola want to meet the man who found their daughter and thank him." Anissa kissed him lightly on the cheek. She blushed again, remembering how her husband, Foley, used to kiss her on the cheek after beating her senseless. She kissed Merlot once more, just to be different from Foley.

"Thank you for that! It's a good thing I can record the game, or else I'd pick you up and carry you back inside and drop you on the sofa so that I can trip and fall on top of you."

He pulled her to him and hugged her causing an emotional skirmish to her insides.

"You're in rare form this evening. No more dirty talk for you. You're making me have hot flashes and I'm way too young for that."

They both laughed as he released her. *Only a matter of time before we get between those sheets.*

He opened the car door and she got in, revealing a hint of thigh as she pulled her legs inside. It was not easy to resist this man. *But oh well. All in good time. A good relationship is more than sex.* She took deep breaths as he walked around the car. He opened the door, unbuttoned his black jacket to reveal a mauve-colored shirt with matching paisley tie, and slid in behind the steering wheel. *My goodness. This man is so fine.*

"You're a hero, you know," Anissa said softly.

"Oh really?" Merlot gazed into her eyes again as he pushed the button to start the car. He was so good at staring.

"Yes, really." She pulled her eyes away and concentrated on the road. Keeping him at arm's length was paramount tonight. She decided to turn a deaf ear to his charming words. But he's so sexy and he smells so good.

Remember Foley. She reminded herself that her ex-husband had been all of those things and more. She'd fallen hopelessly in love with him, missing all of the warning signals. That would never happen to her again.

Anissa and Merlot had seen many plays together, danced the night away at a multitude of fundraising galas and charity balls, sat side by side and crooned to their favorite singers in concert, and walked until their feet hurt in many outside festivals held in Piedmont Park. Even the hikes that they took on Sunday morning were beginning to be intimate. How many times had he taken her hand to help her in a particular slippery spot on that mountain? She was running out of excuses.

Merlot was the kind of man who did everything well—dancing, golf, skating, playing basketball, matching wits. She dared not think too long about what he could do in the lovemaking department. She told herself again to be calm, and not let that smile of his get her all hot and bothered. *Only a matter of time.*

Same Day

Chapter Thirty-Eight

Merlot drove smoothly, navigating side streets effortlessly until they arrived at Fernando Luigi's Primo Italiano Restaurant at 7:55 p.m.—five minutes early for their eight o'clock reservation. Inside they were immediately led to their table. The Canola family, already seated, stood as they approached.

"You look great, Anissa," Louise said, coming forward to meet them. Merlot could not miss the deep sadness in her eyes even though she smiled.

"And so do you, Merlot," Louise added, admiring Merlot's attire.

The two women embraced, Louise holding on longer than Anissa who gave her a big squeeze and patted her back and tried to pull away. “I’m so sorry about Chanel,” Anissa said. Louise released her and then hugged Merlot.

“Mama, Papa, this is my friend, Anissa Strickland, and this wonderful man is Merlot Candy. Merlot, meet my mother, Lausanne Canola, and my father, Theo Canola.”

Mr. and Mrs. Canola both stood up to greet them. Merlot observed that everything about Louise’s facial features were like her father’s. The two men shook hands and Mrs. Canola hugged Anissa, kissing the air on either side of her face. They came apart holding hands, looking at each other, and smiling.

“I want to thank you, Mr. Candy for your excellent work. Louise tells me that she came to see you and you found Chanel the same day.” Theo cast an appraising look at Merlot.

“Please call me Merlot.”

“Thank you, Merlot.” Lausanne took both his hands and pressed them to her cheeks.

“You’re welcome. But it’s my job and I take it very seriously. I’m glad I was able to locate her so quickly,” Merlot said as he pulled out a chair for Anissa.

Once everyone was seated and the server had poured red

wine, Theo looked at Merlot and said, "I want to hire you to find this person who tried to kill my daughter. But first we eat."

Merlot almost choked on his wine. Was he hearing things? Had this man been talking to Dennis? Find the person who killed his daughter? He didn't look for killers! What was wrong with everybody? He didn't know how he was going to say no to this man, but he would decline.

Menus were explained, the specialties of the house were presented, and soon everyone was eating. The food was delicious. After updating them on Chanel's condition and sharing that Louise would donate skin, the Canola family steered the conversation in another direction. The only other comment made was about the length of time before she healed. Over dessert, the best cannoli Merlot had ever had, Theo Canola got down to business.

"Mr. Candy, I am a skeptic by nature. I rarely trust the police even though I've never had need of their services. My daughter tells me she filed a missing person's report late Saturday night and has heard nothing from the police. She visited you once and you found Chanel within a few hours. Someone tried to kill our daughter and I want to know who that person is. I don't care what their reasons are, I don't care if this person is insane and has no reasoning power, I don't care about him at all except I want to know who he is. I want him to pay for what he has done. I am a wealthy man, Mr. Candy. No price is beyond my means. Please find this person for me."

Merlot took a sip of coffee. "Mr. Canola, I am a private investigator. I am not trained to look for murderers or would-be murderers. I look for missing people. I'm good at that. And to be fair to the police, I must explain that your daughter was reported missing in Atlanta, but was found outside of their jurisdiction, near Peach Grove. I have a friend, a homicide detective, who's had suspicions about this killer for a while. He's actively involved. He was at the hospital yesterday, too. He's who you need. He knows how to gather clues, evidence—the whole thing. I can introduce you to him." Merlot shot Anissa a quick look, but no help was coming from her.

"Ah, but you said the word I don't want to hear. *Police.* If this man is your friend, perhaps he can work with you and show you the ropes, so to speak. When you think about it carefully, a murderer at large is a sort of missing person. And as you told my wife, you take your job seriously, your job of looking for missing persons." Mr. Canola sipped his cognac. He could compete with Merlot any day in a contest for holding eye contact the longest—and win. Merlot chuckled to himself. Theo had made a good point, but it was not going to win this little battle.

"I'm sorry, Mr. Canola. I feel that I would be doing myself and all three of you a disservice if I were to accept such an undertaking. I cannot. I will not accept it." Merlot's voice remained calm, with a degree of finality.

"Louise tells me that you are the reason that *Mademoiselle* Strickland is alive today. She tells me that you refused to tell her late husband, who hired you, where to find her. Why is that, *Monsieur*?"

Merlot signaled the waiter. Normally he didn't have after-dinner alcoholic drinks. Especially when he ate dessert, but tonight he would make an exception. The waiter was at the table in a few seconds.

"Yes, sir. May I get you something else?" he asked.

"A cognac please," Merlot said. He surmised that Mr. Canola was not going to easily take no for an answer. The man was addressing him formally in French. Merlot loved

Anissa and he knew that she and Louise were friends. Anissa would understand his need to decline this offer. Of course, Louise would, too. But her parents. What were they thinking? He wasn't a superhero. And he was not a homicide detective. He could not ethically accept what this man proposed.

"Monsieur Canola, je suis désolé, mais ce n'est pas possible." Merlot's French accent was flawless and he knew it.

One of Mr. Canola's eyebrows went up a notch. "Mr. Candy, in Europe, every child at some point is introduced to a fictional Frenchman who is a detective and the main character of many books by a world famous author. He specializes in finding murderers. A private detective," Theo Canola said.

Merlot smiled. This man was pulling out all the stops. "I, too, was introduced to this well-dressed *Belgian* detective who relies upon his 'little gray cells.' Agatha Christie was one of my favorites and it follows that Hercule Poirot was one of my favorite characters."

Again the eyebrow went up a notch. *I can do this all night long*, Merlot thought to himself. The answer was still no. He would never agree to this proposal.

Or so he thought.

By the end of the evening Merlot agreed to try to find the killer. To do the best that he could. He wasn't making any promises. And he felt like he'd been made to do something against his will. But how does a man say no to the parents and friend of the woman he loves while she's looking at him?

As he drove Anissa home, Merlot couldn't help thinking that the last time he accepted a million dollars as a retainer, Anissa was involved. He had to marry her. It was only fair that he spend his money to make her happy.

June 18, 2008

Wednesday

Chapter Thirty-Nine

Dennis Cane sat at his desk. He was frustrated. The incident at Mint Leaf Manor had been mentioned briefly in the *Peach Grove Sentinel*, the article written as though the whole thing had been taken care of—*Nothing to worry about, citizens of our fair city*. He had gone over his copy of the investigator's report twice. Those black threads provided a link he could possibly tie in to this murder attempt if just one had been found. This report contained nothing about threads. He was an experienced crime scene investigator. Maybe he could go back to Mint Leaf Manor and look around. His phone rang.

"Dennis Cane," he answered.

"Dennis, this is Merlot. Did I get you at a bad time?"

"Of course not. What's up?" Dennis was surprised and pleased to hear his friend's voice again so soon.

"Well, it seems I've been hired to find another missing person and I need your help."

"Really? You need my help? This means *quid pro quo.* I help you and you help me," Dennis hoped Merlot would offer to help him in his torch killer investigation.

"I need you to help me get to know your serial killer. You know, as much as you can with the little you have. And if I can say or do anything that might assist you, I will."

Dennis raised his free hand toward the heavens. Maybe Merlot had seen a light or a star in the east. If he was serious.

"I didn't think you got involved with murder. Are you messing with me?"

"No, I'm not. My missing lady, Chanel Franco, is your semimurder victim. I wondered if we could get together and map out something. I have no idea how to proceed. I just want to offer you my assistance and at the same time pick your brain."

Dennis laughed. "It's harvest time in my head, Merlot. When do you want to start gathering this crop?" Dennis couldn't quite wrap his mind around Merlot's change in attitude, but he was ready to do whatever it took.

"Like I said looking for killers is not my thing. I was asked by Chanel's father—a relentless, man who has no faith in the police—to find the man who hurt her. No offense to you. He thinks I can walk on water just because I found his daughter in the hospital the same day that I was hired. He wants justice. And it didn't help at all that the whole time I was turning his offer down, the woman I intend to marry sat across from me at the dinner table pleading with her eyes," Merlot said.

"So that means that you and I are going to work together? I mean, you said *my serial killer.*" Dennis crossed his fingers.

"From what I remember about our conversation the other day, you're convinced that this person has killed more than once and that he will kill again. So let's see if we can by some miracle find him. You and I have to work together because I don't want to break the law trying to be the law. You know what I'm saying?"

"Well I'm ready if you are. Great Scott!" Dennis said, closing the file and placing it inside his desk drawer.

"Great who? Who says that? Anyway is now good for

you?”

“I’ll be at your office in an hour.” Dennis grabbed his jacket, peppermints and briefcase, and then rushed out of his office. Peter Millet, reading his newspapers at his desk, did a double take.

“Where you going, boss? I didn’t fill you in on today’s headlines yet.”

“Later, Peter. If the chief asks about me, tell him I’ll be back later. I’m out in the field.”

“The field?”

“That’s police talk, Peter. Read your newspapers.”

Same Day

Chapter Forty

Dennis sat across from Merlot and Glenn at a long lacquered table in Merlot's conference room. In the center of the table was an open file containing printouts of probability charts Glenn had created, all of Dennis's files that he usually kept locked up in his briefcase, a platter of sandwiches, and an urn of coffee. Each man had a steaming cup and a half-eaten sandwich in front of him. They had been sharing information for almost thirty minutes.

"Since you and I talked on Monday, I've learned the identity of another one of these victims—Clementine Ments who died in Wilder County on June 24, 2007. Their county medical examiner identified her by a knee replacement," Dennis said.

"And that's why I need your input, Dennis," Merlot said. "Who knew it takes almost a year to track down that kind of information? I thought everything was easy to find online."

"Not that kind of thing," Dennis replied. "They said something about the surgery being done overseas. Sometimes those things can get all mixed up when the patient relocates. I'm just happy we know who she is. And the irony of the whole thing is that her parents are my next-door neighbors."

"So you talked to them?" Merlot asked.

"Is snow white? Of course I did. As a neighbor."

"A nosy neighbor. Okay, here is the fact. We don't know who we're looking for. I don't like that. That's not how I do it. And when are you going to show me these files?"

Dennis picked up one of three file folders. It was labeled "Missing Women." He opened it and removed a list of names and dates that he placed on the table so both men could see it. He then removed six fliers he'd snatched from public places where more than one of the same was posted.

"Okay, you guys. Follow along with me please. Meredith Payne, aged 25, blonde, worked as a receptionist, last seen on June 16, 2005."

He placed the flier on the table so that Merlot and Glenn stared into her face.

"We found her," Glenn said. "Only she didn't look that good when we finally located her."

"I told him about her," Merlot said, picking up the flier to take a closer look. "I was hired by some attorneys to find her. An aunt died and Meredith was her primary heir," he said to Dennis.

"Lucy Wren, 27, blonde, a human resources officer for a large Atlanta corporation, last seen on June 24, 2005."

The flier was placed on the table.

"Janet Lilly, 24, blonde, a nurse, last seen leaving work on June 15, 2006; Maggie Brooks, 26, blonde, a nail technician, last seen going into the mall on June 24, 2006; Carrie Lee, 32, blonde, a plumber, last seen walking down her street toward the city lights around 9 p.m. on June 16, 2007; and last: Clementine Ments last seen on June 24, 2007. She's my neighbors' daughter."

All of the fliers were on the table. Dennis folded his

hands under his chin and looked at the two men across from him.

"You'll notice that their bodies were all found on the date they disappeared. Carrie Lee just made it under the deadline. Her body was discovered by the police at 11:58 p.m. on the sixteenth. This killer stays with the routine," he said.

"All of the women are young and blonde. They're all pretty, and if I look close enough, I can see a slight resemblance in all of them," Glenn said.

Dennis opened the second file that contained newspaper clippings with stories that gave locations, dates, and information about how and where each body was found.

"And what's behind door number three?" Merlot asked, glancing at the third file.

"This one has notes I've written to myself. They may not make sense to either of you, but I understand them."

"We still have no clue who we're looking for," said Merlot. I don't like feeling helpless. I like to have a name, a photo, and the last place the person was seen. This I do not like."

"It's not how I like to do it. But we do have a *modus operandi*—this killer likes to burn women to death—and that's a great start. We also know that the killer has a pattern. The women have died on two dates in June for the past three years—the sixteenth and the twenty-fourth. And that he wears a black leotard. We have identified two women from your list of missing persons as victims and the latest attempt failed. We're getting closer. We just have to hope that Chanel is able to talk before the twenty-fourth," Dennis said.

"Okay. That's good, but I know enough to know that we have to find somebody that all of these women have in common. Do you have anything like that, Cane?"

"You know more than that, Candy," Dennis insisted.

"How do you know what I know?"

"Let me put in terms you understand—basketball," Dennis said.

"What does basketball have to do with finding a murderer?"

"I'm glad you asked. It's like setting a screen between the killer and the intended victim. A moving screen is not a foul in a homicide investigation. You have to move because if you don't, you'll never catch the killer," Dennis explained.

"With homicide a moving screen is legal?"

Dennis nodded his head in agreement. "Now you're getting it! You've had it all along. That's why you're so good at finding people."

Merlot looked at Glenn. "I'm good because Glenn is good. In our business, he sets the screens for me," Merlot said.

"Like I said, you know more than you think you know about finding a killer." Dennis smiled.

"Comparing information received from Louise Canola concerning Chanel to information received from the parents of the now identified victim, Clementine Ments, we discovered that both women have attended the same church," Glenn said, shrugging his shoulders with arms bent at the elbow and hands held wide apart like a basketball player who just scored one of those no-way-that-ball-is-going-in shots.

"And Glenn strikes again! When did you make this discovery?" Merlot turned to Glenn with eyebrows raised.

"While you were putting this picnic together." Dennis waved his arms over the sandwiches and coffee.

"What church?" Merlot asked.

"A church in my city." Dennis placed a fact sheet about the Peach Grove Praying Hands Non-Denominational Church in front of Merlot. Merlot read the information and then looked first at Glenn, then Dennis.

"I looked into that church," Dennis continued. "It appears to be solely owned and operated by the pastor. There's no board of directors, no steering committees, no one to tell this man what to do but God. Think about it."

"I have thought about it. I've got some more research to do," Glenn said. "That's my job here, to look deep into anomalies. Another odd thing is that all of the missing women recently moved to Georgia before their deaths. That could explain why no dental records were available locally to help identify them if they were among the burned bodies found."

"That's good thinking, Glenn. The families reported their loved ones missing in the counties where they lived. I guess no one ever thought about checking burn victims that closely and if they did the procedure would have been too costly," Dennis said.

"Dental x-rays would have been less costly, had they

been available. But I wasn't able to track down any dentists for the missing women. Not yet." Glenn turned his attention toward Merlot who held one finger in the air to get their attention.

"If you guys are done talking about teeth I say we move forward with what we know. The church will be our first stop. And we need the help of one of your profilers to give us an idea of what kind of person we're looking for." Merlot leaned back in his chair.

"My profilers? Are you kidding?" Dennis asked, his eyes open wide. "What does a city with no murders need a profiler for? These men usually work with the FBI and they won't get involved unless I have three murders."

Merlot stared through the window behind Glenn, deep in thought. They needed to have some idea of who they were pursuing. Otherwise they could just go out on the street and become suspicious of everybody. That's not how Merlot worked. Minutes later he snapped to attention.

"I have an acquaintance who has lots of friends," he said. "Maybe she knows somebody that can lead us into the light. Right now I don't know if we're looking for a male or female, dog or cat!"

"Fine with me. I like to know who I'm looking for, too," Dennis responded.

Merlot looked at his watch. "Let me make a call while the two of you finish comparing notes on Meredith Payne, Clementine Ments, and Chanel Franco. Glenn's got the info we received about Meredith in one of those printouts over there."

Merlot slid his chair back and walked over to his desk. He pulled out a rolodex and flipped through it, stopping when he found what he was looking for. He picked up the receiver for the phone on his desk and dialed a number.

Miles away, in Powder Springs, Georgia, another suburb of Atlanta, in a beautifully decorated sunroom, the phone rang. Kathy Stockton, sitting on the yellow sofa and sifting through her mail, glanced over at the phone. It rang three times before she moved to answer it.

"Hello?" Kathy sang into the phone. An attractive redhead, aged fiftysomething, she could easily have passed for late thirties. Her green eyes twinkled when she recognized the voice on the other end.

"Hello? Kathy Stockton? Merlot Candy."

"Hi, Merlot! I recognize your voice. How are you

doing?" Kathy said. The two had not spoken in years. Theo Canola thought Merlot was the reason why Anissa was alive today, but he had not met Kathy Stockton. It was she who'd welcomed Anissa into her family home in Manhattan and convinced her the only way to escape from her abusive husband was to disappear in the chaos of 9/11. Kathy brought Anissa home with her to Georgia to begin a new life, with a new identity that one of Kathy's friends helped her establish with legitimate identification papers. Kathy and Merlot had worked together to warn Anissa that her husband knew where she was, and Kathy helped her get out of Boston to New York. She and Anissa became close friends. As a result Kathy warmed to Merlot even though she believed at first that he'd led Anissa's husband to her. She appreciated his kindness and his mind, and told him to call if he ever needed her help.

"I'm fine. Working hard as usual. I called to ask for your help," Merlot said.

"I'm at your service."

"Would you happen to have an FBI profiler in that bevy of friends of yours?" Merlot laughed. "Seriously."

"I just might. I'll look into my little black book and see

who I can find. How quickly do you need such a person?"

"Now, or no later than close of business today."

"I'll get on it and call you back. I talked to Anissa last night. She told me all about the new role you've taken on to track down someone who attempted murder. Good for you. I trust you'll do a fantastic job and we both know how much I don't like men who do bad things to women. Count on me to help in anyway I can, sweetheart."

"Thanks for the vote of confidence, Kathy, but I made no promises. I have no idea what I'm doing or who I'm looking for. But if you can find a profiler for me, that would really simplify things."

"You can do this, Merlot. Call you later," Kathy said as she ended the call. Merlot stared at the phone, and then took a deep breath before rejoining Glenn and Dennis.

"This guy is great, Merlot," Dennis said looking appreciatively at Glenn. "He's just pulled up and printed out tons of information about that church."

"How's about the two of us pay a visit to this church?" Merlot asked.

"When?"

"Right now."

Same Day

Chapter Forty-One

The Peach Grove Praying Hands Non-Denominational Church sat on ten acres of prime property at 3137 Smithstone Boulevard on the southwest end of the city. Merlot read over the church brochure and one of the printouts about the church from Glenn while Dennis drove.

"Do you go to church?" Merlot asked.

"I visit. You don't remember how my mom and dad took us to church three times a week? When I left home I had no plans to ever go to church again."

Merlot laughed. "I didn't know, man. You okay?"

"I'm fine. Since I've been here I go to church on Easter and Christmas. It just seems like the right thing to do. How about you? What church do you call home?

"I can't tell you the last time I went to church. Yes I can. It was my grandmother's funeral. I believe in God, but I don't think my God is really into all of the rigamarole created by so many denominations and churches on every corner. To be perfectly honest I feel uneasy in a building dedicated to the worship of a God who only shows up on Sunday." Merlot glanced over at Dennis as he spoke.

"That's true. A lot of people act like God only goes to church on Sunday. Not me. I pray whenever I want, and until I feel at home in a church, I'll keep visiting."

"I don't even visit. But I guess I'll go when Anissa and I marry. She'll probably want to have a church wedding. I want that too," Merlot said.

"So when am I going to meet Anissa? Sounds like you're serious about her."

"Soon. Look at that!" Merlot said as Dennis turned into the drive to the church. A long winding driveway led to ample parking. Dennis parked near the front. "Man that's a church! That little brochure didn't do this place justice!"

Peach Grove Praying Hands Non-Denominational Church was impressive. Steeples, arched windows with stained glass, and massive wooden doors as the entrance.

They entered the building and stepped on a plush purple runner in the center of marble flooring, which led to a huge marble-tiled wall that seemed to soar. The ceiling was so high the two men had the momentary feeling of being outside. In the center of the wall hung a bulletin board framed in gold and encased in glass. A tall, attractive, regal woman standing nearby turned to greet them. Although she'd averted her eyes when they came in, Merlot was certain she'd watched as they walked up and entered the door. She had one of those faces that looked like someone he'd seen before. A comfortable, familiar face. Her hands filled with papers, she slid the glass door of the bulletin board case to one side, her eyes traveling the length of both men in seconds.

"Good afternoon, gentlemen. God bless you," she said in perfectly enunciated syllables.

"Hello," Merlot began. "We're looking for the church office."

She turned her gaze toward him, and he looked into the

clearest and shrewdist blue eyes he'd seen in a long time. Her eyes seemed to penetrate to his soul. He shivered. He really thought he'd outgrown his fear of people who claimed to be so holy that they had a one-on-one relationship with God—a relationship that allowed them to see into the lives of others. Her hair pulled up in a bun on the top of her head revealed years, at least sixty, but her arms looked toned and she had a nice figure. The pale-pink suit she wore flattered her waistline while the hemline revealed a pair of shapely legs. He imagined she'd been a real looker in her younger days. Her face, with a tiny smile, aquiline nose, and blue eyes, had the look of intelligence.

"I can show you to the office. Do you mind if I ask what your business is with us today? I'm Olivet Wendell, the pastor's wife." She walked forward and extended her hand to Merlot and then to Dennis. She had a strong grip. Both men eyed each other after the handshake.

"I'm a private investigator, and my friend is a homicide detective," Merlot said. "We're looking for some information. We understand you have a singles ministry here, and we wanted to see if you kept some sort of record of who comes and goes to these meetings. We'd also like to speak with the person who presides at the meetings."

"How very interesting that there are two of you. Very interesting indeed. I can't imagine how we can help with homicide, but come this way. I'll introduce you to our singles pastor. Perhaps he can shed some light on your unusual request." She smiled and beckoned the two men to follow her down a long hallway.

Here the floors were carpeted in deep purple. The framed art on the walls did not consist of the more common portraits of Jesus looking upward in the garden of Gethsemane as he prayed at the last supper with his disciples, but rather garden scenes, and modern people on their knees praying. All oil on canvas. Beautiful music from an organ came from somewhere in the building and voices harmonized.

"That's our women's choir that you hear. This is their practice time," Olivet looked back over her shoulder as she opened a door to an office marked Singles Ministry, Pastor Michael Thomas Genner. Inside, the office was elaborate and well furnished. The only occupant in the room stood as they entered and walked from behind his desk.

“Hello, Mrs. Wendell,” he said in a soft, cultured voice.

“Tom Genner, these men will first show you some identification, and then they’d like to ask you some questions about our singles ministry.”

The confident-looking thirtysomething man she addressed wore glasses and was handsome in spite of his receding hairline. Not one to compliment men on their looks, Merlot had to admit this pastor was well built and had perfect teeth. He looked at both men expectantly.

Merlot removed his wallet and produced his investigator’s license and ID, while Dennis produced his badge. Tom Genner’s expression remained unreadable as he nodded to Olivet, who smiled at him.

“Thank you, ma’am,” he said.

Olivet studied Tom’s face momentarily, her blue eyes staring into his, and smiled that little smile again. She looked down at her hands modestly crossed in front of her, and then backed away to the open door behind her.

“I hope you get what you need, gentlemen. I can imagine how distressful a murder can be, although I don’t believe you’ll find anyone with that mindset in our little church.”

Merlot couldn't help but notice that Tom Genner visibly relaxed when she closed the door.

"Gentlemen, please have a seat and tell me what I can do for you," he said, indicating with a sweep of his hands the several options for sitting in the lavish office. Merlot and Dennis chose two navy wingbacked chairs that flanked the desk.

"I don't know if you heard the news," Dennis began, "but an unidentified female body that was found burned beyond recognition last year was found in Wilder County. That body was recently identified as Clementine Ments. Her family tells me that she attended your singles ministry."

"Yes, I heard about that. I actually officiated at her memorial services on June 7," Tom said, his coloring changing as he adjusted his glasses. Merlot recognized the reaction as a signal the man was uncomfortable. It was time to pay attention.

"Chanel Franco," Merlot said in a soft voice. No response. "She was supposed to have attended a singles function here as well. Is that true?"

Tom cleared his throat. "We have a member who keeps up with attendance at the singles meetings. Her name is Etta

Wasp. Her records are kept off site—by special request. I'll be happy to call her and ask."

"If you don't mind we'd rather speak with her personally," Merlot said. "If she keeps records perhaps she'll know if Miss Franco attended on June 7."

"May I have her address, please?" Dennis requested. "And may I ask if you ever noticed Clementine with any men?"

Tom swallowed and his cheeks flushed as he turned his attention toward the computer on his desk. He typed a few keys, picked up a pen, and copied down an address from his screen. He gave the address to Dennis.

"Yes, I noticed. She was always alone," he said to Dennis.

"Thank you," Dennis glanced over the paper Tom gave to him. "Etta Wasp. Mrs. Wasp?" he prodded.

"Yes. Mrs. Wasp. She is a widow and a very nice lady. I'm certain that she'll be delighted to help."

"How long have you been the singles minister?" Merlot asked.

"I've been with the church for three years," he replied, as he turned his blue eyes toward Merlot. "I was sorry to hear about Clementine's death, but there's really nothing more that I can tell you. I didn't know her personally."

Merlot learned years ago how to recognize a "tell"—an unwitting signal that people give when they lie. Tom's tell was a fine line of perspiration forming above his top lip, barely perceptible Maintaining unwavering eye contact allows one to see things appear that were not there before. Could this man be troubled? His conscience uneasy? The singles pastor was not being forthcoming.

Merlot relaxed his gaze and began to take in the office décor. On a bookshelf to the right of the desk were several framed photos. All contained a pretty, smiling brunette, either alone or with two small children—a boy and a girl. An immense print of a seaside covered the wall behind a burgundy couch. End tables, lamps, and a nice rug underneath an oval cocktail table completed the cozy sitting area. The opposite wall was covered with framed certificates, educational degrees, and awards. An impressive collection of trophies to indicate the level of respectability of Tom Genner. And yet he chose to be disingenuous about a single lady who attended his ministry. Why?

"I think that's all I need. How about you, Dennis?" As

Merlot looked at his friend, his peripheral vision observed a subtle relaxation of Tom's muscles throughout his body. Like he could suddenly breathe better. The pressure was off.

"I'm done. If I need anything else, I'll be back." Dennis stood and shook Tom's hand.

Tom stood. "I'm sorry I couldn't be of more assistance. I believe that Sister Wasp will help you. I'll let her know to expect you. This afternoon?" he asked.

"Yes," Merlot and Dennis answered simultaneously.

"I will give her a call immediately. I'll walk you gentlemen out," Tom said, moving from behind his desk.

"We can find our way," Merlot said. "It seemed pretty straightforward."

Tom opened the door to his office and stood to the side as Dennis and Merlot left. He closed the door behind them. They walked back the way the pastor's wife brought them in. Merlot was surprised to find her in the exact spot where she was when they arrived, only this time she wasn't alone. She was joined by a tall, distinguished gentleman with frosted gray hair and pale-blue eyes, and immaculately dressed in a gray suit with blue accessories. He stood by Olivet's side as she faced two elegant elderly women. One of the women spoke with a serious expression on her face as she looked intently at the pastor's wife who was giving complete attention to what was being said. The other woman, standing a little apart from them, looked as though she was in another world, her attention focused on the pastor. He spoke quietly to her until he noticed Dennis and Merlot approaching and turned to greet them.

"Good afternoon. Do you need any help?" he asked.

Olivet turned away from the woman, training her eyes first on Dennis and then on Merlot. Once again Merlot was impressed by the brilliance and illumination of her ocean-blue eyes, and the overwhelming feeling of familiarity.

"These gentlemen are detectives," Olivet told her husband, as she clasped the hands of the woman who had been speaking with her. Merlot noticed a slight change in the woman's demeanor, as if she tightened every muscle in her body in preparation for self-defense.

"This is Martha Smith, a longtime member of the church, and her friend Genevieve Roark, who is also a veteran member. And this is Pastor Gavin Wendell, my husband," Olivet said. "I didn't get your names, gentlemen."

"I'm Merlot Candy." He extended his hand, and exchanged handshakes with the pastor and the two women. When he took Martha's hand, she looked directly into his eyes, her gaze unsettling. He sensed she wanted to say something, but the moment passed.

"Dennis Cane," Dennis said as he grasped Pastor Wendell's extended hand.

"My wife tells me that you gentlemen are interested in our singles ministry. You're looking for someone who attends. Is that correct?"

"Yes," Dennis replied, as he presented his badge. "We have a murder victim whose parents claim that she was member of your church."

"I see. Was Pastor Tom able to help you?" Gavin Wendell was composed—no facial expressions to read, no body language to interpret.

"Yes. He was very cooperative," Dennis said.

"We are all here to serve our Lord and give honor and respect where it is due," said the pastor. "If we can be of further service, do not hesitate to call again."

"Do you gentlemen have a church home?" Olivet asked.

"Not at the moment," Dennis replied.

"No," Merlot responded.

"Come back to visit us on Sunday morning. You may find that you like it here." She smiled.

"Have a nice day, all of you. A pleasure meeting you," Dennis said as they turned to exit the building. Merlot couldn't help but notice that the woman called Genevieve had suddenly entered the earth's atmosphere and looked as if she had something to say, but thought better of it as she smiled and looked expectantly at her friend Martha.

Outside the sun was shining and the warmth felt good after the chilling temperatures they'd just left. The church building had an excellent air-conditioning system. Both men got into Dennis's sedan. On the radio a voice boomed, "*That is our cause in this campaign. And that is the future we can build together if you join me in November.*" This was followed by a barrage of applause in the background.

"Barack Obama, Democratic presidential candidate, speaking from a town hall meeting in Taylor, Michigan, yesterday," said the radio announcer.

"I'll tell you one thing about Mr. Obama. He can certainly deliver a speech. Have you been paying attention?" Merlot said.

"Of course I'm paying attention. I like him, he seems very intelligent." Dennis steered his car into the flow of traffic.

"What do you think about Tom Genner?"

"I think Tom's hiding something."

"Me too."

"How about Pastor Wendell? He's a dandy. He looks like he stepped out of a men's magazine. Like you." Dennis wiggled his eyebrows.

"He does. And he's not ruffled at all about police officers being in his church in the middle of the day. He was super cool."

"He was. God must be proud."

"I don't know, man. Don't get me started again. Not to change the subject, but how about those Celtics? NBA champions!" Merlot said.

"That's exactly what you did. You changed the subject. But I'm so glad those guys won. They fought hard for it. Like we did for the state championship. We were the best team."

"Truer words were never spoken. And I'll never forget that pass you threw in to me from the other end of the court. To this day I don't know how I caught that ball."

They both laughed.

"Not to change the subject, but I'm very interested to hear what Etta Wasp tells us," Merlot said.

"You *did* change the subject."

Same Day

Chapter Forty-Two

Missy was dressed for daytime and evening. After having spent almost forty-eight hours inside, she was ready to get out on the town. Of all the things she hated doing, outside gardening was at the top of the list. And yesterday she'd helped her aunt plant geraniums—not only plant, but hoe the ground to create rows, mulch after planting, and water it all. When they finished it looked great, but Missy had not been that tired since she was pregnant. After a hot bath and a dinner of lamb chops, broccoli and banana cream pie, she went to bed. But that was yesterday.

Today was a new day and she did her nails early. She enjoyed clothing that went from day to night, because once she went out, she stayed out a long time. Today she wore a fitted denim skirt with a split on the side that stopped midcalf. Her top was black with sequins around the three-quarter-length sleeves and along the hem. A pair of multicolored sandals covered her feet—flats, because once she imbibed she would not be too steady on her feet. Her long hair was curled and she wore huge gold hoops. Not much makeup, and a bold red lipstick added finishing touches. Her routine was to leave home while the sun was up and stay out until the wee hours of the next morning—if she got lucky. She took one last look at herself in the mirror, left her room and headed for the kitchen.

"You look nice," Aunt Connie said when Missy walked in.

Aunt Connie sat at the kitchen table across from Etta Wasp. The ladies were having tea. On the counter in front of the two women was a small television tuned to the afternoon news. Missy glanced at the screen where a full facial image of a young woman was displayed. Missy's brow wrinkled with recognition. She'd seen this face someplace before, but she couldn't remember where. The news reporter was asking anyone with information to call the number at the bottom of the screen. Missy took an apple from the fruit bowl beside the TV, thinking that she'd certainly call if she could remember who the woman was and where she saw her. Nothing came to mind.

"The Boston Celtics are the 2008 NBA champions," the sportscaster announced as Missy took a bite of the apple.

"Thanks, Auntie. I'm going out. Don't cook for me because it will be late when I get back," Missy said. "How you doing Miss Etta?"

"I'm fine. How are you?" She knew how Missy was. She either had a hangover or was on the way to having one.

"Just peachy, like all you Georgia gals,"

"Aren't you going to eat more than that apple? I can make you a sandwich," Aunt Connie said.

"No thanks. I'm not that hungry. I'll see you later. Bye, Miss Etta," Missy said over her shoulder as she headed out of the kitchen toward the foyer.

"Not before you show me the flower bed you made yesterday. Connie told me about it. Come on back here and let's have a look," Etta said, coming out of the kitchen.

"Oh, Miss Etta! You know what those . . . what are they called Aunt Connie?" Missy said.

Connie came out of the kitchen. "Geraniums. Come on. Let's go brag. Etta can't ever find the salmon color. Right,

Etta?" Connie led the way to through the archway to the back breakfast room and out the back door. They came out in a line, with Connie in the lead, Etta in the middle, and Missy heading up the rear. Down the steps they went from the sundeck to the patio, which was now bordered by rows of salmon-colored geraniums, with hosta lilies behind them edging the lawn.

"Aren't we proud?" Etta giggled. "This is lovely, Connie. I have to admit, I'm jealous. Where did you find all of these?"

"At that little hardware store on the corner that no one wants to go to because it looks so crowded and rundown. They'd got in a new shipment the day I happened to stop in. I don't know what I would have done without Missy's help." Connie beamed and hugged Missy, who blushed.

"It was nothing at all, Aunt Connie. I sort of enjoyed it." She winked at Etta.

"I'd better get on home," Etta said. "Some police officers are coming to see me about some singles ministry records."

The three women started around the house, walking on the paved stone path that led to the front.

"I'm out, ladies! See you gals on the flip side!" Missy said, trying to stay on the path and get past the elderly women. She made it to the front of the house first.

"Oh my goodness! What's this? Do my eyes deceive me? " Missy gasped as she spotted Merlot Candy and Dennis Cane entering the yard.

"Hot damn!" Missy said as she approached the two men. "What can I do for you two? Just name it." She stood there smiling at them, her body language becoming relaxed and inviting.

"My Lord," Etta said as she appeared around the corner with Connie close on her heels. "You two must be the detectives." Then she turned to Connie and spoke over her shoulder. "They're looking for a missing woman. I told Pearl to tell them where I was." Missy stood there with her hand on her bosom completely bowled over at the sight of two very good-looking men in front of her.

"Hello, young men," Etta said, reaching across Missy to extend her hand to one of them. "Missy, weren't you leaving?" she asked. Missy straightened her skirt and smoothed down the black top, letting her hands linger on her hips.

"I think I'll have a bite to eat before I go. Would you gentlemen care for something to eat or drink? Won't you come in?" Her eyes moving from Merlot to Dennis and then back to Merlot. "You're a hottie," she said.

"You aren't bad yourself," Merlot said. He handed Missy one of his cards and then turned to Etta, shook her outstretched hand, and placed a card in it just as Connie reached them. "Are you Mrs. Wasp?" he asked Etta.

"Yes, I am. This is Connie, my best friend, and her niece, Missy," Etta said.

Connie grasped Merlot's hand and gave it a firm shake. *No soft flab there*, Merlot thought to himself. It took a moment for him to register the fact that Connie, a very attractive woman, had hands that were bigger than his. His eyebrows went up a notch when he saw Missy wink mischievously at him. He told himself not to stare at Connie's hands. He'd seen stranger things before.

"This is Dennis Cane," said Merlot. "He is actually a police officer. I am a private detective. We want to ask you some questions about this young woman." Merlot handed a photo of Chanel to Etta. Missy moved over to glance at the photo and to position herself directly in the line of Merlot, who seemed amused at her actions. Boldness was one of Missy's strong suits when she needed it.

"How do you do, Mr. Cane?" Etta offered her right hand to Dennis and shook it, while using her left hand to take the photo from Merlot.

Etta looked at the photo and gave it back to Merlot. "Why don't we go to my house where we can talk. I didn't think you'd arrive so quickly. It's just right down the street." Etta headed toward the gate and motioned for the two men to follow her. "I'll see you later, Connie. We'll do our thing."

"Okay, Etta. Nice to meet you, gentlemen," Connie said.

"So nice to meet you. Are you gentlemen certain that there's nothing I can do for you?" Missy asked.

Merlot and Dennis looked back at her, then at each other, and smiled.

"Have a nice day," Merlot said.

"Nice meeting you, Missy." Dennis's cheeks were turning red. Missy had both hands on her hips, her red lips parted, and one leg extended in front of the other in a fashion pose. She shook her head from side to side.

"Unh, unh, unh," was the last thing she muttered as Dennis glanced back at her.

"Girl, you are a mess," Connie said to Missy. "Now come on in here and get yourself that bite of food you mentioned to the two gentlemen."

Missy couldn't help but laugh aloud as she followed her aunt back into the house, slipping Merlot's card inside her skirt pocket along the way.

Same Day

Chapter Forty-Three

Seated close together in the center of a baby-blue sofa flanked by pink pillows on each side, Merlot and Dennis waited for Etta to return with her files. On the coffee table in front of each of them sat a cup of chamomile tea in blue Dresden china cups. Cut flowers on the end tables and the center of the coffee table sang praises of Etta's flower beds and rose bushes.

"Here we are," Etta said as she breezed back into the room. "How's the tea, gentlemen?" Her arms were laden with file folders that she stacked on a hassock in front of a comfortable-looking white armchair. She sat down and opened the folder on top.

"Everybody's all gung ho about computers. I like to do things the old-fashioned way, you know? So I can find things when I need them. Computers go down and when they do, it's worse than your car stopping on the side of the road in the middle of the night. Now let me see . . . you want to know about Clementine Ments and Chanel Franco. Let's start with Chanel. I keep things in alphabetical order." Etta thumbed through some pages in the folder and pulled one out. She looked it over and handed it to Dennis.

"And if your records go back to 2005, we'd like to know if Meredith Payne attended as well," Dennis added.

"Yes they do. I'll have to get those records for you, but as you can see, according to the sign-in sheet for Thursday, June 12, Chanel Franco's name is there. We do that speed-dating event on Thursday. And on this sheet you'll see where I made a record of sending her a thank-you note on that Friday. That's one of my duties, you know. Sending notes to let people know that we appreciate them. You'd be amazed at how attendance has picked up since we started doing that. I also take a photo of them, just so I can put the right name with the right face later." Etta handed over a photo of Chanel chatting with two young men, and in the background, a smiling Olivet Wendell.

Opening a different folder, Etta said, "As you can see,

Clementine signed in for every meeting except May 29. You see, every person who has ever attended has their own folder, with a copy of the sign-in sheet, their photos, and notes about my mailings to them," Etta beamed with pride.

Dennis scanned the dates and saw that Clementine attended the meeting on June 24. He pointed it out to Merlot.

"Now you'll have to excuse me while I pull the files for 2005. Would you gentlemen like some cookies?"

"Cookies would be nice," Merlot said.

Dennis and Merlot moved closer to verify they hadn't missed anything. Minutes later Etta came back with a box. She placed it on a table and removed the lid.

"The whole year is in this box, one file per month. Help yourselves. I've got coconut cake if you gentlemen would like some," she said.

Both men accepted her hospitality. Etta went to the kitchen and Merlot took the folders labeled January to March, and Dennis April to June. After almost thirty minutes, two cups of tea and two slices of moist, delicious coconut cake, their efforts were rewarded. Meredith Payne attended the singles functions in January, April, and on June 16, the day she was last seen. She too was shown in a still shot conversing with a young man.

"We've found three of the women we were looking for," Dennis said. Meredith Payne, Clementine Ments, and Chanel Franco had been photographed at Praying Hands Church. It was not a coincidence. Merlot reached for the photo of Chanel.

"That's good. I've got files going back since 2004. I'd be more than happy to dig those out for you too," Etta said.

"This helps a lot, Mrs. Wasp," Dennis said.

"Did Chanel leave with one of these two guys?" Merlot asked, as he scrutinized the photo of Chanel with the two men.

"I didn't notice. We had a full house and I tried to get pictures of everyone. By the time I got around the room she was gone. A few people hung around for refreshments, but the date winners usually pair off and leave and so do the losers." Etta chuckled. "That is the strangest way to get a date that I've ever seen. Well, next to this Internet dating. That's just dangerous!"

"Was Chanel a winner?" Merlot asked.

"No, she only went one round. She talked to the pastor and his wife, and then those two guys. I didn't watch her the whole time, but I have to keep up with the rounds. She really didn't seem to be interested in getting a date, not with that speed option at least."

Merlot looked at Dennis, who took the cue.

"I understand that Clementine was a member of your church," Dennis said.

"Yes. She was a sweet girl. Always willing to help out. I guess you know she was murdered. That's why you're here. Her folks thought she was missing."

"I learned about that recently," Dennis replied.

"Burned to death! Who would do such a thing?"

"I'm working hard to find out, Mrs. Wasp."

"Well my goodness! Her poor parents. Our singles pastor did the eulogy. I understand it was a small service with family and a few friends. They didn't want flowers. I can't much blame them. It was an ugly situation that no amount of blooms or foliage could improve. To die like that, I mean. She was so nice. Faithful to the singles functions. Did you talk to her parents?"

"Yes, but you've given us great information. Was Clementine dating anyone from the church? Had she won one of those dating games?"

"Every time I saw her, she was alone." Etta sat back in her chair and strummed her fingers on the arm of the chair. Dennis and Merlot remained quiet.

"I guess you talked to them about it at the church," Etta said.

"I talked to the singles pastor. He seemed upset."

"I imagine he was. You know, most of the young single women get a crush on Tom. He's got a lovely personality and he's quite handsome. Clementine could not hide her feelings. Nothing would have ever come of it though. Tom has a nice wife and children. He's a family man. Oh well, I don't want to say too much. If I could have those papers and photos back. I'll just put everything away. Would you gentlemen like another cup of tea?"

"Have you attended the church long?" Merlot asked

"Yes, for about ten years now. I knew the first Mrs. Wendell. He and his first wife started the church in a strip shopping center. As I understand the congregation grew very fast. He likes to use the Bible you know. He doesn't do a lot of dos and don'ts. Just reads from the Bible."

"So the woman on the brochure is the new Mrs. Wendell?" Dennis asked.

"Yes, she is. They married so quickly. We were all shocked, but he spent enough time in mourning. I just never expected him to bring in a woman from outside the church. There were plenty women in the church who would have said 'I do' to him. Yessir, Miss Olivet walked into the church as a first-time visitor and took him right to the altar. She's a fine woman. Loves the Lord. And she keeps her eyes on her husband. It won't be easy for someone to snatch him away from her."

Merlot laughed. "We met both of them today. They make a handsome couple."

"Yes they do. A lot of people question the way they run the church. Like a business, some say. But I have no problems with it. Somebody's got to be in control. Too many folks can make a mess."

"So it's true that he's the sole proprietor?" Merlot asked.

"I don't know for sure. I just know that nobody makes decisions except Pastor Wendell. And he's said before the whole congregation that if someone offered him enough money, he'd sell the church and retire to Hawaii."

"That's a good retirement plan," Merlot said.

"Can I get you some more tea? Another slice of cake?"

Dennis and Merlot stood. “No, thank you,” Merlot said.

“Thank you very much for your help,” Dennis added. “If I have more questions later, I may contact you again.”

“I wish you luck, sir. And anyway that I can help, just let me know.” Etta walked the two of them to the door. “Have a nice evening, gentlemen.”

“I think we just got dismissed,” Dennis said to Merlot after she closed the door behind them. ‘And did you notice a change in her mood?”

“I did, but we got what we needed,” Merlot replied, as his cell phone rang. While walking back to the car, he listened to the caller, said a few words, and hung up.

“Let’s get back to my office. Kathy has a profiler to introduce to us.”

“You know we really should have checked her files for 2006,” Dennis said.

“You’re right. And we can always return. Right now we’ve confirmed two bodies and one intended victim who attended the singles ministry. Let’s just go with that for now. Maybe this profiler can come up with a suspect and then we’re really on the ball,” Merlot exclaimed as they reached Dennis’s car, got inside and drove away.

Neither of them noticed the worried look on Etta's face as she closed the door behind them. They couldn't know that talking about the church's business operations was troubling to her. She liked to think that a church home was permanent, and not subject to a fast sale so that the pastor could retire. She began to gather up her files when her sister, Pearl, came into the living room. One of the church brochures that pictured the pastor and his wife on the cover fell to the floor. Pearl leaned over to pick it up and did a double take.

"This is different from the last brochure," she said as she handed it to Etta.

Same Day

Chapter Forty-Four

Missy sat at the bar of the Wasted Barrel waiting for Davinia, a friend she'd met at a support group for divorced women. The two of them connected right away because they had something in common—an ex-husband who was a son of a bitch.

"What are we starting with today, Missy?" asked Lonnie, the bartender.

"The same. You know what they say, if it ain't broke don't fix it," Missy said.

Lonnie laughed. His sense of humor made it easy to talk to him. And even though he was around Missy's age, late thirties, his wisdom made him seem older.

"So Long Island iced tea, brandy on the rocks, red wine . . . what are we talking here?" he asked.

"Red wine sounds good," Missy replied. Wine was a

good starter drink—an appetizer. With a routine that involved drinking for a good part of the evening, it was better to start with something light to delay inebriation before she got into any action. Action always included a man. Anyone watching Missy from afar would consider her a loser—a party girl with no future and probably an even less-than-pleasant past. This observation was partly correct even though her past had been the best days of her life. Until they weren't.

"You ever been married, Lonnie?" Missy asked when he sat her wine in front of her.

"Nope. And I don't intend to either. How about you?"

"Unfortunately, yes," Missy replied, taking a long sip of wine. "To a handsome, kind, honest, intelligent, two-faced mama's boy."

"I love my mother, too. That doesn't make me a mama's boy." Lonnie leaned on the bar, his face close to Missy's. That was all she needed. She felt like talking today.

"His mama and daddy bought a house as a wedding gift for us. His mama furnished it. It was waiting for us when we returned from our honeymoon."

"That was a nice gift. Maybe if I could find a girl with

parents like that, I'd reconsider."

"The gift came with strings attached. My husband, Reese, wanted me to keep the house like his mama."

"I don't get it. What does that mean?"

"Another wine, please, and I will explain." Missy drained her glass and plopped it on the bar.

"Coming right up," Lonnie moved away to get her refill. He was back in two minutes. He placed the glass of red wine in front of Missy and leaned forward again, forearms on the bar, hands clasped beneath his chin.

"Mrs. Reese Kinner. That was me. Had to clean the brand-new house every day—not put too much water on the hardwood floors but make sure they were cleaned daily; the furniture was to be polished, not just dusted, daily; the windows had to remain spotless and the best way to insure that was to clean them once a day; the rugs were not to be vacuumed. They were to be hung on a clothesline and beaten with a broom."

"Okay, that sounds like deep cleaning. Did you have a job too?"

"Of course not! No wife of Reese's worked!"

"And was hiring a maid out of the budget?"

“He could have paid for an upstairs and a downstairs maid. I had to do it because that’s how his mama cleaned their house when he was growing up. An old house. But wait, you haven’t heard the best part.” Missy finished off her wine for the second time. Lonnie, taking the cue, moved away and was back in a flash with a third glass.

“If I didn’t do everything just right he’d go to his room. And lock the door, and stay for days.”

“You’re kidding! He’d isolate, huh?” Lonnie said.

“After the baby, his mother and sisters were around all of the time. Naturally, I couldn’t care for Glenda, our daughter, the way they thought I should—”

“You have a kid?”

“Yes, but he took her and the house. They said I was an unfit mother. I didn’t do things the way they wanted, and I started to drink too much and . . . well, now I have only memories—”

“Water-colored memories? What’s up, trick?” Davinia plopped down on the seat next to Missy.

“My IQ,” Missy giggled, giving her stock answer to that silly question. She was relieved to see her friend. Her trip down memory lane was about to blow her evening.

“Been here long?” Davinia was dressed in black as usual.

“Of course I’ve been here long. Are you ever on time?”

Davinia laughed. “Lonnie, pour me a shot,” she said. Lonnie patted Missy’s hand and went for the liquor.

Davinia was always in a good mood, and seemed to get happier the more she drank. Missy really liked her. Missy had asked her once why she wore black all the time thinking she was into the Goth thing. But Davinia had answered with three letters—PCB.

“PCB?” Missy asked.

“Pasty Chick in Black,” Davinia explained. “I’m so pale that the only color that looks good on me is black!” And that was that.

“What are we doing today, Missy the Brain?” Davinia asked as Lonnie placed the shot glass in front of her. She downed it in one gulp.

“The same thing we do every day. Getting high and getting laid,” Missy answered as Lonnie poured Davinia another shot. No appetizers for Davinia—she went full course right away. It was amazing how much alcohol the woman could tolerate.

Missy rapped the countertop to let the bartender know she was ready for a refill too. It was then that she noticed the big screen behind the bar. She couldn't hear what was being said, but she saw a picture of a woman on the screen—the same woman in the news broadcast back at Connie's— and another message about calling a number to share information. Missy stared at the woman's face as a memory flashed. She was in a house with a purple-accented living room, and there were photos of this same woman all over the place. She suddenly felt uneasy.

"Have you seen that band guy again?" Davina asked.

Band guy?

"What band guy?" she asked as Lonnie placed another delicious glass of wine in front of her. She took a long swig.

"The guy we met Sunday night. You left with him. Remember?"

"Of course not," Missy said. Davinia and Missy could be honest with each other about their blackouts. Both of them drank to such a degree that memory of the nights or days before often escaped one or the other of them. Which explained why they drank together. Safety in numbers kept them both out of serious trouble. Sometimes one of them could remember. It seems Davinia remembered Sunday and the wee hours of Monday morning.

"Was he good-looking?" Missy asked.

"He must have been! Yeah he was. I wanted to know if he had any friends," Davinia said as she frowned from that second shot of bourbon going down.

Another memory flashed across Missy's mind. She saw herself getting out of bed, a man sleeping soundly beside her. She stumbled toward a bathroom noticing photos of a woman on the chest of drawers. And a bathroom where she was attacked by leggings. The photos. *Were they really of the same woman she just saw on the news?* She took another sip of wine. And thought about the good-looking guys who'd come to Aunt Connie's house today. And the photo one of them showed. *It was the same woman in the news!* The taller, extremely good-looking guy gave her a business card. Missy reached into her pocket and pulled it out—Merlot Candy. Specializing in the lost and found.

"You get flashbacks, don't you?" Missy turned to her friend with a grave expression on her face.

"You mean, do I sometimes remember what I've forgotten when I'm drunk?"

"Yes. Do you?" Missy said.

"You know I do. We both do. That's how we get through. What's bothering you?"

"I'm not sure. It's like I know something, but I don't know what it is," Missy replied. "Something is nagging me."

"Well stop drinking for minute and let's talk about it."

"Let me finish my wine. I don't want to waste it," Missy said as she guzzled down the rest of her wine and took a deep breath.

"How do I begin to talk about something when I have no idea of what to say?"

"Let's start from the beginning and you talk until you can't remember anymore and then I'll pick up from there if I can," Davinia said with all her worldly wisdom.

Same Day

Chapter Forty-Five

When Merlot and Dennis entered the reception area of Candy Detective Agency, a middle-aged, gray-haired, heavyset man sat on the couch with Kathy Stockton. He turned and regarded the two men with hazy brown eyes as they entered. Kathy smiled, but the man didn't smile. He stared. Merlot watched him as he studied all of Dennis's features, his clothes, his shoes, his mannerisms, and then back to Dennis's face. The man then shifted to Merlot's clothing, lingering as he took in the whole ensemble, all the way down to his shoes and then back up to his face, meeting Merlot's eyes and holding eye contact with him for several seconds. Merlot tried to fathom what he saw in the man's eyes. He gave no clue of what he was thinking or being. A fact which took Merlot off guard momentarily. He bounced back when Kathy spoke.

"Are you guys finished sizing each other up?" she laughed. She stood and the man followed suit. He was taller than he appeared, about six feet one. He wore a well-made brown-tweed sports jacket and a pair of khaki pants with suspenders. His white shirt was open at the collar. Kathy put one arm around his shoulder and squeezed.

"May I introduce Sterling Templeton, a retired FBI profiler who's been bored for over a month with his present state of departure from the workforce." Kathy smiled at Sterling and put both hands on her hips. "Sterling, I'd like you to meet Merlot Candy, who will no doubt introduce you and me to his friend."

"Pleased to meet you. Sterling," said Merlot as he shook his hand. "This is Dennis Cane, an old high school buddy who is now a police detective with the Peach Grove Police Department." Dennis and Sterling shook hands.

"Dennis, this beautiful lady is Kathy Stockton, who has more friends than anyone I've ever met." Merlot beamed at Kathy who reached out and gave him a big hug. Her nice figure looked even nicer in her purple tailored skirt suit.

"So good to meet you, Dennis," she said, giving him a

big hug.

"The pleasure is mine." Dennis replied.

"Now I've got some shopping to do, so I will leave the three of you to talk." Kathy began her approach toward the double doors, her heels clacking on the marble floor. Her purple suit a lovely blur as she breezed out of the door waving goodbye to Sterling and Dennis and giving Merlot a wink.

"So. How can I be of service, Merlot?" Sterling asked.

"Let's go into my office and Dennis will tell you everything," Merlot replied.

Same Day

Chapter Forty-Six

Michael was in deep thought. Things were still going awry. Although the rain had been an act of God, failing to notice he had dropped the pouch was his fault. And that was unforgivable. He told himself from the beginning he needed to be careful. But this new development! Somehow Chanel had been identified. How in heaven's name had that happened? All of her identification was in a safe place. Her facial features should be totally marred by the fire and she had no police record on file. No reason to ever have her fingerprints in a database, as she lived a life above reproach. Michael had done his research. Yet her photo was being flashed on every local news station, but they were not giving any information. Instead, they were begging anyone who saw her to call in.

That would be me, but I'll never call.

Being caught and going to jail played no role at all in

Michael's plan. Extensive research into serial killers had proven enlightening. Jack the Ripper had chosen prostitutes as his victims. He killed them all the same way by slashing their throats and doing some extractions of organs. And of course was never caught. A killer in Honolulu was never discovered. This one raped, strangled and murdered five women, and tied their hands behind their back. In India a murderer killed homeless victims by bashing their heads with stones. Never caught. And then there was the killer whose victims took their last breaths on February 9 annually.

Michael had considered how police connect victims. Usually by type so he tried to avoid types. All his victims had to be women, had to die by fire, and most definitely had to die in June. To avoid drawing attention, he had chosen different cities to dispose of his victims so that only one police district would be involved with each incident. And until now, Michael had never disposed of a body close to home. But this was to be the last year. After driving by that construction site many times, he had decided it would be a perfect spot to incinerate the next body. But his plan called for the woman to be charcoal before she was discovered. Peach Grove was the perfect place. A police department undergoing change with new personnel, and a city with a new real estate development that wanted to attract new residents—both fit into a unique and well-constructed scenario. Murder would be discouraging and politics dictated that the news in Peach Grove be diluted so that residents could continue to float on their pink clouds. The incident was supposed to be played down, just long enough for Michael to finish his work.

To further complicate matters, a new threat had popped up—one that had nothing to do with Chanel Franco and her survival. This was something he needed to handle quickly and not in the usual manner. No planning—only action. It would have to appear as a random act of violence, in no way related to what was going on already. If the police were smart enough to tie it all together, Michael would be relieved. It would mean that taking a life was not as easy as pie. In spite of the risk involved, this threat had to be eliminated. The time was drawing near to kill the one person who needed to leave this world and nothing could get in the way. The one person that all the other women had to die for. Only then would Michael have peace. But first this pesky little nuisance had to be dealt with.

Same Day

Chapter Forty-Seven

The walls on one side of Merlot's conference room were now covered with what he called various and sundry paraphernalia. In reality it was a collection of newspaper clippings about missing women; Dennis's list of unidentified female bodies found burned to death around the metro area; the fliers he'd taken from public locations; and his notes, thoughts, and scribblings about his theory of a serial killer. In addition there were Glenn's notes he'd translated into his perspective based on what Dennis told him; printouts of articles he'd found about serial killers; information he'd researched about arson; a list of manufacturers of black leotards; the pros and cons of using gasoline as an accelerant; a detailed summary of forensics; and oddly enough, the month of June and the position of the stars. All of this paperwork was grouped together according to categories.

Merlot was amazed at the sheer magnitude of all that had come into his office in only a matter of days. It had never taken so much information for him to find a missing person. All he ever needed to begin his search was a photo and a list of last-known contacts. Of course Glenn could pull tons of data from his computer and narrow it down to a few pages. He often mentioned this fact to Merlot, who never fully comprehended because he saw only the finished report. His head was now swimming with so many lists and notes. Sterling devoured everything, stopping now and then to stare into space or to check something twice. Occasionally he'd fire a question at Glenn or Dennis. Merlot merely listened, observed, and wondered when they would make a move. He thrived on action. After what seemed like hours, Sterling began to speak.

"It certainly appears that a serial killer is at work here. He is what we in the bureau refer to as an *unknown subject* meaning we don't know his name. But I'm beginning to get a picture of him because I've looked at what all of this tells us. I believe the killer is a male. I believe he is acting out of extreme rage. Only rage would push someone far enough to douse a human being with gasoline and then let them burn to death. This killer also has a strong desire for power, because it is a foregone conclusion that the women are drugged first or rendered unconscious in some other manner. I say this because, otherwise, there would have been some signs of a struggle. Maybe even an escape."

"How can you possibly know that they didn't struggle? Or that they weren't knocked in the head with some blunt object?" Merlot asked.

"Glenn has documented here that he talked to someone in the trauma unit who confirmed that Chanel Franco suffered no head trauma. That's usually where a fight to incapacitate someone would begin. They did, however, find Rohypnol in her blood. I think that's his MO. Drugged them, moved them to the crime scene, and then committed the final assault of flames with a live victim, as is evident with Ms. Franco."

Merlot had no idea Glenn had spoken with hospital staff. He walked over to the wall and found Glenn's notes.
Sure enough, he found documentation of a conversation with Sal Carter, an emergency room technician.

"Is that all you have?" Merlot asked turning to Sterling.

"He is strong—he has to be because all of our victims weighed over 125 pounds. I also note that all evidence is destroyed, and yet this time he chose to commit murder in a public place with the same *modus operandi,"* Sterling said.

"For that I am grateful," Dennis said. "It gives me all the authority I need to investigate the hell out of these murders."

"Do you really have a case of murder though, Cane?" Merlot asked. "Maybe attempted murder—"

"Will you please stop reminding me of that?!"

"If I may continue, "Sterling said, as he looked from one to the other.

"By all means," Merlot replied.

"Leaving a body at the construction site was deliberate, which means he doesn't care if we know about him. And that his attempt failed and we still have no idea who he is shows our killer is organized and that his plan was well thought out. He has taken all kinds of forensics countermeasures. He hasn't chosen a particular type of woman—their ages as well as their employment histories and the locations vary. They all resemble each other in that they were blondes and they were new to the area with no dental records on file. This killer seems to know a lot about his victims. He is in pain and he's sure of himself; he thinks he's smarter than the police. He's covered all bases, and he won't stop until he's caught. Unless he's mission oriented. If so, once he completes his mission, he can fade away into the sunset and we will never hear from him again.

"What I'd like to do now is go to the scene of the crime in Peach Grove if you gentlemen will join me. I won't look at the scene the way that you do. I look to get a feel for the killer. To imagine myself in his shoes, to enter his mind, and see what he sees," Sterling said.

"Sounds like a plan," Merlot said. He looked at Dennis who nodded his head.

"I'm ready when you two are," he said.

Merlot, taking in Sterling's every word as he spoke, agreed with everything he'd said. Except the part about seeing what the killer saw. But if Sterling had the power, he should do so. And quickly.

Same Day

Chapter Forty-Eight

The woman stood on her porch and surveyed the smallness of her yard—its dash of grass, sprinkling of petunias, and one whole tree. She then turned her head toward the west as the sun made its way on the horizon. Her gray hair gleamed like silver in the late afternoon light. Her tired hazel eyes still had that twinkle of youth—that twinkle which gazed upon life with the belief there was good to be found in everyone and everything. She smiled to herself. She'd done the right thing. She'd told someone what she saw. She moved gracefully from the porch into her living room and settled herself in her comfortable old green chair. On the end table beside her sat a silver tray with a silver coffee pot she used for tea, and a china cup and saucer. The silver sugar bowl and creamer nestled beside them. That silver set had belonged to her mother and she cherished it.

She reserved this time every day for pampering herself; and as she poured the still steaming mint tea, she began to silently thank God for her life, her health, her strength, and her wisdom. She sat back and took into view the scene in front of her. She had sat in that chair for many years looking out of the window that faced Mimosa Street undetected by anyone. She'd seen things from windows all over her house. But she had taken steps. Everything would be all right now. She sighed as memory forced her to face the fact that one could indeed predict the future. Not as a fortune teller. Her mother had warned her about those people—possessors of evil spiritual powers that were to be avoided because it was dangerous to believe in them.

No she was neither a soothsayer nor a diviner. She saw herself as someone gifted with the power to discern the truth. Now it was time for the truth to be known by all. She had spent considerable time thinking about how to make the truth known. She'd made a plan and decided to just do the deed and worry about repercussions later. Many people would be surprised. Some would not believe and would accuse her of being senile or worse yet a liar. Unless she had proof. And she did—indisputable proof. The proof was indeed in the pudding. She closed her eyes and took a long swig of her tea. It was delicious. She thanked God again that at last justice would be done. She felt happier than she'd felt in years. So intent was she in her joy she did not hear the sound of the footsteps as they approached her from behind.

Her last thought in this world was that God could not have chosen a better vessel than herself to wage his war of vengeance. Tenacious and unerring, she knew what she had seen. She leaned forward, unknowingly exposing her back to the knife in the hands of the intruder who stood behind her. The sharp blade plunged and struck home to her heart, silencing her. She could only gasp as the knife was pulled out and plunged in again. And again—twisted and then wrenched out as she slowly slipped away, her mother's precious china cup slipping from her hand.

Michael plunged the knife four more times. He waited and watched until he was certain she was no longer breathing. Just to be sure he touched his finger behind her ear and felt for a pulse. Her skin was still warm to the touch, but no heartbeat could be detected. Satisfied, he relaxed.

Seven times was enough. Seven was God's perfect number. And now an inconvenient truth has been eliminated.

He smiled wickedly as he slipped the knife into its case.

This is a really good knife. It moved through flesh like butter. I didn't have to use a lot of effort.

He walked back to the kitchen where he'd entered the house, placed the knife case inside his briefcase, and snapped it shut. After exiting the house, he retraced his steps through the backyard of the house he'd just left and the backyard of the house behind it. He continued around the side of a house that waited for its occupants to return home after a day's work, and onto the sidewalk of the street that ran parallel to Mimosa. He removed his gloves as he walked. By the time he reached the car, Michael had once again become a nondescript entity that no one had reason to fear.

Same Day

Chapter Forty-Nine

Sterling Templeton stood in the area above the drainage ditch where Chanel Franco's body had been found. The scene had not yet been released from police custody and was still roped off. He stared at the photographs taken before her body was removed to the hospital.

"Who discovered the woman?" he asked.

Dennis and Merlot looked at each other puzzled

"If you look on page one of the report, you'll see that we never identified the person who called in," Dennis said. He had already mentioned the anonymous phone caller, and was beginning to wonder if this guy was a sharp as he should be.

"I mean, was the person male or female?" Sterling locked eyes with Dennis. "The person who discovered this woman is a key witness. In fact they could be our killer. If not, whoever it was may have seen the killer—"

"Which is why I have a protective detail on Chanel Franco at the hospital as we speak," Dennis said. *Did this guy listen?*

"This space is too wide open, even though isolated, for the suspect to have undressed her and then wrapped her in a tarp at this location. He chose this place. Was the caller male or female?" Sterling asked again.

Dennis gave Merlot a look of exasperation. *Really? Was the guy senile and that's why he retired?*

"It was a female," Dennis said. All of these questions had been answered before they left the office. Maybe Merlot had confidence in this guy, but Dennis was losing it by the second.

"And this was around 4:30 a.m. So this female could have been a lady of the evening, a lady who enjoys night life, a lady who works an odd night shift, or . . .?"

Dennis had asked himself these same questions trying to determine what kind of female was out at that time of morning and what was she doing at the construction site. Shrugging his shoulders, he replied, "There have been some complaints of people breaking through the construction barriers at the site to get to some main streets on the grid. I believe it was someone taking a short cut home, because the call originated from a pay phone at an all-night convenience store on the street behind this construction." Dennis pointed in the direction of the street in question.

"From a pay phone there. That means that the female caller left the scene and then made the call."

Sterling looked toward the direction Dennis indicated and seemed to go into a trance. He stood like that with his eyes closed for a few seconds and then opened them.

"Why would the caller use a pay phone? Doesn't everybody have a cell phone these days? I mean, I have a cell phone," Sterling said.

Merlot raised his eyebrows at Dennis as if asking the same question.

"I don't know." Dennis said. He rummaged through his pockets and found a piece of peppermint, unwrapped it, and popped it into his mouth. "Maybe the caller is still in the dark ages and doesn't have a cell phone. Maybe the cell phone died. That's a question only the phone caller can answer."

"Now would be a good time to tell both of you that I am good at asking rhetorical questions. I don't expect you to answer. The questions are for me," Sterling said. He looked down at his notes again, walked over to ditch where Chanel was found, and peered down into it. Closing his eyes, he backed away from the ditch in line with the trajectory of the street Dennis had named. He opened his eyes and turned around. Merlot and Dennis followed suit.

As the three of them stood there, each looking for something—anything— a young man appeared, walking toward them with a backpack. He had earphones on and his head was down. He veered around the police tape and continued. Giving no hint he was aware of their presence, he bobbed his head to the music of whatever tune he listened to. He walked in the direction of the street, two blocks away, where the anonymous call originated. He was taking a shortcut.

The three men watched the young man continue on his way; and then, as if on cue, all three turned back and headed toward the direction the young man had come from, with Sterling leading the way. Through the crime scene tape, and then continuing through the entrance of Mint Leaf Manor. When they crossed the street, Sterling walked to the right a few feet and then back to the left a few feet until he stopped.

He stepped off the street, entered the underbrush, and disappeared in the trees behind it. Dennis and Merlot nodded at each other and then followed.

Once inside the area, they could see a faint path. They continued along the trail until they entered the huge backyard shared by two houses located in a cul-de-sac. By this time Sterling was ahead of them, heading around to the front of one of the houses. He continued out to the sidewalk, and made his way to the end of the short street. Several young children were out, some riding tricycles or bikes; others playing basketball on the driveway, one of the little guys going up for a jump shot; and two little girls sitting on the curb with a handheld electronic device. Sterling ignored them all while they did likewise. Merlot and Dennis took in the view as their newly acquainted profiler turned and walked back in their direction. He passed them and went to the house numbered 1427.

"This is her home," he said, looking down at the papers he held in his hand. Dennis and Merlot shot puzzled expressions to each other.

"Whose home? The anonymous caller's?" Dennis asked.

“Chanel Franco lives here,” Sterling said. Mumbling to himself, he walked up the steps and rang the doorbell. He waited a beat and then turned to leave when the door flew open.

A young man stood in the doorway. His face showed a slight curiosity, but he seemed completely at ease.

“What’s up? Do you need some help?” he asked.

Dennis was ready to read him the riot act, when Merlot rushed up the steps with his hand extended.

“Pierre Canola. I’m Merlot Candy, the detective hired by your father to find the person responsible for Chanel’s injuries.” Merlot shook Pierre’s hand. “This is Sterling Templeton, and Lt. Dennis Cane,” he continued, turning toward Dennis with a smile.

Dennis joined them on the porch and extended his hand. “Good to meet you,” he said as he felt his hand gripped with the vise-like hand of Pierre Canola.

“So this is the home of Chanel Franco?” Sterling asked.

“Yes, in fact it is. Come in, gentlemen.” Pierre stood aside and waved the men inside. As the three men entered the living room, they all picked up on Chanel’s preference for purple.

"Have a seat," Pierre said. Dennis and Merlot sat but Sterling remained standing.

"We have determined that our witness or the person who found your sister could possibly have come from this house. I understand that your sister has not been heard from since Friday morning. And she was found in the early hours on Monday, and, as I understand it, not said a word. Could she have been here on Sunday night, entertaining maybe?" Sterling asked.

"No, she was not here entertaining; however, I was. I met a girl and brought her here. She left before I woke up," Pierre said.

"What was the name of this girl?" Sterling asked, his eyes scanning the room.

Pierre blushed. "She was a full-grown woman, and I'm sorry, but I don't remember her name. It was one of those one-night stands."

"I understand. Did she drive herself here?"

"No, I drove us here. She left on foot, I guess. When I woke up she was gone. She told me that she lived within walking distance when we got here."

"And where did you meet her?"

"At the club. I play in a band and we had a gig there. The Floor Stopper on Ponce.

"Can you describe her?"

"I'm sorry, man. All I can tell you is she must have been cute and sexy. I had a lot to drink and so did she."

"And yet you got behind the steering wheel?"

Pierre's brow furrowed and his expression changed. "Is there anything else I can help you gentlemen with?"

"I apologize for my bluntness," Sterling said. "It can sometimes rub people the wrong way. You've been a great help. I'm sorry about what happened to your sister. We will do our best to find the person responsible," he said. He walked to the door and opened it, and Dennis and Merlot stood to follow him.

"Thank you, Pierre. It was good to meet you and I'm sorry it had to be under these circumstances," Merlot said, extending his hand. Pierre grasped it with a firm handshake.

"Good to meet you, too. I hope you find this bastard."

"Sorry to disturb you," Dennis said with a smile.

"No problem. I really want you to find out who did this to her and why." The three men nodded and left, while Pierre stood in the doorway, watching as they walked around the house.

After returning to the crime scene via they path they'd followed, Sterling, once again, assumed a trancelike state as he looked at photos and then at the lay of the land. He took a long time, and then turned to Merlot.

"Let's go back to your office. I have an idea."

Same Day

Chapter Fifty

Missy and Davinia walked into the Floor Stopper Lounge just in time for the end of happy hour. All of the bar seats were taken, but they were able to find a table near the stage where a live band usually set up. The sight of the stage triggered a memory as soon as Missy looked at it. She saw herself leaving the club holding on to the arm of a good-looking musician from the band. They walked to his car and got in. He drove to a house on Trammel Court—the house with all the purple. She remembered waking up and staggering to the bathroom. She remembered leaving. She remembered leaning against the tree. She remembered the headlights. The car. The driver. The fire. The woman in the ditch that she uncovered. *The same woman in the news that the authorities wanted information about!* And she remembered the fanny pack.

Missy felt her breath coming faster. She remembered the rain. The mud. She saw herself walking to the phone and dialing 911. *So I called someone?* If that was true, she'd done her bit for giving information. She didn't need this guilt that came out of nowhere as she remembered. The news reporter said the woman had been burned. The face on the news was perfect. No sign of scars or bandages. And then Missy felt the ton of bricks hit her. The woman was the same one in the photo that the good-looking detective showed to her at Aunt Connie's house. He was looking for her. Missy had to do something. *But what?* The only thing left to do was go home.

"Davinia," Missy began. "I've got to cut the night short. There's something that I have to do and I don't need to keep drinking and risk blacking out right now." She spoke as sincerely as she could, noticing how Davina, who was already in the zone, gave her a fuzzy look.

"Okay, girl. Do what you gotta do. I don't have nothing to do so I'm gonna stay here and have fun. Okay?"

Missy got up and walked as steadily as she could out of the exit. Once outside she realized it was still daylight. The fanny pack had something in it. Where had she put it? She strained to remember, but nothing came. Knowing herself well, she believed she would have at least opened the fanny pack or even carried it with her. She knew she would have been nervous because she was nervous now just remembering what she saw. She had to go home and eat something and drink some coffee or something. She'd had only three glasses of wine this evening so she was not drunk. It was not a good idea to drink anymore tonight. She'd go home, watch the news, and maybe somehow she'd remember what she did with that fanny pack. It could be important.

And then another memory came. She remembered putting something inside her purse.

The fanny pack! Where was that fanny pack?

Same Day

Chapter Fifty-One

Merlot, Dennis, and Sterling got off the elevator on Merlot's floor. Glenn, who had also been busy, had agreed to wait for their return. Almost simultaneously, as if on cue, the other elevator door opened and the delivery man from Merlot's favorite Japanese restaurant stepped out with their food. His timing was impeccable and that combined with the superb cuisine guaranteed that customers would keep coming back. Every time Merlot was within thirty minutes of his building and phoned in his order, the food always arrived just as he did. He paid for the food with a generous tip, and then the four men gathered in the conference room.

They sat at the end of the table with the least amount of paperwork, being careful to stack what little was there neatly away from the food. Each had double portions of the *chawan mushi,* the egg soup, edamame, and the Japanese mushrooms, as well as noodles. Dennis and Sterling ordered sushi, while Merlot opted for grilled salmon with *nasu dengaku*—grilled eggplant. Glenn had sea bass and king crab. They ate in silence, each man contemplating what they'd learned in the past few hours.

Merlot was convinced that progress had been made. It was now believable that someone had discovered Chanel while taking a shortcut home. So the killer must have fled the scene. They'd learned where Chanel lived and established that Pierre had brought a woman home with him to Chanel's house. That woman left on foot. Could she be the anonymous caller? If so, who was she? Pierre remembered nothing about her except she must have been cute. Merlot stopped thinking and concentrated on his food. An hour later, all of their appetites satisfied, they cleaned away any remaining food and Sterling took the floor.

"Okay, gentlemen. As I stated earlier, this killer has suppressed rage. It is this rage that is pushing him. But why? Why is he enraged? When we have the answer to that question, we will have a motive. He has become comfortable with taking lives. I don't know what is catapulting him forward yet, but believe me it is personal."

“We need to look at the one man we know of already—the singles pastor at the church—who would have had contact with these women. The two victims that we can identify went to that church and I believe that is not a coincidence. Unfortunately, too many people, with their own personal interpretation of God’s will, hide behind good standings in a religious organization. From that pious vantage point, they convince themselves that they can do no wrong,” Sterling continued.

“I’d like to add that I did some more digging while you all were gone,” Glenn said. “Tom Genner has been the singles pastor for only three years. He took the position in January of 2005.”

“How do you know that?” Dennis asked.

“I found the story in news articles from that year. It was one of those feature stories to introduce the new pastor to the city in an indirect way. He moved to Georgia in the summer of 2004 and joined Praying Hands Church. He’d been a singles pastor at his old church and according to the article ‘just seemed to feel at home at Praying Hands.’ He is supposedly a family man, with a wife and children. He is well educated, and dedicated his life to the ministry at an early age. He mentions some misdeeds when he was a teen that helped to turn his life around," Glenn said.

"That's a huge bombshell you just dropped!" Dennis said. "Let's suppose for the moment he took the position and then started killing six months later. Do you think the strain of having all those good-looking young women around was too much for him?"

"Tom Genner is a handsome man, maybe even a weak one," Merlot said. "He's only human. He slips and then decides to get rid of the one person who could reveal his infidelity. Only he didn't stop. He kept going? Is that what you're going with?"

"I'm going with whatever I can get! Etta Wasp all but said that he's a ladies' man," Dennis said.

"He's also married with a family. I'm certain he wouldn't want to ruin that with a little infidelity. But killing the women? Why would he do that?" Merlot asked.

"And there you have the question that profilers work to answer," Sterling said. "Unfortunately, there is always a logical reason in the minds of these types of killers. The one thing about this killer that's on point is his method of ending the lives of these women. The fire represents something.

And this something could very well be tied to religion—hellfire and damnation. Tom Genner is a religious man."

"What about mercy and compassion—those things that church people are supposed to have in abundance? That's a horrible, merciless way to die," said Merlot. "And there is some danger involved for the killer himself, especially since he uses gas as an accelerant, and yet he's willing to risk everything. It just doesn't fit. I mean, if anything it fits too well."

"Sometimes the simplest answer is the correct one," Dennis added.

"If I may continue," Sterling said. "This suspect has become quite proficient at destroying DNA and extinguishing life without impunity. He leaves no trail. And yet he decides to dispose of his victim this time in public. Let's not forget that."

"I cannot approach Tom Genner in a legal capacity without more to go on. My city protects its upstanding citizens. The only thing I can do, now that we suspect him, is pay close attention to his activities without him knowing it." Dennis straightened his shoulders and sat back in his chair.

"And that's why I think my idea will work," Sterling said. "The fact that Chanel has an identical twin is pivotal. If we leak to the press that Chanel is alert and ready to talk and somehow imply that we will soon have a break in the case, we could draw this murderer out. He doesn't know how long the fire burned or how much damage was done to Chanel's body. He just knows she survived and is presently in intensive care, which is what every other person knows from the news reports. Let's trick him. He'll have to do something if he thinks she's talking. He knows she can lead us right to his door," Sterling finished.

"You set a screen?" Merlot asked, winking at Dennis, who nodded enthusiastically. Sterling's look of confusion could not be mistaken.

"I'm afraid we'll have to commit a foul here. This trap will be a moving screen violation." Sterling laughed for the first time since they'd met him. "I'm a basketball fan, gentlemen."

Merlot laughed. He was delighted to know the man could focus on something other than figuring out the identity of a killer.

Same Day

Chapter Fifty-Two

Dennis and Merlot stepped out of the elevator on the third floor of Grady Hospital. They had arranged to meet with Dr. Salada for a few minutes to discuss the plan with him first, knowing that cooperation from some of the burn unit staff was tantamount to its success. They needed Louise to look like a patient.

"So you want us to bandage Louise, place her in a bed here in the hospital, and you're going to photograph her? Am I getting this correct?" Dr. Salada asked, his tone of voice skeptical.

"We want the suspect to believe his identity is about to be revealed. He can't afford for that to happen. We're hoping he'll try to do something about it," Dennis explained.

"And how do we guarantee that he doesn't carry it out? I can't be responsible for such a thing," Dr. Salada said.

"I will take full responsibility. I've got enough officers to protect her," Dennis said.

"Have you discussed this with her parents?"

"No, Dr. Salada. We wanted to get you on board first."

Dr. Salada looked at Merlot and then Dennis. "I'll help in any way I can," he said.

"We need to move quickly. I'll get in touch with Louise and her parents," Dennis said.

* * *

Theo and Lausanne did not hesitate to show their willingness to set a trap. Louise presented herself to the staff a short time later to get ready for her new role as her sister.

The plan called for photographing Louise wearing a blonde wig, bandaged to her waist as she lay in a bed in a patient room. It didn't take long to get her ready and for Dennis to snap several photos. After the mock photography was over, she returned to her house to wait with her parents until time to return to the hospital for admission.

Dennis contacted members of the press to alert them to a short conference to be broadcast on the eleven o'clock news that night. The reporters, eager for any news about the victim, agreed to show up. Dennis would hold the photo as proof of her recovery at the press conference and announce a possible break in the case resulting from questioning of the patient. Now all they had to do was wait. Dennis posted another officer outside Chanel's door to ensure that she was protected round the clock. He also assigned three other officers to remain on the floor at all times.

Just as they were congratulating themselves on the trap they were setting, Dennis's cell phone buzzed inside his pocket. He pulled it out and excused himself from the others.

"Dennis Cane," he answered.

"Cane, there's been a murder. You need to get to 4241 Mimosa Street immediately."

Same Day

Chapter Fifty-Three

Dennis Cane stood in the living room of Martha Smith—now dead, her body peacefully reposed in a blood-soaked armchair that was once green. The blood oozing from her wounds covered the fabric with crimson splotches that spilled over to the floor around her feet—and a broken teacup. Her face looked familiar, but he couldn't place it. Someone had done a nasty job on her with overkill. Seven knife wounds, apparently inflicted from behind as she sat drinking tea. According to the medical examiner, the time of death appeared to be late afternoon. Someone had killed her in her own home in broad daylight in front of a window. A fearless individual with no regard for human dignity or his own life considering the fact that someone could have seen him in the act through the huge window.

Dennis assigned several of his officers the task of talking to onlookers and canvassing the neighborhood. He walked around the chair several times, noting the only direction from which someone could have approached without being seen was from behind. It must have been a sneak attack as there were no signs of struggle. He stood behind the chair and backed away—out of the living room and into the hallway, to the left open archway and into the kitchen. The back door was there. Unlocked. The killer had to have come in that way. He looked across the backyard as far as the floodlights afforded a view and knew immediately the killer had escaped through the yards of the residential subdivision that backed this one. He would have exited on the next street over. He either walked away or drove away in a car left parked there. Someone needed to canvass that neighborhood as well to see if anyone saw anything.

He sighed as he watched the forensics team working tirelessly. So far they had found nothing incriminating. No fingerprints, no footprints, no fibers.

"Who found the body?" Dennis asked one of the officers.

"A neighbor," was the response.

"Do your best, fellows. There's got to be something here," Dennis said. He rubbed his forehead. A main course had suddenly been added to his plate—a bona fide murder with an intact corpse. What was going on? Now he had two unknown suspects to find? The only good thing of the past twenty-four hours was Sterling's idea of setting a trap—or a screen in basketball vernacular. Perhaps when all was done, they would have a lead to the torch killer.

The medical examiner was finished which meant it was time to remove the body. Dennis walked to the front porch and looked out at the small crowd of neighbors that had gathered. He couldn't see all of their faces in the dark so he decided to join the group. When he was close enough, he spotted one of his officers talking to Olivet and Gavin Wendell. Both were wearing bathrobes over their pajamas as if they'd gotten out of bed to come over. Olivet looked at him with tears running down her face, and Dennis walked over to where they stood.

"Good evening, Mr. and Mrs. Wendell. Did you know the victim?"

The pastor turned toward Dennis. His face was puzzled at first and then slowly registered recognition. "You're one of the police officers that came to the church," he said.

"Yes, I'm Lt. Dennis Cane." As Dennis extended his hand, he noticed Tom Genner, the singles pastor, just beyond the Wendells, praying with a small group.

"You met Martha just yesterday, at the church," Olivet said, dabbing at her eyes with a tissue. "Life can slip away just like that. Who would want to do such a thing to Sister Smith? She was a kind woman, always ready to lend a helping hand." Olivet turned to her husband and buried her face in his chest.

That's why the murdered woman's face was familiar. She and another woman were talking with Olivet and Gavin as he and Merlot left the church. A small world, getting tinier by the minute.

"We don't have any idea who's responsible. It's early yet," Dennis said before turning to complete his mission for coming outside.

"Ladies and gentlemen, if I could ask you all to please return to your homes," Dennis said in a loud voice. "We need to keep the area around this house cleared. A lot of personnel are going to be moving in and out of here. This is now a crime scene. Please. Let us do our jobs."

Genner ended his prayer with a loud "Amen" and slowly the people began to move away. The Wendells and Tom Genner got inside a Lincoln SUV and pulled away from the curb.

Feeling tired and overwhelmed, Dennis reentered Martha Smith's home. He couldn't believe what was happening. He'd finally found credence with Merlot and his team about this serial killer, and now another wrongful death was dropped into his workload. He couldn't let the torcher's trail go cold for another year. He had to focus on the plan that he, Merlot, Sterling, and Glenn had decided to follow. Tom Genner as the suspect. Uncanny that he was at the scene of this murder. Could they somehow be connected? What was Genner doing here? The pastor and his wife Dennis could understand. But Genner? Perhaps Martha Smith was a member of the singles ministry. Didn't Etta mention that some of the members were a little older?

He needed sleep. But first the news conference. He had to be in time for the eleven o'clock news.

Same Day

Chapter Fifty-Four

At exactly 11:00 p.m. Dennis Cane stood outside Grady Memorial Hospital surrounded by members of the press. He was dressed in his best detective suit—gray with a white shirt and black tie. This, he hoped, would be his finest hour.

"What can you tell us about new developments in this case?" a reporter near the front asked.

"I can tell you that we will talk to Chanel Franco tomorrow morning after her bandages are changed and hopefully have the identity of the person responsible for this attempt on her life." Dennis spoke and looked into the cameras with confidence.

"Why wait until tomorrow?" another reporter shouted out in the back.

"The doctors have asked us to wait. They don't want our presence with her to create a setback."

"What is her condition?" another reporter asked.

"She'll be able to talk for the first time since she came in. Her condition is guarded as you can see from this photo." As he held up the image for them to see, he imagined camera lenses zooming in and putting Chanel's face in the center of television screens. "That's all I have at this time. As I said before, we hope to have a suspect in custody soon." Dennis turned and walked away to the sound of reporters screaming questions, and then reentered the hospital where Merlot and Sterling waited.

"I've got my officers on duty, but I've got to get some sleep. I'll talk to you fellows tomorrow," Dennis said.

Same Day

Chapter Fifty-Five

Michael sat ramrod straight as the photo of a smiling, wide-awake Chanel Franco filled the television screen. He'd almost missed this news broadcast because he'd planned to go to bed early. It had been a busy day, but something prompted him to turn on the television in time to catch a recap and be blown away by what he heard and saw.

How can this be?

He had done everything he'd practiced for the last three years. He stripped her naked. He drugged her. He poured gasoline all over her body and then rolled her in the tarp . . .

Did I forget to pour gas over the tarp?

He thought back to that night. Of course he had poured the gas over the tarp. No one could avoid getting burned severely under those circumstances. The rain may have extinguished the fire, but not before damage from the flames was done. She should at least have third- and fourth-degree tissue damage. And why would they put someone in a coma who looks that good? Should he trust the news? Michael had read all kinds of books on burn injuries. He'd done Internet research, too. She should be in critical condition. And yet there she was, her face hardly damaged at all, smiling for the camera. That just could not be possible!

And yet it appeared to be so.

He had to do something. Chanel was able to talk. Maybe she didn't suffer the same symptoms as anyone else given the Rohypnol. Maybe she was someone God had plans for, which meant she couldn't die before her time. God would perform a miracle to save her. And even if she couldn't remember anything now, eventually she would remember. The most innocent and unlikely thing could trigger a memory.

But I was chosen, too. And this is my mission, my purpose.

If she were one of the select few, God would never have allowed her to be taken. But he had made it possible for Michael to take her easily. These circumstances were not working out for Chanel's good; instead, they were a test for Michael. To show that he would not give up, that he would not judge by outward appearances, that he would keep the faith until he was victorious. And indeed he would claim the victory. He would finish the task. He had put a lot of thought into this and was prepared for any contingencies.

Everything changes. Even his plan had gone through some reconstruction. He'd never set out to murder more than one woman. The first one was supposed to be at trial run, where he went to the edge but not over it. But Meredith Payne saw his face and her reaction had not been good. So she had to die. But it was so easy to leave the house burning with her in it. He never got the full effect, so he felt like it was expedient to try it again. After the second time he was so nervous he almost ditched the whole idea. But after a whole year passed without one single police official showing up at his door, he had to keep going.

That's when it occurred to him that more was really less. The more women found in different jurisdictions, the less likely the trail would lead to Michael. This new development was only a distraction, but he needed to sleep before making his next move.

* * *

Thursday morning, June 19, 2008

Hours later, the alarm sounded and woke him up. It was 1:00 a.m. He got out of bed, went to a hidden recess in the walls, pulled out the bag with the hospital uniform and the generic white shoes he'd had delivered, and dressed quickly. As a finishing touch he clipped the ID badge to his waistband. He went to his closet, pulled out a shoe box, and selected a syringe. Then he went to the kitchen and removed four vials of insulin from a container in the back of the refrigerator. He remembered plastic gloves just as he opened the back door to the garage. He stopped and did a quick mental inventory.

He was ready. Minutes later the dark sedan sped south down I-75 south. Destination: Grady Memorial Hospital.

The interstate highway traffic was light at this time of morning. But Michael, tired and sleepy, had to force himself to concentrate. The last thing he needed was to fall asleep behind the steering wheel. Yesterday had been a long day and this day's events could extend into the late evening as well. And he was determined to finish what he had started. Everybody and their friendly neighborhood member of the press wanted to know who was responsible for trying to burn Chanel Franco to death. They didn't care about why. They thought they did. They called the suspect a psychotic maniac. They had no idea what it took to go through years of pain and heartache. Not one of them would be able to stand before their maker one day and know that if they heard the words *Well done, my child,* it would be because they'd gone above and beyond the call of duty—that they'd given their all.

As he anticipated, the hospital parking lot was practically empty. He drove the rental car into a parking place close to the exit and not far from the elevator. He straightened his hospital-issue uniform and clipped the identification badge to the bottom edge of the top. He had no concern about the badge having been reported stolen or missing because he'd stood near the nurses' station long enough to hear that A. D. Huff was on vacation and and had left in such a hurry that the badge was forgotten. Of course A. D.'s friend and roomie would bring it home in time to permit Huff to enter the hospital when the cruise was over. It was such an added advantage that the badge was not necessary for exiting—only entering. Michael walked into the main entrance, past the empty reception area, and got on the elevator. Oh the joy of drowsy employees and early morning hours. If anyone had any questions, they'd see only a nurse making rounds. By the time someone in human resources realized that A. D. Huff reported to work during time off for vacation, Michael would have moved on to other pastimes.

The halls were quiet. Michael kept his head lowered and strode with purpose toward his destination. He'd noticed that if he walked in the direction away from the double doors, he could enter the burn unit without telling anyone why he was there. He suspected police would be there, but his plan was to walk straight into the patient's room. If she was doing so much better, she'd probably not be in intensive care. And if she was, he'd just walk in during an off moment, because off moments happen with people.

Same Day

Chapter Fifty-Six

Mira Dream's next task was dressing changes for Jane Doe; although she tried to remember not to refer to her patient as Jane when she was in the hospital, it was to no avail. Dedicated to her job and to putting forth a good impression, Mira thought first and foremost of her patients. Her first duty was to each one of them, and then to the family. She didn't work hard to inspire confidence; it came easily because of her honest approach and sincere concern for the health and well-being of those under her care. Chanel was a much prettier name than Jane anyway. But as the bard once asked—*What's in a name?*

"Her name is Chanel," Mira said aloud to herself as she stepped off the elevator and turned right.

Chanel was scheduled for skin grafts later this morning and this upcoming session of dressing changes was critical.

It was imperative that Mira document what she saw underneath those bandages—unhealthy tissue or infection—and remove as much dead tissue as she could. Sometimes bacteria would create an infection in spite of the massive doses of topical antibiotics applied directly to the wounds. So far her injuries were coming along nicely, but things could change overnight. Mira got down on her knees to pray this morning and she was expecting to see nothing that would hinder moving forward with the grafting.

Louise Canola would be admitted to the hospital by 9:00 a.m. and then the ball would start rolling. What a blessing she was! God had come through better than Mira could ever have imagined. A huge burn like Chanel's could result in disfigurement, huge scarring, and even spindly limbs due to lack of skin to repair the damage. A twin sibling who was willing to donate the skin needed was like manna from heaven.

Mira's stomach felt a little unsettled. She'd had a late dinner and gone to bed before the food had time to digest. Not to worry. She'd become accustomed to the odor of the wounds, but she didn't want to take the chance that something simple could increase the discomfort she felt and result in her being less than her best. Just to be safe a stop at the employee lounge for an antacid and a last-minute bathroom break would do the trick.

Still completely engrossed in her thoughts, Mira nodded her head to acknowledge a colleague, barely paying attention as she continued on her way. Arriving at the door of the break room, she entered and ten minutes later came out, ready to begin. A nagging thought tugged at the back of her mind, but she shrugged it off. She'd think about it later.

Same Day

Chapter Fifty-Seven

Michael passed only one other employee in the hallway. Nothing was said. Nothing was done. As he reached a break in the hallway, he noticed a door marked Conference Room. The door was cracked open. He could hear a man's voice. Michael stopped in his tracks as he heard the name.

"Chanel Franco's twin sister will be officially admitted later this morning. We should be underway by noon. Any questions? Comments?" the male voice asked.

Michael resumed walking past the conference room until he came to another break in the hallway that allowed him to retreat.

Twin sister! That was her twin sister on the newscast! This is a trap. And I almost walked into it. Thank God I dodged that bullet. Oh well, like my mother always told me, believe half of what you see and none of what you hear.

Minutes later, Michael drove the rental car out of the parking deck and headed home. He wanted to take a hot shower and then make a pot of coffee. In his bathrobe, with slippers on his feet, he would sit in his comfortable chair and watch the charade unfold. The nerve of them! Did they not know by now that he was no fool? It would be interesting to see just how far they'd go to try to lure him in. He would be two steps ahead. He had a job to finish. Only one more little darling to snuff, and he could disappear into the sunset, leaving them scratching their heads.

Same Day

Chapter Fifty-Eight

As Mira entered the intensive care area, she called out to the nurse on duty to signal her arrival, and then dressed for the next occasion by putting the plastic protective covering over her body. Next she donned the huge arm protectors followed by a pair of latex gloves. She slid the head covering over her short hair and then snapped her nose and mouth cover in place. Her cart was fully stocked with the necessary supplies. She took a deep breath, grabbed the cart, pulled back the curtain of Chanel's assigned area, and entered the hot, humid interior, which in this enclosed area felt like a steambath. Mira smiled. The best way to get through the labor-intensive procedure would be to imagine spending time in a sauna.

She began to remove bandages, tossing them into the bandage receptacle as she carefully inspected all areas of the burn. Everything looked good—no infection. Her body was still bloated by the edema, but some of the swelling was subsiding.

Once all the bandages were removed, she poured a bottle of sterile water into the bowl and began to gently wash each wound.

Nearly two hours later, Mira emerged from the steamy room, her job finished. As she began to discard the protective clothing, her thoughts returned to normal. As she stooped to tighten the laces of her shoes she thought about her friend Dee Dee. *Something had been different this morning. What was it?* She shook her head to clear her mind. She had other patients to care for now.

Same Day

Chapter Fifty-Nine

It was 6:45 a.m. and Dennis Cane had a decision to make. What would take priority? Martha Smith's murder or the serial killer that he had just set a trap for? He wanted to be at the hospital if the bastard showed up. But investigative reports had to be filed. His incident report was laid out in front of him on his desk. He decided to read it again even though he'd already gone over it twice. Looking for a link, a clue, anything out of place. All he needed was a break.

Thirty minutes later, Dennis still sat huddled over the report, sniffling constantly. He'd been moving around so much, he hadn't noticed that he was coming down with a cold. The air-conditioning vent in his office was closed and yet he still felt chills. If he ever got to the bottom of these killings, he vowed that he'd take a vacation. Concentration was getting impossible. He walked over to his coat closet and rummaged inside looking for his old red sweater. No luck. He looked over at the coat rack in the corner. No sweater. That sweater had to be somewhere because he never took it home.

"Great Scott! Where is my sweater?" he asked in exasperation as he headed toward the lobby and reception area. Gladys was so efficient that if any item of clothing was left by staff anywhere in the building, she'd somehow find it and hang it up.

"That blasted rain has to be the reason for this cold," he muttered to himself. He'd spent almost twenty-four hours wet on Monday; that was enough to give a person pneumonia. He walked over to the closet for the general population and slid the hangars to the right, inspecting each garment. He frowned at the gray hoodie, the black jacket, the plaid shirt, and then he spotted it. His red sweater. He eagerly pulled the oversized pullover from the hangar and plopped it over his head, snatching it down his chest in one motion, as he turned triumphantly to Gladys's workstation. But she wasn't there. She was probably on the prowl for other discarded outerwear to neatly hang in the closet. He returned to his office determined to be warmer.

He closed his door, sat down, and stared down at the report for Martha Smith. There was nothing in her murder to tie it to those patterns he'd attributed to an unknown serial killer. Not one blasted thing. The intercom on his desk buzzed.

"Yes," he answered.

"There's a lady out here that says she needs to talk to someone in charge," Gladys said in her raspy smoker's voice.

"Send her to the chief," he responded. He didn't have time to deal with anyone now, and he was not in the mood for complaints. Not today.

"The chief hasn't come in yet. He's at the mayor's office. She says she'll wait all day if it takes that long to talk to someone in authority. I told her you were the closest authority figure we had in the building right now."

His first impulse was to let her wait, knowing the chief might not get in until after lunch as he was probably being drug across the carpet about that press conference. Dennis had received at least three calls this morning from the chief that he'd let go to voice mail. That thing with the press had been a rogue operation, but desperate times called for desperate measures. The mayor was probably laying the ground rules about publicity and its impact on future residents of Mint Leaf Manor. That kind of pressure could lead an emotional and slightly unstable person like the chief to have a few drinks, which meant that by the time he returned to the precinct, he would either be mellow or ready for a fight. What the heck? He would take the heat when it came. Maybe it was wishful thinking to believe that he'd catch the Torch—a killer who left no traces of his identity behind.

He stood and then sat down. He removed the sweater, which was just beginning to warm his body, stuffed it in the bottom desk drawer, straightened the collar on his white shirt, and checked the knot in his blue-and-white striped tie, satisfied the dimple was still in place. He took a deep breath.

"Send her in," he said, steeling himself for whatever or whoever walked into the door. He'd listen, make apologies, and then send the woman right back to Gladys to file a report.

Same Day

Chapter Sixty

When the door to Dennis's office opened, the most beautiful young woman he'd seen in his life —and he'd seen quite a few—walked in. Her simple black dress draped softly, showing every curve. Her dark-brown hair was long and wavy. She smiled, revealing even white teeth as her violet eyes met his. She carried a purse and pulled a carry-on bag behind her as she walked toward him.

"I'm Michelle Chalk," she said, extending her hand.

Almost forgetting his manners, Dennis rose to move toward her and grasped her hand, noticing it was warm and soft. Her perfume entered the room with her. It smelled of hibiscus. Her full lips were covered in a glossy orange shade of lipstick.

"Lt. Dennis Cane. please . . . what can I do for you?" he

managed.

“I’m not certain that you can help me at all. I’m here with a story that has no foundation of evidence and could be construed as a lot of malarkey and an old woman’s fantasies. Unfortunately, you’d have to know my aunt to be reassured that what I’m about to tell you is not fantasy. My great-aunt, Martha Smith, was a very intelligent woman.”

Dennis came down to earth at the mention of Martha Smith’s name. He’d spent all morning poring over his investigative report of her murder. He was all ears now.

“She called me early yesterday morning,” Michelle continued, “to warn me that she could be murdered. At first I wondered about her, but then I had to realize that she was completely rational, as usual. So I listened to her, made all the appropriate remarks to urge her to get those thoughts out of her head, said goodbye, and promptly decided that maybe I needed to come visit her. But when I got a call last night informing me that she had in fact been brutally murdered, I took the first flight from Charlotte, North Carolina. I have no idea who did this, but I know what her last words to me were. I’m hoping that you people can make heads or tails of it,” she concluded, those violet eyes still focused on Dennis.

His heart began to race, and he felt himself breaking out into a cold sweat. "Please continue," he said.

"She said, and I quote, 'Michelle, I've always tried to live a godly life and mind my own business.' She went on to say she's seen things that let her know there is a killer hiding in plain sight in her church. She gave me the feeling she'd spoken to the person because she mentioned she'd persuaded this person to go to the police or else she would. But she was afraid she might die before she could do so. And she told me where to find the proof."

"Where is the proof?" Dennis asked, wanting to bear-hug this woman. *Could this be the break I desperately need?*

"At her house. If you will drive me there I will get it for you."

Same Day

Chapter Sixty-One

Anissa undressed slowly in front of the full-length mirror on the wall in her bedroom. She had to see the effect of a seductive disrobing. Her body was in good shape, thanks to time spent in the gym. Her breasts were not perky, but they didn't sag either. She put her hands on her hips and leaned forward, noticing that her bosom shifted slightly with her movement. She turned to the left and then to the right. Finally she turned her backside toward the mirror and peered over her shoulder. The effect was not good. She got a hand mirror from her dresser in order to see her rear. It was still well defined. She giggled, suddenly feeling silly.

She'd had a female version of a wet dream last night. In

the dream Merlot was with her, both of them naked. He was on top of her, and just as she felt him enter her, she woke up. That pleasure was short and sweet. Enough to convince her that the time had come to end the waiting. She would bring him home with her tonight and lead him to this very bedroom where she intended to make love to him as long as he could hold out. It had been so long for her that she knew she'd behave like a full-fledged nymphomaniac, but she really didn't think Merlot would mind.

She walked toward the bathroom to get into the shower when the doorbell rang. She stopped and listened. Sometimes the delivery person would ring once to signal his arrival and leave the packages near the door. It rang a second time. She grabbed a robe and went to the door. She leaned against it and peeped through the hole. She saw no one, nor was she expecting any deliveries. Suddenly the top of a head appeared and a cracked voice made an announcement.

"I have registered mail for Anissa Strickland," the voice croaked.

Anissa sighed with relief and opened the door, expecting to see a short person standing there with an envelope and a clipboard for her signature. Instead she saw the flash of a hand as it reached toward her. And then felt a prick in her neck. She looked at the person, her eyes opened wide in disbelief as she instantly crumbled to the floor.

Same Day

Chapter Sixty-Two

Michael quickly stepped over Anissa's body and dragged her back inside the apartment. Looking around and seeing no one, he reached down to retrieve his bag. He closed the door behind him and turned the deadbolt to a locked position. He wanted to dance around with glee. He wanted to shout to the heavens with joy. At last! He had her! The one person he'd killed all those other women for. The one person who counted. Now it would soon be over. But first he wanted to sit down and look at her in her helpless state. To relish in his victory.

Anissa. There you are, my pretty.

Three years ago he saw her at a gym, laughing and full of life, and knew instantly that he would kill her. But with no clue as to how to kill and get away with it, he needed to do some research. And he needed practice. He didn't want to botch it. She absolutely had to die once he took her. He'd had no idea that killing could become addictive. He couldn't count the times he'd had a sudden urge to kill someone outside of his time frame. Each time he would remind himself of his purpose, which included two deaths and two dates per year. His only failure had been Chanel Franco.

The brilliant idea to substitute Chanel's twin sister had forced him to move ahead of schedule. And Anissa lying unconscious on the floor was the consequence of their deception. Their lies had created a necessity, but everything was in place for him now. In twenty-four hours the police would have a suspect in custody and soon the case would be closed. And Michael would be gone.

From this city. From this state. Never to return again.

Such a lovely room.

He crossed over to a comfortable armchair with a pale-peach floral pattern and sat down. He looked around, admiring the peach drapes and the white sofa with toss pillows done in the same pattern as the chair. The soft peach rug underneath the oak cocktail table. The art on the walls, the absence of personal photos. He felt a strong urge to go into her bedroom and take a look around, but he didn't have time. He had to get her out of this apartment and into his car.

It was fortunate that she lived on the ground level with a back door from her kitchen that led out to a small patio. From the patio it was a short walk to the curb of the street that ran from behind the building to the dumpster, and then circled back out. Today was not trash collection day. All her neighbors were working people. Michael knew it well. He had sat right outside her door for hours on many Thursdays and never seen a soul. Today would be the same.

He opened his bag and pulled out the thick tarp and a syringe filled with Rohypnol. He slid the cocktail table back and spread the tarp on the floor. As he removed Anissa's robe from her body, he couldn't help but smile at the irony of her being naked. Nothing much for him to do. He injected her upper arm and then sat back and admired her beauty. Then he rolled her up into the tarp and secured it with plastic ties on both ends.

We don't want you to fall out.

He pulled the wig off, removed a baseball cap from the bag and a hooded long coat. He put the hat on and then the coat, buttoning it all the way. He closed the bag, slung it over his shoulder, and then reached down and grabbed one end of the tarp. He drug Anissa's inert body across the wooden floors, through the kitchen and to the back door. He opened the door and peered out.

Just in case.

Not a creature was stirring. He pulled her out of the door, closed it, and drug her across the patio, across the small lawn to the back of his sedan. After opening the trunk, he lifted one end of the tarp where Anissa's head was, and leaned it against the right side of the trunk compartment. He then pushed her body forward. Moving it slowly toward the left, he lifted and pushed her until she was wedged inside the trunk. He slammed it shut and kept his head down as he approached the driver's side of the car. Opening the door and throwing the bag into the back seat, he got in and closed the door. Only then did he lift his head to look around. Still no one in sight. He turned the ignition and drove slowly forward, making the U-turn near the dumpster. He then drove back down the street, allowing Anissa to pass her residence for the last time.

Easy as pie.

Once again a perfectly executed abduction. No witnesses.

Of course Michael didn't know about Stan.

Same Day

Chapter Sixty-Three

Stan Causey was a veteran of the United States Marine Corps who lost his legs when he stepped on a land mine during the war in Iraq. He lived in the building across the street behind Anissa's townhouse. From the windows of his dayroom, he enjoyed a perfect view of her back door and patio. He'd often watched her water the flowers or sit in a chair and read a book. She was good eye candy and he looked forward to seeing her outside. Especially through the crosshairs of his sniper's rifle that sat on a stand he'd put together and placed in the room.

He loved that rifle. Keeping it set up allowed him to practice his skills honed on active duty. The gun was unloaded, but peering through the scope was like looking through a pristine magnifying glass. Scoping out his surroundings kept his mind off of his injuries and his inability to walk. So far, he'd declined being fitted for artificial legs. From his wheelchair, he positioned himself so he could watch the squirrels, the chipmunks, and the few people who ventured outside. That's how he passed most of his days—looking down the barrel of his rifle with a bottle of whiskey beside him. Other days he waited for hours at the VA.

He sat back from the rifle and took a long swig, thinking about what he'd just seen. That person had driven down the street for the past few months. Always on Thursday. Always at a slow speed as though looking for something. And never the same car. That's what caught Stan's attention. A sniper is trained to see what others can't see.

The driver wore different clothes and always with hats, but the shoulders, the steering wheel grip, and the gloved hands were the same. Always the same. Only today was different. Today he got out of the car and went around to the front of the building.

Even though he had never met his neighbor, Stan knew she ran in the mornings. Her daily routine was to come around the corner in what seemed like a cool-down jog. She'd stop about midway, walk to her patio, and then remove her shoes before doing some stretches. She'd done so earlier today. She was inside the house now because she'd not locked the sliding glass doors like she always did when she left home.

Through the rifle's scope, he saw her go to the door in a robe and then suddenly fall to the floor. He watched as the stranger pulled her inside the apartment and out of sight. That was strange behavior. If he had been on military duty, that kind of behavior would have called for alerting his fellow troops.

Enemy encroachment.

Stan liked his privacy and respected the privacy of others; but something was not right, so he sat up and paid attention. When the stranger appeared dragging something behind him toward his car, he knew something was amiss. At first he thought it was a rug, but upon closer inspection, he could tell a body was wrapped inside from the way one end of it lolled backward as it fell inside the trunk. He had seen enough bodies being moved to recognize one even though it was covered.

He would have to do something.

He rolled over to the table where his cell phone rested and made a call to 911.

Same day

Chapter Sixty-Four

The news about Chanel's ability to speak with the police about her attack had the burn unit staff abuzz as they reported to work. All wondered how it could be possible, considering the protocol for heavy sedation for a burn patient with third- and fourth-degree wounds. Dr. Salada met with several people in the employee lounge to explain what was going on.

Mira Dream stood with the staff and listened as Dr. Salada spoke.

"Chanel Franco is still under heavy sedation and will have a skin graft on her left leg this afternoon as scheduled. Her sister Louise has been admitted to the hospital as well," Dr. Salada said as he looked into the faces of his staff. "A heavy police presence is to be expected for the next twenty-four hours, but we are all professionals here. We will work around it."

Mira left to check on Chanel when it suddenly occurred to her what it was that was off with Dee Dee. Angela Diane Huff, affectionately known as Dee Dee to her friends, was on a cruise ship to Jamaica. And Mira had passed her ID badge this morning hanging on a stranger's hips.

She walked to the reception area, surprised to see Claire in place. Mira picked up the phone and dialed security.

Same Day

Chapter Sixty-Five

Merlot had tried unsuccessfully for the past hour and a half to reach Anissa on her cell phone. He knew she ran every morning, but should be in her apartment by now. He was supposed to meet her for lunch, a decision they'd made that morning when Anissa called him prior to her run. It was unlike her to not answer. She usually took her phone when she was out jogging. Even if she was in the shower, she should have noticed that he'd called several times. He was a little concerned.

The only other reason he could think of for her not returning his call was some exotic preparation for the dinner at her place that she'd invited him to tonight. He was certain he had not imagined the promise of a sexual encounter in her words.

"You ready to show me what I've been missing?" she asked.

"Anytime," he'd responded, knowing she never played around when it came to that sort of thing. The closest they had come to sex was the time he lost himself between her breasts, sucking her left nipple into his mouth. She had recoiled as though touched by a flame and immediately asked him to leave. He'd been a good boy since then.

"How about tonight? Come for dinner around seven. And come hungry. The main course is me," she'd said with a laugh.

"I'll be there with chimes on. The bells are out of order. Are you sure about this?"

"I've never been more sure about anything in my life."

He'd been in a dream world since then. He was more than ready for whatever she had planned for tonight. He just wanted to hear her voice.

He decided not to leave another message but go to her place instead and make sure everything was okay. He'd been so busy with this attempted murder as well as with Dennis and his enthusiasm about Sterling that he'd let too much time pass without spending quality time with her.

"I'll be back after lunch," he said to Maude as he breezed past her and out the door. While waiting for the elevator, it occurred to him that Anissa could be at the hospital. Louise was having surgery. And so was Chanel. He pulled out his cell phone and dialed Louise's number. As the phone rang, he looked up impatiently and saw that the elevator was stopped on the 21st floor. The elevator to the left was going up. He counted the floors as they lit up in passing—18, 19, 20— when suddenly he heard a voice answer on the other end of the line.

"Louise?" Merlot began.

"No. This is her mother. She cannot talk right now," Mrs. Canola responded.

"Hi, Mrs. Canola. This is Merlot Candy. I'm trying to reach Anissa. Is she with Louise at the hospital?"

"No, Merlot. But the police are here. They believe the person who tried to kill Chanel has been here."

Merlot had to run what she said through his brain twice.

"The killer? What makes them think he's been there?"

"One of the nurses reported seeing a stranger wearing a coworker's employee badge on the floor. The burn unit is on lockdown and the police are searching everywhere," she answered.

"I certainly hope they find him! And you haven't seen Anissa?"

"No. She told Louise she would be here this afternoon."

"Thanks, Mrs. Canola. I'll be in touch," Merlot responded, his head down and eyes focused on what appeared to be a stain on his pants.

The killer went to the hospital, he thought. Their little ruse worked. Surely the police would capture him now—they'd have a description of him. The elevator door opening snapped him back to attention as he moved forward and nearly collided with Missy Kinner.

"I need to talk to you. It's important. My aunt found the fanny pack!" she said.

Same Day

Chapter Sixty-Six

Dennis and Michelle sat in the bedroom of the late Martha Smith staring at the screen of a laptop computer. Martha had uploaded a video into a file that she'd nicknamed "Pudding." She told her niece "the proof was in the pudding." She then directed her where to find the laptop, gave her the password to unlock it, and identified the file name. Martha had taken every precaution she knew to protect the information she'd gathered.

On the screen a dark sedan moved slowly down the street. No headlights were illuminated, but based on what Dennis had seen of the neighborhood, he knew it was the street that ran in front of Martha's house. It was hard to see the make and model of the vehicle because the streetlight stood to the left of Martha's front yard. The camera followed the automobile as it turned into the driveway of a house two doors down from Martha, on the opposite side of the street. Martha's upstairs bedroom window provided a perfect view of the driveway and the entrance to the garage of this house.

They continued to watch as the car pulled up to the closed garage and stopped—brake lights came on. The view here was better. To see why, Dennis glanced out of the window and saw that another streetlight stood about fifty feet away from the house on the same side of the street as Martha's residence. He turned back to the computer screen as the garage door lifted. A tall, dark figure exited the car and entered the garage. Minutes later a white van backed out and stopped beside the sedan. The driver exited the van, and then drove the sedan inside the garage. As the door began to lower, the driver climbed into the van and began to back out. Dennis could tell from what he saw next that Martha ran downstairs with her camera. Her breathing became louder, the lens shaking as she moved, displaying the hallway, the stairs, and her passage through the living room. He watched as the focus went from a chair to the window where the van was passing in front of Martha's house. She caught the side panel of the van this time, thanks to the streetlight. The imprinted words Praying Hands Non-Denominational Church, Singles Ministry showed clearly in large letters.

The video stopped on a still shot of the license plate. The date and time stamp was June 24, 2005, 4:47 a.m. In a few seconds the video started up again, with the identical scene sequences repeated—time and date stamp, June 16, 2006, 4:30 a.m. The video started up again, repeating the same scene, time and date stamp, June 24, 2006, 4:17 a.m. The video started three additional times, with time and date stamp registering June 16 and 24 in 2007, and June 16 in 2008. The night Chanel Franco was set on fire. The driver, though blurred and out of focus, was around the same height as Tom Genner. And the fact that the van belonged to the church was damning.

"My aunt mentioned that the house belonged to the church. Said it was used by the singles ministry," Michelle said.

Could I get a search warrant based on this video? If not

a warrant, I could certainly bring him in for questioning. But would that be premature? Would it tip him off and stop him before I have enough to arrest him? Dennis couldn't take that chance. He had to do something. He had no idea that things were coming to a head and all of his questions would soon be answered.

Same Day

Chapter Sixty-Seven

As Merlot led Missy toward his office, he held the phone to his ear and listened to Anissa's line ringing on the other end. He stood aside to allow Missy to go ahead of him as once again the call went straight to Anissa's voice mail. He didn't bother to leave another message. He'd already left seven. She always returned the call within minutes because she checked her messages so often. She always kept her phone nearby because she said there was no need to have one at all otherwise; landlines were for people who were too busy to keep their cell phones handy. He told himself not to get upset, but this whole thing about a killer and Chanel's near-death experience had put his nerves on edge.

He'd given Missy ten minutes to tell him whatever she thought was so important. As he passed the receptionist's desk, he gave Maude a wink that was her signal to buzz him in five minutes with an emergency. A very private, phone call—their system for getting rid of unwanted guests.

Missy swished her hips from side to side as she walked in front of Merlot. He had to give it to her—the body looked great. But so did Anissa's, and that was the only body he was interested in at the present moment. His door was open and as Missy hesitated, he waved his hand to give her permission to enter. She sat on the couch and patted the seat next to her for Merlot to sit, but he sat behind his desk. She crossed her legs and smiled at him. She was actually quite pretty.

"I'm listening," Merlot said.

"The woman you were looking for when you came to my aunt's house has been found, hasn't she?" asked Missy.

"Yes, she has."

"I didn't remember at the time—I drink a lot—but I saw her get dumped at that construction site," Missy said.

"You saw her get dumped?" Merlot stared straight into her eyes.

“Yes. And the person who dumped her had to be a woman.”

Merlot relaxed. She hadn’t seen anything. She just admitted she drank a lot. This was an excuse to get into his office. He didn’t want to flatter himself, but he knew he was good-looking and he knew she’d been attracted by his looks. This kind of thing happened to him a lot—women creating excuses to see him. He stood up abruptly. He didn’t have time for this.

“That was a good effort, Missy. That’s your name, right?”

“Yes, that’s my name. And it’s the truth. It was a woman. I saw her boobs! And she dropped this.” Missy pulled the fanny pack from her oversized purse and threw it over at Merlot. It landed on top of his desk where the only other objects on the surface were a pen and a notepad.

“What’s this?” he asked as he reached for the little bag. Unzipping it, he raised his eyebrows when he saw the contents—a box of matches; a torch lighter; a torn, scrunched piece of paper; and a lip gloss. He took the paper, straightened it out, and saw that it was two halves of a small envelope. He turned them over and put the pieces together, forming an offering envelope for Praying Hands Non-Denominational Church. He looked up at Missy who smiled from ear to ear.

"And you didn't say anything about this the day we came to your house?"

Missy looked sheepish. "I told you. I'd been drinking and I didn't remember. Alcohol does that to everybody. My aunt found it under my bed and asked me about it."

"Did you also make the 911 call?" he asked, his curiosity burning.

"Yes, but how did you know that?"

"And did you use an iron pipe to pull the tarp away from her face?"

She hesitated, looked upward as if trying to think.

"Yes, I did. I just wanted to see what it . . . I mean she—"

"You saved a good portion of her face from burns. And you saved her life," Merlot said. He shook his head and looked at her with admiration. She had no idea what she'd just done. Who could have known? This was turning into a good story for someone to tell years from now, but he needed to move. He had to go to Anissa's place and he had to call Dennis.

"Thank you, Missy. You're the gift that keeps on giving," he said, standing to lead her out while punching in Dennis's number.

Chapter Sixty-Eight

Michael had just passed one of those variable-message signs on I-75 that provide information such as traffic alerts and the time and distance to the next exit. This one had an Amber Alert with a description of the car he was driving and the license plate number. It was wrong. The number 1 was in the place that the letter I should have been. But it was too close for comfort. He didn't take a second to even think about how they knew. He simply took the next exit, Moores Mill Road, looking in his rearview mirror to see if someone was following. No one in sight. He was now forced to do something completely irrational and there was risk involved.

But he couldn't get caught with Anissa still alive in his car. Everything would be ruined.

Time for plan G—Get out of Dodge.

He waited patiently for the light to change to green at the end of the exit ramp. He turned right and then right again, moving left to the center turning lane so as to turn into the strip shopping center. As usual the parking lot was crowded. From the street he spied an empty parking space, hoping that no one would beat him to it. He reached behind for the can of gasoline on the floor. While waiting to turn, he let all the windows down, opened the can, and began to pour gasoline all over the floor of the front seat. He felt so proud he'd followed his instincts about bringing the gas along with him this time.

When all lanes were clear, he turned left and zipped into the waiting parking space right between a red truck and a gray SUV. A few people milled around. Most were on the sidewalks in front of the various shops. He unbuttoned the long coat and removed his hat. He leaned over through the bucket seats and poured the remaining gas on the back floor, careful to slosh some across the backseat after retrieving his bag. Once the can was emptied, he dropped it on the floor.

The fumes were strong even with the windows down. Working quickly, he unzipped the bag, pulled out another bag, a pair of sunglasses, and a lighter. He put on the sunglasses and got out of the car, casting a casual glance around the area. No one looked his way. He ran his fingers through his hair, and walked around the front end and then between his car and the red truck. He flicked the lighter and held it for a second before tossing it into the backseat, and then continued on his way. It was all that he could do and it had to work. He'd planned for such a time as this.

Michael crossed the parking lot and then down the sidewalk to the bank that sat nestled among crepe myrtle trees. He didn't look back. If the flame went out, then so be it. He entered the bank and walked to the service counter. He took out a counter check, filled in an amount and took a place in the line of waiting customers. Just as he was called to a teller's window, he noticed that the people entering the bank were talking excitedly. And then he saw an employee rush outside.

Something must be going on outside. What could it be? Of course, a car is burning.

Michael watched as the teller counted out his cash, placed it in an envelope, and handed it to him.

"Have a nice day," Michael said with a smile, as he placed the envelope in his bag. He left the bank and continued down the sidewalk away from the direction of the shopping center, listening to the screams and loud voices. He'd walked only a short distance before he heard sirens approaching from afar. Then he heard the explosion. It was too late for Anissa.

Michael hailed a taxi and got inside.

Same Day

Chapter Sixty-Nine

Merlot arrived at Anissa's apartment to find three police cars parked nearby and one officer with police tape busily outlining the front entrance. He pulled onto the nearest curb and ran a full sprint to the door of her apartment where inside more police officers roamed. One of the officers was older than the others.

"You can't come in here, sir," he said, moving in front of Merlot to block his entry.

"My girlfriend lives here. Anissa Strickland. Has something happened to her?" Merlot pulled out his identification.

The older officer's face lit up in recognition. He nodded to the others and turned to Merlot.

"We believe she's been abducted. We got a 911 call from a neighbor who saw someone put a person in the trunk of a car right outside the door to her patio. It looks like she was getting ready to shower because the water was still running, her clothes are on the floor in her bedroom, and a robe was here near the door. We put out an Amber Alert on the vehicle and just got a radio message that the car has been found. It's on fire." The officer reported the incident like he was talking about a load of hay that caught on fire, not the woman that Merlot loved.

"What about Anissa?!" he screamed.

Same Day

Chapter Seventy

Dennis managed to talk a judge into issuing a warrant and after a thorough search of Tom Genner's home, office, car, the church van, and the house on Martha's street that belonged to the singles ministry, enough evidence was found to put him away for life. ID from the missing women, torch lighters, a storage shed filled with containers brimming with gasoline, and boxes with new pristine tarps. And a black leotard that Dennis was certain would contain the same fibers he'd found at the scene of the burned victims the past few years. The clothing that the women were last seen wearing, an old juvenile report that showed Tom having been arrested as a juvenile for starting fires. His computer showed a file of emails to various women who'd attended singles functions—including emails from all the missing women in Dennis's file.

Dennis couldn't believe his luck. Everything he needed to put this man away was there. It was perfect.

Too perfect. And then he noticed the message on his phone. He listened once and then replayed the message from Merlot, the phone on speaker so he could hear what he thought he heard loud and clear.

"Dennis, this is Merlot. I just talked to the woman who made the 911 call about Chanel. She saw the perp and she swears it was a woman. Just wanted to let you know because I have to go find out why Anissa hasn't answered her phone. Call me when you get this message."

Dennis stared into space. *A woman?*

He looked at Tom Genner in the backseat of a police cruiser. Definitely not a woman. And yet all of the evidence made a strong case against him. Dennis felt in his gut that everything had dropped into place too easily. Almost as if someone planned it that way. What killer plans to get caught? The only anomaly in this thing was Martha Smith and her video. Martha told her niece that she had talked to someone at the church. Was it Tom? Who else could it have been? That video alone had no chance in court because the driver could not be seen clearly enough to identify. This whole thing was beginning to stink.

Same Day

Chapter Seventy-One

Etta Wasp sat at the dining room table eating a salad when Pearl came into the room. Unlike Etta, Pearl had salvaged her figure. She stood a foot taller than Etta, dyed her hair to cover the gray, and enjoyed her makeup. A puzzled expression crossed her face.

"Now I know what's bothering me," she said.

Etta put a fork full of lettuce into her mouth and looked curiously at her sister.

"The woman on the brochure," Pearl began.

"What woman? What brochure? What are you talking about?"

"Your church brochure. The one that fell on the floor the other day. I know that woman!"

"What woman?" Etta put the fork down and waited.

"Get that brochure." Pearl said.

Etta got up and went into her office with Pearl on her heels. There was no need to try to eat until this drama was ended. Pearl didn't know when to stop. Etta pulled out a drawer of her file cabinet, thumbed through it, and pulled out the church brochure. She handed it over to Pearl, who pointed with her finger as she held the brochure for Etta to see. Her finger was directed at the face of Olivet Wendell.

"That woman! I know her. Her name is Lacy Larson. I went to high school with her when I lived with Grandmother," Pearl said.

For the four years Pearl attended high school, she lived in Tennessee with their maternal grandmother who was alone in a big house after their grandfather died. Etta stayed with their parents. It was during that time she learned not to be so dependent upon her older sister.

"Are you sure? We know her as Olivet Wendell," Etta said.

"Of course I'm sure. She looks five hundred times better, but that's her. We all thought she was nuts. And could she hold a grudge!"

"Her name isn't Olivet?"

"No. Her name is Lacy. She married before graduation. Some of the girls who knew her well said he was filthy rich. Money made that change in her looks. But Lacy had problems. She had a nasty mean streak; and if you ever crossed her, she'd find a way to make you pay. Brogdon! That was the last name of the man she married. Her new name would be Lacy Brogdon. And now she's calling herself a pastor's wife when she was the biggest heathen ever? She never stepped foot inside a church when I knew her!" Pearl said.

Etta was mystified. Why would this Christian woman pretend to be someone or something that she wasn't? Etta liked to mind her own business, but her church family was a part of that business. Did Pastor Wendell know that his wife of three years was using a false name? What did he really know about her? He'd told the congregation that she'd never been married. Something didn't make sense.

Those detectives coming to visit had caused consternation but now this? This was downright upsetting. One needed to be able to trust church leaders. Should she do something? One of the detectives was with the police and one worked privately. Perhaps the private detective would appreciate any information that showed duplicity. He had left a card with her. Etta opened the desk drawer and found the card. She would call him right now.

Same Day

Chapter Seventy-Two

Michael, known in the scriptures as the one who is like God, gazed at the scenery from the window of a Greyhound bus as it moved through the streets of Atlanta toward the Interstate. Bible scholars are familiar with Michael, the arch angel, the chief prince, who appeared to Daniel in the Old Testament. Michael who appeared in the book of Revelations to fight Satan. Michael who came to help. And create distress, sadness, and destruction to save a holy one. Michael who was sent to do the will of God.

Lacy Olivet Larson Brogdon, a holy one, leaned back in her seat and marveled at the glorious works of God. She had often mourned the years before she came to know him. She wandered in darkness until her redeemer shed his glorious light upon her and made her paths straight and clear. A friend in time of need, God was there to fill every void, mend every flaw, right every wrong. Oh the things she could have done in her earlier years. Now she walked with the God of her understanding and nothing was impossible for her. She was Michael. She was like God.

When FJ, her only son, died, a part of Lacy died, too. No mother rests easy when death claims one of her children. Mothers expect to be buried by their children. She couldn't eat, sleep, or even get out of bed for days. No matter how many sedatives, anti-anxiety pills or shots of booze she took, she got no peace. She went to New York and stood in the middle of the street on the spot where he died. She talked to police, she talked to the people who owned businesses along that thoroughfare, and she learned about the SUV that hit him and knocked him into the path of the bus. And to whom that automobile belonged. She learned who the bus driver was. The last thing he said before he died, at Lacy's insistence as she held the syringe to his throat, was that he should have been watching where he was going.

Lacy's husband—Foley, Sr.—had to die as well. He was in the way. He watched her too closely and he was a heathen. It was a shame he was accident prone, falling down the stairs and breaking his neck. With a little push from behind from her. Once he was gone Lacy was free. She cried out to God for help and he sent Michael to her, just as he'd done for Daniel. And she began to wait. When Gavin Wendell wandered across her path she seized the day. Always a beautiful woman, it wasn't hard to get the man to fall in love with her. Her days and nights of poring over the scriptures paid off in a big way. Gavin was convinced he had found himself a godly woman to stand beside him to help lead his flock. And indeed she was.

Atlanta was where Lacy needed to be because that's where Anissa was. Anissa Strickland who was responsible for the death of Lacy's one offspring. The only person in the world she had ever really loved.

She could not believe it when FJ announced he was marrying Anissa after only a few months of dating. Everything about her was wrong. Loving her son more than life itself, she allowed it to be so. He was such a beautiful, innocent boy who grew up watching his father abuse his mother. He didn't know how to be any other kind of husband. Lacy had endured the abuse until she learned of God and put a stop to it. But Anissa was weak. She couldn't take the abuse. She tried to escape because she didn't trust God. FJ became a broken shell of a man after she left him. When he learned she didn't die on 9/11, the deception was too much for him. It made him crazy.

It was Anissa's fault that FJ was on the streets of New York. He went there to bring her back home. He died a horrible death; therefore, she had to die a horrible death. Lacy prayed and read the story in chapter 10 of the book of Daniel over and over. She became Michael.

She married Gavin and then began research on the men in the church. That's how she found Tom Genner, who'd been a closet arsonist in his youth. He was caught setting two fires that caused minimum damage, mostly to his reputation. His records were sealed, but fine Christian man that he was, he confessed all to her. She told him his past didn't matter. God had forgiven him. All boys are mischievous, but Tom's mischief came in handy. Fire was Lacy's weapon and someone had to take the fall for it. So Tom was appointed singles pastor and Lacy began to prepare.

She took care of her body—her temple. She spent time in the gym with strength training so that dragging bodies around would not be difficult. She began to practice by actually killing. Selecting the girls became a simple matter of seeing a resemblance to Anissa. Especially the blonde hair. Getting the women to come with her was as natural as addressing her Sunday school class. Telling them a young man wanted to meet with them with her, the pastor's wife, as a chaperone was textbook.

It was easy to kill them, but the thoughts afterwards were not so pleasant. Unless she prayed. Lacy held on to the shoes and clothing of all her victims and a supply of filled gasoline containers, new tarps, and the black leotard. She'd hidden all of it where it could easily be found. All left in that house down from Martha that the church had originally allowed the singles ministry to use. At a moment's notice, everything was in place to incriminate Tom.

That silly fool Martha Smith! She came to Lacy at the church with her suspicions. The church! Lacy tried to smooth things over, promising to look into it. And she had—with a knife. She knew Martha snooped, but she had no idea the idiot would approach her. She had been careful to disguise herself in the black leotard so that her face or skin could not be seen. She deliberately drove slow enough for Martha or anyone else to see the church van coming and going on those early mornings. A second witness added credibility to the notion that Tom could be a killer. The best thing of all was that, in her stocking feet, she and Tom were around the same height.

Tom knew his good looks were unsettling to the young single women who came to the church. He basked in it, and flirted even though he had a wife and children at home. He committed adultery in his heart and he deserved to pay for those sins. He was only reaping what he'd sown.

Lacy had actually expected the person who lived in the house on the end of the street to be the witness, because he worked an odd night shift. She never expected Martha Smith to be up so late at night. She almost choked the life out of her as she simpered and purred.

"I'll give you time to repent and go to the police," she'd said.

"Thank you, Martha. But tell me, how can you be so certain that it's me you saw?"

"Why, Olivet. Your bosom is one of your most obvious features. And the way you walk. Who else could it have been?"

When those police officers appeared, Lacy almost lost it. She'd expected the simpleton to try to tell the police what she knew then. But instead Martha had looked at her reassuringly like the idiot she was. Lacy lived her life to inspire confidence and her husband preached love and forgiveness. Martha left her alone to do the right thing. And the right thing was to shut Martha's mouth forever. Little pest! Now she'd have to tell the people she met in the next life. Loose ends always had to be tied.

Anissa and FJ married on June 16, 1998, and FJ died on June 24, 2002.

Till death do us part.

They were joined together as one. It was preordained that Anissa should die on the same date, but a series of unfortunate events culminating with the police setting a trap caused her to die today. It was ahead of schedule. Lacy had intended for Anissa to die in 2009. Seven years after Foley took his last breath.

Seven. God's perfect number.

Death would reunite them. FJ could have his revenge in the afterlife. He wanted Anissa so much he risked everything trying to get her back.

Anissa would certainly be dead when the twenty-fourth of June arrived. An eye for an eye.

Lacy ran her fingers through her hair and relaxed, thinking of her next move after the long trip ahead. She was on her way to New York.

Judge Orella Bookings, the driver of the SUV that hit FJ and sent him flying in front of the bus just in time for it to crush the life out of his body, was next in line to meet her maker.

Maybe I'll use that nice sharp knife on her.

Same Day

Chapter Seventy-Three

Merlot sat in Anissa's living room and listened as the police communicated with an officer on the scene. It was where the car Anissa was suspected to have been abducted in was found. The site was completely chaotic. Several bystanders injured. Multiple automobile totalities. The whole area was cordoned off as emergency vehicles entered and exited. The fire was out. A body was found inside the trunk of the vehicle that exploded. The evidence was inconclusive but probable.

A female.

Deceased.

Burned beyond recognition.

Heartbroken and confused, Merlot left without another word.

He got into his car and began to drive. He had to get to someone who could positively identify the remains before he would believe she was dead. This couldn't happen. She'd been through enough. It was time for life to be good to her. Not to be destroyed by a psychopath. He wouldn't believe that Anissa was gone. His phone rang. At first he wanted to ignore it, but changed his mind. Someone could be calling to wake him from this nightmare.

"Hello," he answered.

"Mr. Candy?" a timid female voice asked.

"Yes," Merlot replied.

"This is Etta Wasp. You came to my house with a police officer? Asking questions about the singles ministry at my church?"

"Yes, I remember," Merlot said, wondering about the reason for the call. Her timing was really bad.

"My sister, who doesn't go to church with me—ever even visited—says that Olivet Wendell is really a woman named Lacy Brogdon. I didn't know—"

"Did you say Lacy Brogdon?" Merlot's heart sank. There was no doubt in his mind now that Anissa was dead. The name Brogdon brought everything into focus. Now it made sense that Anissa had been taken. This was a vendetta because of Foley Brogdon, Lacy Brogdon's only son and Anissa's ex-husband.

"Yes, my sister says—"

"Thank you so much, Mrs. Wasp." Merlot disconnected. He then dialed Dennis's number. As the phone rang, Merlot's thoughts raced. Lacy Brogdon! That's why she looked so familiar. Foley Brogdon was the spitting image of his mother.

Why didn't I see the resemblance? Merlot was tormented. If he'd only looked closer, maybe he could have prevented all of this. Foley Brogdon died underneath a bus in Manhattan with his head crushed. His whole family had to be nuts, but Merlot had thought Foley the craziest of all. Obviously Lacy was insane. She had to blame someone for her only son's death. In her twisted mind Anissa was at fault. Beautiful Anissa. All she'd done was marry an abusive son of a bitch.

What had Glenn said? Merlot thought back to the day Dennis laid fliers of all those missing women on the conference table. He'd said that they were all blonde, that they resembled each other. *They resembled Anissa too!*

Merlot had to get to that church and confront her. Dennis would come along to back him up. With all the technology available, there had to be away to convict her.

For Anissa's sake.

July 22, 2008

Chapter Seventy-Four

Merlot, Dennis, Sterling' Glenn, and Kathy Stockton sat around the table in Merlot's conference room. A month had passed since the day Anissa died. A memorial service was held, her apartment cleaned out by her sister, and her ashes would be scattered in the Seine River in Paris as she'd requested. Merlot would take them as soon as he felt like he could let her go. She had come through so much just to die before her life could begin anew. With him. He could not release her until her killer was dead or behind bars.

Chanel Franco had gone through three successful skin graft procedures, the most challenging one had been her facial reconstruction. But all had gone as expected. She would not look the same, but her face would not be hideously scarred. Naturally, she had a long period of healing ahead and some physical therapy, but her outlook was excellent. Louise was on the mend as well, although she too mourned the loss of Anissa. Mr. & Mrs. Canola were looking for a house large enough to accommodate the family while their daughters recuperated.

Chanel had no memory of her lost weekend. She vaguely recalled being given a drink by someone and feeling a sharp prick in her wrist when she reached to take it. Dr. Salada insisted that memory loss leading up to a traumatic experience was normal. And the fact that memory of the gasoline, the tarp, and the fire was completely erased was a blessing in disguise.

Lacy Brogdon was in the wind. The five of them were together today to finalize their plan. They intended to track her down and one way or another get all of their questions answered. Merlot had asked Dennis to join his team and rename it with the catchy title Candy Cane Agency. They were not taking on new clients at the moment. They had one person they were determined to locate. Glenn had worked his magic and learned that the owner of the first car that knocked Foley Brogdon, Jr. into the bus's path was Orella Bookings, a family judge in Brooklyn. As it turns out, Orella was also a good friend of Kathy's. Now Kathy's stakes in this mess had increased. Anissa was her friend and what she liked to call her first success story. She had known Orella since college. A victim of abuse herself, Kathy was more than willing to finance the whole operation to bring Lacy to justice before her trail got cold.

Sterling agreed to work with them as well. Although he was embarrassed that his profile had been wrong, he remained confident that his profiling ability and his knowledge of killers would help them to reach their goal. He wanted Lacy in prison. According to Sterling, a murderer who killed for revenge would pay his victims back in order of the injustices committed. Lacy Brogdon had used a different chronology to eliminate her victims.

Glenn informed them that the driver of the bus that killed Foley had died under suspicious circumstances, but his death was not considered foul play. He would have been the first offender. Next should have come Orella Bookings, but instead Lacy had chosen Anissa.

There was no way that Orella would not be in danger. Not if Lacy was fighting a one-woman blood feud. Orella was warned by Kathy and sent to another Stockton property in Miami. She would be safe there.

Tom Genner had been released when the DNA found on the black thread at the scene of the first murder—Meredith Payne—did not match. It did match DNA taken from hairs in the brush used by Lacy Brogdon aka Olivet Wendell. In addition Tom had alibis for all the dates indicated on Martha Smith's video. A thorough investigation of the church van produced no evidence against Tom. The clothing of all the victims found in Genner's possession contained fibers with DNA that matched Lacy Brogdon. The woman Missy Kinner saw dumping Chanel's body was dressed in a black skin suit or leotard, but the leotard they found had never been worn. All of this "evidence" seemed to have been planted to incriminate Tom.

Lacy Brogdon was now their prime suspect. They were meeting to finalize their relocation plans to Kathy's family home in Manhattan, where they would dedicate all of their energy to finding Lacy.

"Shall we get this show on the road, gentlemen?" Kathy asked.

Acknowledgements

I am able to realize my dream of writing novels because of the gift of creativity from my higher power and the support of my loving family. I am so grateful to God, Butch, and my special admirers: Shakes, Bibbit, and Dragon.

I want to thank my sister, Nancy, who always finds one more error in the manuscript.

Thank you, Elayne Morton, for being my best friend and my voice of reason. You go girl!

Thank you to my editor, Patricia Peters.

And without Alisha Thomas, I'd never have a cover for my novels. Thanks, Alisha! You're the best!

Special thanks to Gail Stiles and Brenda Ceo for your help. You are getting me to the next step every time, ladies.

I so appreciate the ladies of my book club: Charmaine, Yvette, Ann, Joy and Susan. Your inspiring words give me confidence.

I want to thank Ulysses Musgrove for his invaluable input in police procedure.

I want to thank Barbara Ravage for writing the book "Burn Unit: saving lives after the flames." It helped me to get it right. And a special thanks to the nurse at Grady Memorial Hospital who recommended it to me.

A very special thank you to all of my readers!

Coming Soon

Back Court

By

Kris Allis

***

Find out if Orella Bookings will finally pay the piper.